DEATH OF A
SUPERTANKER

Antony Trew

COLLINS
St James's Place, London
1978

William Collins Sons & Co Ltd
London · Glasgow · Sydney · Auckland
Toronto · Johannesburg

First published 1978
© Antony Trew 1978
ISBN 0 00 222474 7
Set in Times
Made and printed in Great Britain by
William Collins Sons & Co Ltd Glasgow

It was a complete act of treason, the betrayal of a tradition which seemed to me as imperative as any guide on earth could be. It appeared that even at sea a man could become the victim of evil spirits.

Joseph Conrad
The Shadow Line

Chapter 1

From the wing of the bridge the second officer searched the distant haze for the land he knew was there but could not see. Ahead, towards the sun, the view was dominated by the main-deck, a vast expanse of red coated steel, nearly a fifth of a mile of it reaching out from the foot of the superstructure on which he stood. The bridge was more than a hundred feet above the water-line, the height of a ten-storey building. Though he knew they were there, the bluff, rounded bows of the supertanker, the bulbous ram of her forefoot, the huge hull beneath the waterline displacing hundreds of thousands of tons of water every minute, were for him invisible, remote and commonplace.

More real was the sub-tropical sun which lay hot upon the ship, flecking the ruffled sea with dancing points of light and gilding the wings of seabirds which wheeled and swooped over the broken water astern. He saw that it was almost 1240; time to set about fixing the ship's position. He checked the distance from the coast by radar. It was thirty-one miles. At the Decca Navigator he noted the lane co-ordinates and identified them on the chart. At their point of intersection he drew a neat circle, wrote against it the time, 1240, and entered the position in the deck logbook. 'She's on course,' he muttered to himself. 'North Sand Bluff abeam.' With dividers he measured distances on the chart: the ship was 31·3 miles offshore, 85 miles from Durban. The electric log above the chart-table gave speed through the water as 15·3 knots, whereas the distance between the noon and 1240 positions showed it to be only 14·7. To avoid the Mozambique current which swept to the south-west they kept off the land on the voyage up the coast. But even out there, he decided, they were feeling some of it.

He moved along the foreside of the wheelhouse and from long habit, almost unaware that he was doing so because his mind was busy with other things, checked along the systems consoles: the gyro compass, course and speed indicators, the Decca Arkas auto-pilot, the bridge-engineroom controls, ship condition and

7

alarm systems, the radar sets, communications panel and much else.

These routine things done he looked across to where the quartermaster – free of the wheel since the ship was on auto-pilot – polished a wheelhouse window with the slow but steady rhythm of a man who has time to spare.

'Eighty-five miles to Durban, Gomez,' said the second officer.

The Cape Verde Islander stopped polishing, turned, grinned, strong white teeth prominent in the brown face. 'What matter, Mister Foley. We not stop in Durban. How far now for the Gulf?'

'Five thousand miles, give or take a few hundred.'

'Is how many days?'

'Seventeen.'

'Ah. Seventeen. Too much. Thirty-six hours in the Gulf to load. Afterwards, six weeks more sea before Rotterdam. It is not a good life, sir.'

'You chose it, Gomez.'

'Life chooses, sir. Not me. Must have money for wife and children.' He turned back to the window and got on with the polishing.

The second officer's thoughts were interrupted by a sudden piercing blast. It was steam exhausting from the funnel and the sound of it was compounded by an unusual metallic clatter from the engineroom. Alarm signals sounded, warning lights on the bridge console glowed red, and he realized that the main turbine was tripping. The RPM meter indicated a rapid fall in revolutions and finally stopped. As if to emphasize its message, all hull vibrations ceased.

He reached for the phone to the engineroom but his intention was pre-empted by its flashing light and persistent buzz. He picked up the handset. 'Bridge here. Foley speaking.'

Above the shrill blast of escaping steam he recognized the hoarse voice of Jerry Whitelot the fourth engineer. 'We've a problem, Two-Oh,' it said. 'All hell's let loose.'

'Sounds like it. What's up?'

'Turbine coupling's packed up. Jonah is shutting down. The HP rotor's probably had it.'

'Sounds traumatic. Would happen to Jonah.' Jonah was Jonathan Malim, the third engineer.

'You said it, mate. Days more than hours to fix this lot. Let

8

the Old Man know right away, will you? 'Bye now.'

'Will do. 'Bye.'

Foley heard the phone click off, and at once dialled the Master's suite. At that moment Captain Crutchley himself appeared on the bridge, a solid squarely built man with weathered features rendered expressionless by dark glasses.

'I was dialling you, sir,' said the second officer. 'There's trouble in the engineroom. They've had to shut down. The coupling between the turbine and the gearing has packed up.'

The Captain was a silent, withdrawn man who seldom if ever showed emotion. Now his mouth tightened and he frowned his disapproval of what he'd heard as he went to the bridge console.

Soon afterwards Freeman Jarrett, the chief officer, arrived in the wheelhouse. 'What's the trouble?' he asked the second officer in his challenging probing way. Jarrett was breathless. Typical of the man, thought Foley, that he'd run to the bridge. Never missed a trick. Had to be in on everything. Foley and Jarrett had two things in common. Their dislike of each other and their admiration for Sandy. The last emotion had a good deal to do with the first because Sandy was Foley's wife; one of four women making the round voyage in *Ocean Mammoth*.

Briefly, in an undertone, his eyes on the Captain because he disliked the chief officer's stare, Foley explained what had happened. Jarrett was muttering something about why had he not been informed immediately, when the Captain interrupted. 'Bring the ship's head twenty degrees to starboard, Mr Foley.' Without turning to look at the chief officer he added, 'Mr Jarrett. Tell Cadet Middleton to report to the bridge at once.'

The chief officer went to the phone while Foley turned the knurled knob of the auto-pilot and soon the gyro-repeater began ticking off the degrees as the ship's head swung to starboard. A few minutes later Foley reported, 'She's twenty degrees to starboard now, sir. Heading zero-four-two.'

'Good. Steady her on that. She'll carry steerage way for five or six miles.' The Captain didn't explain that he wished to get the ship further away from the land and the drift of the Mozambique current, but they knew that. Now he stood in the centre of the bridge, hands clasped behind his back, silent, massive, looking straight ahead. A sallow youth with dark untidy hair arrived on the bridge and he and the Captain went round the screen to the chartroom. The officers knew of the Captain's insistence that

9

Middleton should always be on the bridge with him, whatever the time of day or night. The young man was due to write his DTI examination for Second Mate in a few months' time and the Captain was said to be giving him every opportunity of experience on the bridge.

The chief officer had his own ideas about Captain Crutchley's motives.

By two o'clock that afternoon much had happened. At a conference in the Master's suite with Benson the second engineer and the chief officer present, the chief engineer, Hamish McLintoch, had explained the problem. The coupling between the main turbine shaft and the gearing had failed. The cause of failure appeared to be a collapsed bearing.

'In Malim's watch.' The Captain was thoughtful. 'Was there no warning?'

'He says not.' McLintoch narrowed his eyes. 'But I have my doubts.'

The chief engineer went on to explain that failure of the bearing had fractured the coupling. This had resulted in overspeed of the turbines during which the HP rotor had stripped its blades. No doubt the casing blades would also be damaged. In other words, a major breakdown had occurred and the ship was without power on her main engines. There was a spare coupling on board, and spare casing blades, but a new HP rotor would have to be flown out from Europe. Fitting of the new coupling, the rotor and casing blades would have to be done in harbour.

The Captain asked if the ship could reach Durban under her own power. The chief engineer said she could steam at about seven knots using the LP stage of the main turbine only, but that would entail blanking off the HP stage and by-passing it with temporary steam lines. It was a complicated operation and would take several days. It was then agreed that since the ship was less than eighty-five miles from Durban, an ocean-going tug should tow her in. Captain Crutchley knew that the costs would be borne by the marine underwriters.

His next move was to talk by radiophone to Durban's Port Captain. He reported that his ship, the VLCC *Ocean Mammoth*, bound for the Persian Gulf in ballast, had experienced a major breakdown. He gave the ship's position and asked if a salvage tug was available to tow her into Durban.

The Port Captain said there was, but added, 'What is your length, draught and tonnage?'

'Three hundred and fifty metres,' said Captain Crutchley. 'Draught in ballast ten point three metres, gross registered tonnage one hundred and sixty-two thousand, dead weight tonnage loaded, three hundred and twenty thousand. Complement, thirty-six crew, four passengers.'

'And you are entirely without power on your main engines?'

'That is correct.'

There was some delay before the Port Captain continued. 'I can't permit any ship of that size, without power, to be towed into the harbour. You'll understand, Captain, that the risks are too great.'

'I appreciate that, sir. We will over the next few days blank off the damaged HP stage and steam on LP. That will give a manoeuvring speed of seven knots. All we need. These ships handle well. If you can let us have tugs to assist, and the weather's fine, there should be no problems.'

It was agreed that on arrival off Durban the ship would anchor within the precincts of the port until her engineers had restored power to the main engines. Then, with the assistance of tugs, she could enter harbour and berth at No. 1 Pier on Salisbury Island.

'Have you finished cleaning your tanks?' enquired the Port Captain.

'Yes. They've been cleaned and inerted so there is no risk of explosion.'

'Thank you, Captain. Who are your agents here?'

'Lars Hammarsen and Company.'

'Right. I'll be in touch with them. In the meantime please ask them to arrange for the services of the salvage tug. They'll have to see to guarantees and so forth.'

'Certainly,' said Captain Crutchley. 'I will do that.'

They discussed a number of other matters including a safe anchorage. The conversation ended with expressions of mutual esteem, the Port Captain having remarked that *Ocean Mammoth* would be the largest vessel ever to enter Durban harbour.

Captain Crutchley next put a call through to his marine-superintendent in London, discussed the breakdown and reached agreement on the steps to be taken. That done he informed the Durban agents by radiophone of what had transpired and asked them to arrange for the despatch of a salvage tug.

11

He and his officers then settled down to wait while their new ship, outward bound on her second voyage from Rotterdam to the Persian Gulf, lay helpless and drifting on a calm sea under a hot sun, her crew as listless as the weather.

Down in the engineroom the ship's engineers were already busy by-passing the damaged HP turbine. The chief engineer had told them they would have to work day and night until the task was completed.

In the office which formed part of his ample and luxurious suite, Captain Crutchley was writing a report on the day's events. He wrote slowly, stopping often to wipe his eyes and clean his glasses. The report was addressed to Nicolas Kostadis, marine-superintendent of Inter-Ocean Crude and Bulk Carriers Ltd., the man in London to whom he had just spoken. A strange company, reflected Crutchley, registered in the Bahamas, operating offices in London, directors and financial control in Zurich, and each ship of the modern fleet – four supertankers and six bulk carriers – registered in Famagusta, a port they would never use though they flew the Cypriot flag. It was very much a flag of convenience. *Ocean Mammoth*'s officers and engineers were British, the remainder of the crew Cape Verde Islanders except for the Goanese stewards.

Captain Crutchley sighed. It was difficult for a seaman to comprehend the complexities of modern ship-owning. One thing he did understand, however, was the crew mix. Britain was well down in the European maritime pay league, indeed only just above Spain. It would have cost the owners a lot more to operate their ships with German, French, Scandinavian or even Greek crews. He consoled himself with the thought that he was very much better paid than he would have been in a British ship. Money was important to Captain Crutchley.

At half past four that afternoon the Port Captain reported the departure from Durban of the *Seahorse*, one of two deep-sea salvage tugs stationed on the South African coast, the most powerful of their kind in the world. He gave the tug's estimated time of arrival at the tanker as eight-thirty. Captain Crutchley thanked him and said the ship would in all respects be ready to be taken in tow when the tug arrived.

At the Captain's request, Foley – the ship's navigating officer – gave him the times of sunset and moonrise. The sun would set at

1803, the moon rise at 0313. The Captain, impassive and formidable at his desk, nodded acknowledgement. Foley, knowing the tow would have to be passed during the hours of darkness, wondered how the Captain felt about it, but since Crutchley said nothing and the dark sun-glasses masked his eyes there was no way of knowing. Strange man, thought Foley. Within the protective cocoon of his stateroom he led the life of a semi-recluse. Yet when a decision had to be made, when sound judgement was needed, when firm control was essential, he never failed. To the men the Master's silence, his apparent unawareness of those around him, was strange, almost awesome.

As the second officer turned to go the Captain spoke for the first time. 'Navigation and not-under-command lights to be switched on well before sunset, Mr Foley. When the tug is sighted the maindeck is to be floodlit. The third officer is to report to me when these things have been done.'

Chapter 2

A number of officers were having their evening meal in the saloon when Tim Feeny the radio officer appeared at the door. He looked round hesitantly before going over to the chief engineer to whom he spoke in a low voice. McLintoch showed surprise, got up and went with Feeny to the adjoining lounge. There they had a brief conversation. When Feeny had gone, McLintoch went to the door of the saloon and beckoned a steward.

The man came across. McLintoch said, 'Ask the third engineer to come to my office right away, please.'

They'd had a real showdown that morning in the engine control-room. It had been an abrasive, stupid row and Malim knew he'd gone too far. He still had a vivid picture of McLintoch rushing into the control-room shouting, 'What the hell are you up to now?'

Partly because he was absorbed in shutting down the engines and partly because he resented being shouted at, particularly in front of subordinates, he'd ignored the chief engineer and that had been disastrous. With a warning growl McLintoch had come up to the control position and pushed him aside. Malim, anger overcoming fear, had seen red, lost his temper and retaliated by shoving McLintoch away and re-establishing his position at the controls. A white-faced, enraged McLintoch had turned on him. 'By God, Malim. You'll answer for this.'

Jerry Whitelot, the fourth engineer – in the control-room by chance when the breakdown occurred – quickly explained to McLintoch what had happened while Malim, his mind now blurred by the row, went on with the shutting down assisted by a junior engineer. Soon afterwards McLintoch had left without a word to either of them, presumably to report to the Captain.

Whitelot said, 'You must be out of your mind, Jonah. He'll clobber you for that. Christ, you can't shove the Chief about in his own engineroom.'

Malim knew that his behaviour had been stupid and childish

14

and he bitterly regretted it. Nevertheless he was determined to defend himself. 'You heard him shouting at me. Shoving me off the console like that before I had a chance to explain.' His voice was still shaking with emotion. 'Okay. I've been a bloody fool. I know I was crazy. But I couldn't take it. Especially with you and that fiver looking on.'

Whitelot shook his head. 'You can't win, Jonah. You know the Chief's temper. Blood pressure or piles or something. He's got it in for you, so why give him the chance. He'll make mincemeat of you.' Whitelot's laugh was a hoarse croak. 'Jesus! I thought you were going to thump the old sod. So did he. That's why he cleared out.' He paused, wiping his hands on a piece of cotton-waste. 'You know he's never forgiven you for that condenser balls up last voyage. It's that and his complex about all the other problems we've had in the engineroom.'

Malim had nodded vigorously. 'You're right. It *is* that. But this is a new ship. For Christ's sake, what does he expect? Bound to be teething troubles. Anyone can make a mistake. That's no excuse for persecution. He's made my life a bloody misery.'

Now, on his way up to the chief engineer's office, Malim stopped on a landing for a moment to recover his composure. He tried to recall how it had all started. He'd been in the control-room when the breakdown occurred. The alarm systems had given absolutely no warning that the bearing was about to fail. That was typical of his luck. Things always seemed to go wrong in his watch. This was by no means the first time there'd been a breakdown in it, though before it had been auxiliary machinery and not the main engines. But *Ocean Mammoth* was a new ship and troubles were inevitable. Why didn't McLintoch make allowances for that? The tension between them was no secret. The Chief had on two previous occasions shouted at him in front of other engineer officers, and except for Jerry Whitelot there wasn't, he knew, much sympathy for him. It was not for nothing, he reflected, that his shipmates had corrupted his Jonathan to 'Jonah'.

Malim was a very worried young man. McLintoch would not only hold him responsible for the breakdown, but would probably submit a written report to the Captain about the incident in the control-room. One way and another he was bound to come off worst. Gloomy, introspective, with few friends, he felt helpless and

15

insecure. As so often happened when he was under stress, the muscles in his stomach contracted and his head throbbed.

'Take a seat, Mr Malim.' The chief engineer was a very formal, proper sort of person, who seldom used first names. He cleared his throat and regarded the third engineer sternly. 'I have an unpleasant duty to perform.' He spoke in an awkward, hurried way.

Malim looked up. There were little pools of sweat in the pouches under his troubled eyes. 'I expected this, Chief. And I apologize for losing my temper.' He shrugged his shoulders. 'There was no warning whatsoever. The alarm system failed . . .'

McLintoch held up a hand much in the manner of a policeman on point duty. 'It's not that, Mr Malim. It's personal news. Your wife . . .' He stopped then to give the younger man time to sense what was coming.

'My wife?' Malim's apprehensive eyes lifted again to meet the chief engineer's. 'What about her? It's not . . .' His voice trailed away, but it was apparent from the way the muscles in his face worked that he was beginning to understand.

The chief engineer stood up, went round the desk and laid a hand on his shoulder. 'Road accident, laddie.' It occurred to him that he'd never called him that before. 'She was crossing the street. A car ran into her.'

The third engineer blinked as if he'd been struck in the face. He was silent for a moment, running his tongue over his lower lip. 'She is . . . she was . . . five months pregnant.' He fell forward on to the desk, head on hands, his shoulders shaking.

Despite his reserved manner and quick temper, McLintoch was a warm-hearted man. Conscious that his relationship with the third engineer had for some time been under severe strain; that he, McLintoch, had provoked the undignified and absurd row in the control-room, he felt a personal sense of guilt as if he were in some way responsible for Mrs Malim's death. With an awkward rather self-conscious gesture he patted the young man's shoulder. 'She knew nothing, laddie. Killed instantly the message said.'

Malim pushed the chief engineer's hand away, pulled himself together, got out of the chair and left the office without a word.

At 1830 the *Seahorse*, then thirty-seven miles distant, spoke to the tanker by voice radio. The two captains discussed details of

16

the tow, the manner in which it would be passed and secured, agreed that the weather conditions were good and signed off. Not long afterwards the tug's steaming lights were sighted.

Captain Crutchley was informed and at once went to the bridge. Cadet Middleton was already there. The ship's floodlights had turned night into day and those on the bridge, looking along the vast maindeck could see, far ahead in the bows, a party of men making ready for the tow. With them was the chief officer whose place on the bridge had been taken by Foley. The Captain had discussed with the chief officer what was to be done and had every confidence it would be well done. Freeman Jarrett was a capable man, good at handling crew and dealing with emergencies. It was a pity, thought Crutchley, as he moved out to the port wing, that the chief officer so often talked of leaving the sea. Bad for morale, particularly among the junior officers and cadets. He shrugged away the thought and spoke to Middleton. 'How is the tug bearing now?'

The cadet moved the azimuth ring round the gyro-repeater and put his eye to it. 'Two-seven-three, sir.'

'Good,' said the Captain. 'Now remember that bearing, Middleton. If it does not change we're on a collision course. Since she is making for us and we are stationary it should not change.'

'Yes, sir.'

With the cadet following closely, the Captain went back to the wheelhouse and moved along the bridge consoles until he reached the radar units. 'Now, Middleton, check that bearing on the anti-collision radar and get the tug's distance.'

While the Captain was speaking the chief officer arrived in the chartroom. He walked past Foley who was at the chart-table and stopped at the break of the screen separating chartroom from wheelhouse. There, in semi-darkness, he watched the Captain and Middleton. The cadet was leaning forward, looking into the display hood of the AC radar, his hand on the range switch. A moment later he reported, 'Bearing two-seven-four, distance fifteen miles, sir.'

'The ship's head?'

'One-eight-eight, sir.'

The chief officer moved up alongside the Captain. 'We're all ready up forward, sir,' he said. 'Shouldn't be any problems in this weather.'

Captain Crutchley continued to look straight ahead. 'Thank

17

you, Mr Jarrett. The tug should be with us soon.'

Jarrett hesitated. 'Would you like Middleton to come forward with me, sir? Good practical experience.'

'No,' said Crutchley. 'You already have Cadet Price. Middleton will remain on the bridge. There's plenty for him to profit from up here.'

Jarrett said nothing but in the darkness he looked at the Captain in a speculative way, as if trying to read his mind.

Chapter 3

The night was dark when shortly before seven, *Seahorse* arrived and without delay manoeuvred her stern under *Ocean Mammoth*'s bows. Lines were passed, a three-inch wire messenger from the tug was taken to a winch-drum on the tanker's windlass, and the work of winching it in began. It would be followed by the main towing wire; a heavy nine-inch rope of tensile steel.

The chief officer stood in the bows on the starboard side of the towing fairlead. He was in touch with both the supertanker's bridge and the salvage tug by R/T walkie-talkie. Cadet Price was to port of the fairlead with a standby set. The *Seahorse*'s stern was now a couple of hundred feet ahead of the bows of the tanker.

'Belay winching,' warned the salvage tug's captain by R/T. 'The eye of the nine-inch has just gone into the water. I'll move ahead another half-cable and take up the slack on the messenger. Don't begin winching again until I give the word.'

'Okay, *Seahorse*,' replied Jarrett. 'Message received and understood.' He called to the men at the capstan. 'The tug's going to move another half-cable ahead. Take a turn off the winch-drum and be ready to let that wire surge handsomely if necessary.' The men at the capstan acknowledged, the tug moved dead slow ahead, one of her searchlights trained on the bight of wire which was just beginning to show on the surface.

Moments later the man tending the wire on *Ocean Mammoth*'s winch-drum lost control as he took the turn off and let the wire run. It fouled a deck fitting, jammed and parted, one end whipping to port with a crack like a rifle shot. It struck Cadet Price's legs and hurled him over the side.

Jarrett at once broadcast, 'Man overboard, port bow.' He passed his R/T set to the bosun and ran across to the port side. The sea beneath the tanker's bows was lit by the tug's searchlight and in its beam, far below, he saw the crumpled heap in the water.

He grabbed a heaving line, secured the inboard end to a stanchion, and threw the coil over the side. Climbing on to the bulwark he lowered himself down the line, controlling his descent with gloved hands. When he reached the water he let go, got rid of the working gloves and his shoes and swam the thirty yards or so to where the lifeless shape bobbed in the sea.

He gripped the body, turned it on to its back and lifted the head clear of the water. A life-buoy splashed close by, but Jarrett ignored it. He was a strong swimmer, the Indian Ocean was agreeably warm, he was enjoying his role, and he knew that more practical help was not far away.

A few minutes later an inflatable skimmer from the *Seahorse* arrived with a sound like tearing linen and picked up both men. Before long they were back on board *Ocean Mammoth*.

It was close to nine-thirty when the tow was finally passed and secured and *Seahorse*, barely making way through the water, moved to starboard on a course almost at right angles to the line of *Ocean Mammoth*'s keel. The salvage tug was pivoting the supertanker to avoid a direct pull against the enormous inertia of the ship at rest. The long towing wire took the strain, lifted from the sea momentarily, a quivering arc from which water streamed like liquid silver in the beam of the searchlight. There was no danger now of the wire parting; the tug's winches were self-adjusting for tension and would render before breaking point was reached.

With infinite care and patience the tanker's bows were coaxed round. Then, gently but surely, *Seahorse* showed her strength and the big ship began to move ahead almost imperceptibly. As way was gained, the tug began a slow turn on to the course for Durban.

Foley had picked up the helicopter on radar long before they saw its lights blinking in the distance. It came steadily towards them and when they heard the sound of its jets floodlights were switched on and men went forward to the white-circled landing area. The helicopter came in close, rotor blades shimmering, jets screaming, and stationed itself above and to port of the maindeck.

The batman waved his neon wands, the helicopter crabbed sideways and hovered for a moment before dropping on to the deck. The rotors kept turning, the dimension lights blinking, as a door slid open. Two men stepped out, bending low and running clear. Soon they reappeared, accompanied by crewmen carrying

Cadet Price in a Skyclimber stretcher. It was loaded into the helicopter, the doctor and his assistant got in, the batman waved his wands and the machine lifted away in a steep climbing turn, the roar of its jets and the beat of its rotors a noisy reminder of technology's importance to Cadet Price's survival.

It was after four o'clock in the morning when Foley got down to his cabin, having been relieved by Jarrett. He found his wife in the day-cabin, propped up on the settee reading *Cosmopolitan*, a magazine of which he did not approve because he felt it gave her ideas she'd have been better without. But since he was dominated by a desire to please her, to hold her at almost any cost, he'd not made an issue of this; any more than of her extravagances and ambitions – ambitions quite incapable of fulfilment by him.

Foley was very much in love with his wife but uncertain of their relationship which to him seemed insecure. She was, he knew, an unwilling passenger in *Ocean Mammoth*. It had taken much persuasion to get her to come: only the knowledge that they had let their flat for six months and would save money – half of which would be hers – had clinched the deal.

He was twenty-six, she twenty-eight. They'd been married for five years and there were no children. Her favourite taunt during heated arguments was: 'I should never have married you. You caught me on the rebound.' The rebound was, he knew, the result of an unhappy love affair with a married man. Foley's perpetual nightmare was that there would be another love affair, when he was away at sea. At those times he would acknowledge the mistake he'd made in marrying a woman so attractive, intelligent and ambitious.

The moment he entered the cabin and saw her lying on the settee in black bra and pants, her body deeply sun-tanned – she spent hours each day beside the tanker's pool – he'd felt the irresistible pull of her sexual attraction.

'Hullo,' he said. 'Still awake. I thought you'd be in bed.'

She put down the magazine. 'I'm not tired. Too much excitement. The breakdown, the tug coming out. Peter Price's rescue. The helicopter. And now the tow. It's dreamy. And weeks in Durban to come. You always told me what a super place it was. Isn't that marvellous?' Her eyes shone. 'What time do we get there?'

'I'm glad. That's great, Sandy. I told you interesting things

21

could happen in a supertanker.' He laughed happily. 'Our ETA is 0830 – another four hours. But we'll be at anchor for two or three days before we can go in.' He stooped over the settee, gave her a long kiss, his hands exploring the sun-tan. 'We've lots of time,' he whispered into her hair.

She pushed him away gently. 'No, George. Not now. Please. I want to talk. There's so much to talk about.' She sat up suddenly, folded her arms round her knees and looked up at him with dark intense eyes. 'Tell me. How's the tow going? How was poor Peter Price when they took him off?'

He forgot his disappointment. It was difficult not to respond to her enthusiams. No one could be a more interesting and affectionate companion if she chose. He sighed, slumped into an easy chair, clasped his hands behind his head. 'The tow's going well. Making a steady seven knots.' He yawned noisily. 'Sorry. I'm tired. Been on the bridge for more than ten hours.'

'Tired? Poor George.' She looked at him in an absent-minded way. 'But tell me about Peter Price. How was he when he went?'

'Sorry. I forgot. Pretty bad. Both legs broken by that wire. Probably some internal injuries too. His back got it when he was thrown against the bulwark. And he was half-drowned. Jarrett gave him a shot of morphine soon after they got him back on board. He was still out when they put him in the helicopter.'

'Poor boy. He's lucky to be alive, isn't he? If it weren't for Freeman Jarrett he wouldn't be. Wasn't that marvellous, George? So brave. Plunging in like that. In uniform and knowing the Indian Ocean's alive with sharks. At night, too.'

George Foley raised a querulous eyebrow. 'Brave? You must be joking. Sea calm and warm, ship stopped, tug close by, the place lit like Piccadilly Circus.' He made a rude noise. 'And *uniform* . . . for God's sake . . . he was wearing tropical kit . . . shorts and shirt . . . what could be better. No *plunge* about it either. Lowered himself down on a heaving line.' Foley sat upright in the chair to lend emphasis to what he was saying. 'And all for what? The tug was there, wasn't it? They'd have had Price on board in no time.'

She smiled knowingly, a contrived smile which she knew irritated him. 'You're jealous, George. It *was* brave. And quick and decisive like Freeman always is. That boy would have drowned by the time the tug's skimmer got there.'

Foley sensed a row coming, tried to check himself but couldn't.

22

The bravery of Freeman Jarrett, real or imaginary, was not a subject he was prepared to keep quiet about. 'Rubbish, Sandy. No risk at all. Pure exhibitionism. He loved it. Typical Jarrett scenario. He ought to have been on the stage.'

'My God, you *are* jealous, George.' She frowned, made a face. 'It's a nasty characteristic. Freeman is an outstanding man. Everyone knows it. He'll be in command soon. Master of his own ship. You mark my words. And only thirty-two.'

Foley stared at her. 'You married the wrong man, didn't you? Well, let me remind you that Jarrett can't wait to leave the sea. Always telling us the great things he plans to do ashore. The city tycoon. Financial whizz kid extraordinary. You must have heard him laying that on the line.'

'Maybe he *will* be a tycoon. He's the sort of man who would succeed at anything he puts his mind to.'

Foley shrugged his shoulders. He'd had his say. She always had to have the last word. He was too tired to argue. He could have pointed out that he had an Extra Master's Certificate – the highest qualification for a deck officer in the Merchant Navy – whereas Jarrett hadn't. But she knew that, and would only be sarcastic if he mentioned it. He picked up his shoes and went through to the sleeping cabin. He disliked Freeman Jarrett intensely. Their relationship was one of continuing tension. The chief officer, secure in his seniority, tended to bear down on him. What Foley found particularly humiliating was his wife's admiration for Jarrett who in turn made it clear that he found her attractive.

What Foley didn't know was that she saw the chief officer as a romantic figure, tall and handsome in a ruggedly masculine way. A dashing, debonair, somewhat reckless man, in a sense indispensable, since he made bearable the monotony of a tanker voyage in the company of people she didn't really care for. And he was divorced, which made him even more interesting from her point of view.

The *Seahorse* arrived off Durban with her tow during the forenoon of the following day, and with the assistance of two harbour tugs manoeuvred *Ocean Mammoth* into the anchorage recommended by the Port Captain. *Seahorse* and one of the harbour tugs then re-entered the port, leaving the other to stand by the anchored ship until such time as she was able to use her engines.

To motorists along the Marine Parade, and others looking out to sea that morning, the ships at anchor were so dwarfed by the huge bulk of the supertanker that they seemed to have shrunk overnight.

It was not long before launches came out with health, immigration and customs officials.

Others who visited the ship that day were Lars Hammarsen the agent, who was accompanied by a large red-faced man who turned out to be a marine surveyor, and representatives of the ship repair firms which had been asked to quote for the work to be done. Representatives of the media telephoned the ship on a number of occasions but Captain Crutchley refused to make any statements or give interviews until his ship was safely berthed alongside. Photographers came out in a hired launch and took pictures of the ship, but they were not allowed on board.

By and large it was a busy day and by evening both Captain Crutchley and Mr McLintoch had had enough.

The sea remained calm, the wind light and the weather fine throughout the next two days. Late in the afternoon of the third day Captain Crutchley was able to inform the Port Captain that the ship would have power on her main engines by midnight. It was agreed that she should enter harbour on the following day.

At eight o'clock next morning a pilot cutter came alongside *Ocean Mammoth*, a pilot boarded, the anchor was weighed and as the ship gathered way three tugs took up station, one on either bow, the third astern, and the supertanker headed for the harbour entrance. Before long she had begun her slow but purposeful journey down the dredged channel between the Bluff and the Point, moving under her own power but with the tugs ready to assist as necessary.

On the bridge Captain Crutchley stood rocklike and impassive, the very symbol of command. In fact it was the pilot who was exercising that command, issuing wheel and engine orders and at times engaging in monosyllabic exchanges with the tug captains by voice radio.

To those in the wheelhouse who watched him, the Captain's gaze behind the dark glasses seemed fixed on some distant object ahead. As was his custom he said little, other than occasionally to ask Middleton a brief question put, it seemed, to test the cadet's

24

perception of what was taking place, and he gave little appearance of being aware of the pilot's presence, making no attempt at conversation but answering his questions about the ship's handling characteristics with abrupt precision.

The pilot, not lacking in experience of sea captains, got on with the business of conning the ship, the biggest he'd ever handled. He knew pretty well what was going on in Crutchley's mind: the resentment of a Master that he was required to accept responsibility for the safety of his ship while it was to all intents and purposes under the command of a stranger; a stranger who had less than thirty minutes earlier come on to the bridge for the first time.

As *Ocean Mammoth* moved slowly down the harbour between the ships berthed alongside at the Point and Addington, and those at the bulk-handling facilities beneath the Bluff, then on towards Salisbury Island, past the ships at the Island View and Fynnland oil sites, Captain Crutchley was the victim of a deep depression. The rhythm of the voyage, of his life, had been interrupted by the breakdown. God knows, he thought, how long we shall be here and to what it may lead. He had no desire to be in port or in touch with the shore. It was far better, infinitely safer, to be at sea. A ship at sea was now the only environment with which he was totally familiar, the only one in which he felt secure and unexposed.

The harbour they were entering, its placid waters basking in the warmth of sub-tropical morning, the quays and ships alongside beginning to hum with activity, the long low ridge of the Berea looming over the concrete towers and blocks of the city skyline, the palms fringing the Esplanade stirring in the breeze, the distant clamour of traffic, the sounds of a city moving into high gear for the day ahead . . . these things, far from pleasing, filled him with foreboding.

He and his ship had already suffered enough: the humiliation of breakdown; of submitting to a tow; the three dismal days at anchor outside the port with a tug standing by because the ship was without power; the invasion of his privacy by the busybodies who'd come out to the ship for one purpose or another – that had been the first assault. Now came the second: the pilot on his bridge, the tugs ahead and astern emphasizing the impotence of his command; in half an hour, when the ship had berthed alongside, there would be a third assault: more port officials,

25

ship's chandlers, marine surveyors, engineering contractors and consultants, shipping agents, workmen, and of course the media ... SABC broadcasts from Durban were already carrying reports of the breakdown; of the impending entry into Durban of the biggest ship ever to visit the port; of the serious pollution caused by tankers along the South African coast and in the Southern Ocean, and the particular threat posed by VLCCs – the super-tankers – should they meet with disaster. It was old hat to Captain Crutchley but its regurgitation was disturbing ... all these people, he reminded himself, would soon stream aboard, bringing with them new problems. Sooner or later they would want to see him, to ask questions, to have documents signed, to justify their existence in one way or another, even if it were no more than to pass the time of day in the expectation of a drink. There would be strange faces, unfamiliar voices, unusual situations to be contended with each day. What, he wondered, lay in store for him and his ship?

Others on the bridge – Simpson the third officer, and Middleton the cadet, for example – felt rather differently. For them the breakdown was a welcome variation of a boring routine: an exciting beginning to the uncertainties and adventures which the minds of young seamen always associate with the shore.

McLintoch and Benson, like the Captain, resented the enforced visit. The breakdown had already involved them in a lot more work and worry than usual, and they had no doubt there would be more to come.

For the Cape Verde Islanders the interruption was an unwelcome or at least a dubious event. They were at sea to make money, to support their families in the harsh poverty of their tropical islands. 'More days more dollars', was their philosophy. But they were seamen and there would be, they knew, the customary attractions of a big port – women and drink – and that meant spending money. At the back of their minds lurked another less pleasant reality. They were dark skinned and would be up against the problems and humiliations of apartheid. So, too, would the Goanese stewards.

Captain Crutchley moved to the starboard wing of the bridge and remained there while the pilot and tug captains, working as a well-drilled team with maximum skill and minimum fuss, edged *Ocean Mammoth* into her berth at No. 1 Pier. Heaving lines were thrown, nylon pennants snaked down to the jetty followed by steel wires, dock hands slipped them over bollards, the super-tanker's mooring winches began to heave, the tugs to push, and the massive hull was inched slowly alongside.

The group of waiting men on the jetty far beneath the bridge wing, their faces turned upwards, their briefcases at the ready, suggested to Captain Crutchley that his gloomy forebodings were not unfounded.

Chapter 4

The Zurich offices of Inter-Ocean Crude and Bulk Carriers Ltd. were in what had once been a large private house in a side street off Seefeldstrasse. The only indication of its changed character was the discreet brass plate on the wall beside the front door.

The boardroom – it had been a drawing-room – was at the back overlooking a pleasant old-world garden of lawns, trees, flowering shrubs and a fountain. It was an elegant room, the highly polished mahogany table at its centre and the tall chairs round it reflecting light from crystal chandeliers set in a rococo ceiling. The tranquillity of the garden seen through french windows was in marked contrast to the tense atmosphere of the boardroom.

The chairman, an elderly German from Frankfurt with iron-grey hair and a deeply lined face, sat at the head of the table; the managing-director, Kurt Raustadt, on his right; the deputy-chairman on his left. Three other members of the Board were present and two officials: the marine-superintendent, Nico Kostadis, who had flown over from London that morning, and the managing-director's secretary, a good-looking woman of indeterminate age.

'So Hammarsen and McLintoch now agree, do they?' The chairman tapped impatiently with a gold pencil on the blotter in front of him.

'Yes. I phoned them again this morning,' said Raustadt. 'They recommend acceptance of the lowest tender: Marinreparat. They are well-established ship repairers with plenty of experience. Head office in Hamburg, but they've had this South African subsidiary for some years now.'

'What's their estimate of the time necessary to complete repairs?'

'Five days from receipt of the new HP rotor delivered on board in Durban. They say they can . . .'

The deputy-chairman, a bald hunched man with a rasping voice, interrupted. 'When will the rotor arrive there?'

'That's the problem. There isn't one immediately available. The intention is to cannibalize a laid-up VLCC which has the

28

same turbines. This means a delay of about a week.'

The chairman leant forward, his jaw thrust purposefully towards the speaker. 'It's five days since the breakdown. So we're talking of a delay of, say, nineteen or twenty days in all. Right?' He resumed his pencil tapping. 'You know what that means, gentlemen. *Ocean Mammoth* cannot now arrive in the Gulf before the OPEC price increase. The charter party specified completion of loading in Bahrain before the fifteenth. There is no possibility of meeting that deadline.'

'So?' The deputy-chairman pursed his lips, turning his head to regard the chairman with tired red-rimmed eyes.

'So we inform Akonol that we cannot comply. Circumstances beyond our control. That still leaves us with the problem of *Ocean Mammoth* broken down halfway to the Gulf. And no prospect now of getting a cargo.'

'We're covered against any claim from Akonol.' The managing-director said it smugly, smoothing his sleek black hair with the palm of his hand in a way which suggested sensual pleasure. 'No performance through breakdown clause. And of . . .'

'Yes, yes.' The chairman interrupted with sudden irritation. 'We know that. And we're covered by the underwriters for towage and repairs but not for loss of earnings – and that item runs into millions of dollars. The central difficulty remains. The breakdown simply underlines it. We have an acute cash flow problem. We ordered the four VLCCs when the market merited such a decision. The ships have been delivered, two are employed, one is already laid up – now we have *Ocean Mammoth* stranded in Durban without any chance of picking up a cargo in the Gulf. We shall have to get her back to the UK and lay her up. May I remind you that we borrowed two hundred and fifty million dollars to pay for those ships. Since their delivery the tanker market has collapsed. The ships can no longer earn the money necessary to service the loans, let alone repay them.' He spread his hands in a gesture of despair.

'I warned against this possibility when first we discussed building them,' said the director from Paris, a thin birdlike little man with yellow skin. 'I warned then of the consequences if the market should fall. But you reassured me.' He paused, his tone hesitant. The chairman was an influential man. He had no desire to offend him.

'That market has not fallen, my dear le Febre. It has collapsed.

29

A somewhat different matter, and something no one could have foreseen. Of course I reassured you. I always do, because you have no heart for decisions and that is sad in an entrepreneur.' He smiled thinly, pleased with the courteous nature of the rebuke. 'However, recriminations do not help. Let us get back to the point.'

The Frenchman made small grumbling noises, sat back and prepared a cigar for lighting. During the subsequent discussion it became clear what the point was . . . the breakdown of *Ocean Mammoth* had provoked a crisis in the affairs of Inter-Ocean Crude and Bulk Carriers Ltd., whose finances were already stretched by the servicing and repayment of loans for the new supertankers. The company's principal creditor, a consortium of Swiss banks, had a few days earlier exercised its right to increase the rate of loan interest. The breakdown was, in a sense, the final nail in the coffin unless the loan could be reduced substantially. The Board had bleakly to admit that the prospects of that happening were remote.

Immediately after the meeting the chairman and the deputy-chairman, with Nico Kostadis and the managing-director, met in the latter's office. There they engaged in long, earnest and confidential discussion before deciding that nothing could be done until Kostadis had assessed the situation in Durban. It was agreed that he should fly out to South Africa the next day. In the meantime the chairman undertook to approach the consortium to ask for less onerous terms for servicing and repaying the loan. It was appreciated that the chances of his accomplishing anything were precarious now that the news of *Ocean Mammoth*'s breakdown was out. But delaying action had become imperative.

Time, reflected the chairman as he went out in the cold wet night to the waiting Mercedes, time was what they were gravely short of. Kostadis would have to work fast.

Five days after the breakdown, life on board *Ocean Mammoth* in Durban had acquired a not particularly agreeable pattern of its own. The days and nights were unseasonably hot and humid and though this made little difference to the air-conditioned accommodation, it was sticky and enervating in the engineroom and other parts of the ship. Communication with the shore was not easy for the crew. An indifferent bus service, or taxis which were

30

expensive and difficult to get, involved an eight-mile detour round the southernmost reaches of the harbour. Captain Crutchley had arranged with the agents for a launch service to cover the comparatively short journey between the Point Ferry Jetty and the ship, but it was a limited one and the last trip was at eleven-thirty each night.

The sounds in *Ocean Mammoth* and the feel of the ship had changed. The hum of the turbines, the straining and creaking of the hull, the noise of the wind and sea, and the slow majestic roll had gone. Now the ship was still, small noises were amplified by the background of silence, so that footsteps on deck, the sound of crewmen laughing and talking as they worked about the ship, had become noticeable. There was an intermittent but distant banging and hammering in the engine spaces where the shaft coupling and damaged turbine were being dismantled by the contractors, and ship's staff were using the opportunity to do maintenance work on auxiliary machinery; and in the accommodation radios and stereos poured forth endless streams of 'pop'.

Though the ship was in ballast the smell of oil fuel hung over her, pungent and acrid, like an unseen mantle. By the fifth day the interest, and for some the excitement, of an unexpected arrival in a new place had worn thin. The confined life on board, the sense of isolation from the city and its community, so close at hand yet so distant, were beginning to tell; tempers were fraying and friction among the men was affecting the behaviour of the women. They became touchy, bitchy, and tension between them grew steadily.

Sandy Foley opened the door, came into the dayroom and stopped for a moment to frown at her husband who sat at a desk writing. He wore nothing but a pair of shorts and, irritated though she was, she thought how fit and strong he looked.

'Why do they have to empty the pool now of all times?' With an impatient gesture she threw a bathing towel into a corner, slipped off her bikini and stood in front of a window looking over the harbour towards Congella. He sensed that a storm was coming from the way she ran her hands down her hips as if smoothing away invisible creases.

'Ask Freeman Jarrett. He made the decision.'

'No he didn't. I've just asked him.' She picked up the *Cosmo-*

politan and lay naked on the settee, the depth of her sun-tan revealed by the whiteness of the skin where it had been protected by the bikini. 'It was Benson,' she went on. 'He said it was ƙeaking and had to be done.'

'Well? What's wrong with that?'

'I don't believe it was leaking. It's absurd. There's nothing to do in this lousy ship but for that pool.'

'You can still sunbathe.'

'Next to an empty pool. What's the point?'

'Well, for God's sake don't take it out on me.'

'I'm not.' She rolled over on her stomach. 'Think I'll go ashore after lunch. Swim at the beach.'

'Why not. You've done that most days anyway.'

She looked up frowning. 'What d'you expect me to do? Sit in this wretched old tank all day chatting up Doris Benson and company? Well, I'm sorry. That's just not on.' With a sudden change of mood she turned her head, smiled provocatively. 'Anyway, why don't you come with me?'

'Sorry,' he said. 'Your boy friend Jarrett wants me on board. Nico Kostadis arrived in Johannesburg this morning. Due here mid-afternoon. Everybody has to be around.'

'Why?'

'To create a good impression. To show Kostadis what a great guy he is, etcetera.' He left the desk, went to the refrigerator and poured himself a Coke. 'Want one?'

'No thanks. And he's not my boy friend. I wonder what Kostadis is like?'

'Human dynamo. Rat-racer, they say. Tell you what. I'll come ashore in the six o'clock launch. Meet you at the Royal at six-thirty. We'll have dinner and do a flick.'

'Oh, super.' She rolled off the settee, stood up, put her arms round his neck and kissed him. 'Darling. That's nice of you.' She wriggled, pressed her body against his. 'Love me, George,' she whispered. 'Please love me.'

He picked her up, took her to the sleeping cabin, put her on the bed and lay down beside her. He kissed her breasts and whispered, 'Know what . . .'

The R/T on the cabin table blared unexpectedly. 'Two-Oh. Two-Oh. Come in.' It was Jarrett's voice.

Foley swore, went across to the table, picked up the set. 'I read you, Mate.'

32

'Come along to the cargo control-room, Two-Oh. Make it snappy. We've a problem.'

'Okay. I'll be along.'

Foley groaned, put on his shirt, shoes and hard hat, and hung the strap of the R/T round his neck. 'That bloody man,' he said fiercely. 'Can't stop chasing me.'

'This goddam ship,' she agreed. 'Isn't it typical? Not a shred of privacy. That R/T never lets you alone, day or night. Can't you do something about it?' She picked up the magazine again. 'Sorry, darling. Not your fault. But it drives me berserk.'

He looked at her in despair, shrugged his shoulders and left the cabin. When he'd gone she stopped reading, lay staring at the deckhead. Next time, she was thinking, next time I'm alone with Freeman Jarrett he'll hear about this. She gave a little chuckle and turned on her side.

During the afternoon a launch came out to the ship from the Point Ferry Jetty. In it were Lars Hammarsen the agent and Nicolas Kostadis the marine-superintendent. He had arrived from Zurich that day. They were met at the head of the gangway by the chief officer and at once taken to the Master's suite where Captain Crutchley and Mr McLintoch were waiting for them.

Since both men knew the marine-superintendent well, the formalities of greeting were soon over. Kostadis lost no time in explaining the Board's concern at what had happened, emphasizing that the breakdown could not have come at a worse moment, a fact well known to his audience. They proceeded then to discuss the cause and explicit nature of the breakdown, McLintoch expressing the view that it would not have occurred had the third engineer kept a sufficiently sharp eye on the systems-state consoles. Kostadis questioned the chief engineer about the work so far done by the contractors. McLintoch told him that Marinreparat were adhering to the schedule prepared in consultation with him. Work was going ahead steadily and the task of fitting and testing the new rotor when it arrived should not exceed the estimate of five days. During this discussion the Goanese second steward, Figureido, arrived with tea, served it quietly and left as unobtrusively as he had come.

After tea, at Captain Crutchley's suggestion, McLintoch took Kostadis to his own office where they went more thoroughly into the technical aspects of the repair work. Later they joined a number of ship's officers in the bar-lounge, Kostadis having expressed a desire to meet them.

The marine-superintendent was a lean man with deep-set eyes in a long pale face, thick greying hair and a prominent nose. He combined a relaxed manner with darting eyes and an unusually quick mind. Before coming ashore to take up the duties of marine-superintendent he'd served in the company's ships as a chief engineer. He had, while at sea, sent a confidential report direct to the chairman – whom he'd not met – alleging certain malpractices by the then marine-superintendent. Not long afterwards that official was dismissed and Kostadis took his place.

In the years that followed he'd established a close relationship with the chairman. This had not only enriched him materially but made him a man to be admired, cultivated and feared by those who worked for the company. Among the facets of this complex character, was an ability to be as charming as he could be ruthless when occasion demanded.

Talking to the officers and their wives in the bar-lounge that afternoon he was all charm. Those who had not met him before felt that many of the stories about him must have been less than fair.

It was not long before they heard him utter the boast for which he was famous: 'For me,' he'd said with an enigmatic smile, 'there's only one loyalty . . . the company. What is good for the company is good for those who serve it. That's why its interests must always come first.' He used the word 'company' with a sort of religious fervour, as if referring to a higher entity.

He did not add that a man who shared those convictions was Kurt Raustadt, the managing-director.

Chapter 5

It was a fine autumn day, cold and crisp, with streaks of cirrus hanging like fractured vapour trails in the blue sky. Looking down from the pine-covered slopes of the Adlisberg over to Uetliberg the lake in the valley between lay dark and tranquil, its further reaches stretching up to Rapperswil. Clustered around its northern end the bustling streets and crowded buildings of Zurich, the elegant shops, discreet banks, well-dressed women and sleek cars along the Bahnhofstrasse, suggested an opulence, an almost limitless wealth somewhat out of character for this bastion of Protestantism at the time of the Reformation. To the chairman of Inter-Ocean Crude and Bulk Carriers Ltd., neither the view nor the limitless wealth was impressive. On the contrary, he was displeased with both for only that morning a consortium of Swiss banks had refused, courteously but unequivocally, to renegotiate the terms of the loan. Thus he looked over the Zurich See with a jaundiced eye while the managing-director lined up a putt on the eighth green and stroked the ball towards the hole. It came to rest just short of the lip.

'Right,' said the chairman. 'I give you that.'

Raustadt picked up the ball. 'And they refused absolutely?'

'Absolutely.' The two men set off down the path between the conifers to the next tee. 'Now we have no option.' The chairman paused. 'When do you see him?'

'Tonight. He's staying at the Baur au Lac. Came in this morning.'

'You must not be seen together.'

'No fear of that, it'll be dark. He'll be waiting in Belvuestrasse, near the lake. I'll drive past, pick him up and we'll go to Rehalp. Park in the woods there and talk.'

'You are certain of him, Kurt. Reliability? Discretion?'

They arrived at the next tee. 'Still your honour,' said the chairman.

Kurt Raustadt teed up, took a practice swing, settled his stance and struck the ball.

'Fine drive, Kurt. Are you sure of him?'

'Yes. Quite sure. Don't forget, he stands to make a lot of money.'

'Of course.' The chairman bent down to tee his ball. 'Now let's see,' he muttered, steadying himself as he addressed it. His swing was stiff, uneven, without the grace and suppleness of the younger man's. The ball went into the trees. 'For God's sake,' he complained. 'Why do I have to do that?'

'Play a provisional,' suggested the managing-director. 'And slow down the swing. Keep your head down.'

The chairman drove a second ball, straight this time but no great distance. They left the tee and made for the fairway. They came to where the ball lay. The chairman said, 'I'll play this one. Can't be bothered to look for the other.' He took an iron from the bag. 'Has Kostadis decided yet?'

'He has made a short list of three. When our . . .' Raustadt checked himself. 'When he gets there he alone will make the final choice. Kostadis will not know who it is.'

'Good,' said the chairman. 'That is very sensible. Now let's see if I can play a decent shot for a change.'

They finished at the ninth hole and went up on to the terrace of the Dolder Grand. The chairman was spending the night there before returning to Frankfurt. A waiter came to the table. 'Two Scotch-on-the-rocks,' said the chairman.

'Very good, sir.' The waiter flicked ash from the table with a napkin, emptied the ashtray into a carton and took it away.

'Make them doubles,' the chairman called after him. He turned to Raustadt. 'Don't say anything at the meeting tonight. I'll tell them we're approaching the Liechtenstein banks. That until we have their decision we can do nothing. That should keep le Febre and company quiet for a while.'

Raustadt lit a cheroot, threw away the match with an exaggerated flourish. 'Of course,' he said. 'I shall not say a word.'

'When will . . .' the chairman hesitated. 'When will he go?'

'When Kostadis lets me know. In a few days probably.'

'The sooner the better,' said the chairman. 'We haven't much time.'

Nicolas Kostadis's days in Durban were busy. Each morning he went out to *Ocean Mammoth* to discuss the repair work and to attend conferences on board with the people from Marinreparat

36

and the ship's staff. Each day he visited the agent's offices to see Lars Hammarsen, to maintain contacts with the port authorities, the marine surveyors, and others involved in getting the ship back to sea.

He spoke daily by phone to Kurt Raustadt in Zurich and to the company's operating offices in London, exchanging news and progress reports. He constantly urged London to exert pressure on the suppliers of the new HP rotor to speed up its despatch. He entertained often, kept late nights, yet was up early and never seemed to tire. To those on board who had not known him, it soon became apparent why he was known as a human dynamo. The man bubbled with energy, and his quick mind and ready wit made him many friends in *Ocean Mammoth*. Each day, his duties in the ship completed, he would be found in the bar or in officers' cabins, talking and drinking. It was noticeable that the Captain and the chief engineer, the two men who knew him best, though polite and co-operative, remained gently aloof and avoided familiarities.

The deck officers whom Kostadis saw most of were Jarrett and Foley. He had already entertained them to dinner at the Oyster Box, the hotel outside Durban where he was staying. Quick to sense the hostility between them he'd not invited them together. Foley had come with his wife on one occasion, Jarrett alone on another.

It had not taken him long to sum up these men, to see into their minds: Jarrett, ambitious, talented, restless, tired of the sea, eager to make a career ashore; Foley, intelligent, conscientious, lacking in humour, content with life at sea but worried that he could not give his wife the sort of life she wanted. Kostadis found Sandy Foley attractive in a physical, sensual way. A little too provocative, perhaps, but very much the sort of woman men wanted. Foley, he conceded, had a problem. Jarrett was a vital amusing man; Foley himself, though competent, struck Kostadis as rather a bore.

Captain Crutchley was busy in his office writing. He did this slowly in a large hand on ruled paper, stopping at times to peer at what he'd written. He finished a letter, sighed deeply, looked at the time and went through the bedroom to the bathroom. There he took off the dark glasses, bathed his eyes in a solution of warm water and metallic salts, inserted drops from a small blue-capped bottle and massaged the eyeballs with his fingers. These tasks completed he cleaned the dark glasses and went back to his desk.

From a drawer he took a rectangular magnifying glass and re-read the letter. It was to his wife in Farnham – his second and very much younger wife. He'd recorded what little had happened since last he'd written, told of the progress of repair work, of Kostadis's daily visits – *I still mistrust the man and disapprove of an engineer in the post of marine-superintendent. It is essentially a seaman's job. But he is capable and popular, so it must be prejudice on my part.* – He complained that neither Kostadis, Lars Hammarsen, London nor Zurich was yet able to tell him the movements of the ship once repairs were completed – *We've lost the cargo we were chartered for.* – He asked after the two boys at Lancing – *it's good to learn from you that they are well and happy. I could wish that Bobby's results were better. He's certainly intelligent so it must be that he's a late starter or just plain lazy.*

It was then that Captain Crutchley came to the matter so much on his mind: *You ask about my eyes. I'm afraid the news is not good. The conjunctivitis shows little sign of clearing up. I intend to see a specialist here if the trouble continues, but would prefer to wait until I get home. I heard yesterday that Middleton is to be transferred to one of our homeward-bound bulk carriers due here shortly, while young Price is still in hospital and will not be fit for sea for several months, if ever again. This, as you will appreciate, confronts me with a difficult situation. Who knows what the end may be. But do not worry. I'll find a solution.*

He wondered if he would and, if so, what it would be.

There was an unseasonal wind blowing, its gusts rustling the leaves of solitary palm trees, chasing dust and old bits of paper along the roads behind the warehouses at the Point where the launch left the Ferry Jetty on its last trip of the night to thud and splash its way over the dark waters of Natal Bay. Freeman Jarrett, the Foleys, two junior engineers and the catering officer and his wife were crowded together in the sternsheets with a number of crewmen. Some of the Cape Verde Islanders had had too much to drink and the journey soon became a noisy one.

The launch was well on its way and the men had just finished a sad mournful song of the islands when a row erupted suddenly. There were sounds of a scuffle, an exchange of oaths. Though most were in Portuguese, some were sufficiently international for

Jarrett to shout, 'Cut that out, there are ladies on board.' It was dark in the sternsheets and he couldn't see who the troublemakers were. 'I like sleep with the ladies,' announced a cheerful but drunken islander. There were cheers, more scuffles, followed by a hoarse, 'Yes, you like do that, Gomez. You not good Catholic, hey?'

A deep throaty voice which Jarrett recognized as that of Fernandez, the senior quartermaster, delivered a rebuke in Portuguese and the chief officer's heart warmed to the sound of the blow which followed. Fernandez was one of the old hands, a God-fearing man with whom the chief officer had sailed before. The mouthers of the obscenities fell silent and the singing began again, this time a fisherman's song. It stopped when the hull of the tanker loomed up above them like some great mountain growing out of the sea and the launch bumped alongside the foot of the gangway.

Jarrett nudged Foley, spoke in a low voice. 'Let the crewmen go up first. No good standing on ceremony with these drunks around.'

The second officer agreed, whispered to the others, and the crewmen clambered out, struggled up the steep gangway, shouting and laughing. They were followed by the two engineers, then Jarrett, Foley and the catering officer and their wives. As Jarrett got towards the top he heard shouting. He reached the floodlit maindeck to find the way aft blocked by men who'd formed a ragged circle round a fight. He watched for a moment, saw one man fall and lie huddled on the deck as his opponent kicked him. Jarrett forced his way through the circle and grabbed the kicker. The prone man struggled to his feet, drew a knife and staggered towards them.

'Stop him,' shouted Jarrett sharply, but the onlookers showed no desire to become involved. The chief officer hesitated, pushed aside the man he was holding, and kicked the knife wielder in the groin. The man grunted and let the knife go as he fell. His adversary at once jumped forward and began booting him in the face. Once again Jarrett pulled him back. The man broke loose, swung round and struck him. Jarrett, rugged, powerful, shook his head, measured the distance coolly, and let fly a left hook which lifted the man off his feet and landed him on the deck. There he lay, flat on his back, twitching and groaning.

The chief officer picked up the knife, threw it over the side and turned to the onlookers. 'Get those men to their cabins and see there's no more trouble. I'll deal with them in the morning.' A trickle of blood came from his mouth.

Jarrett reached the lift to find the Foleys and the catering officer and his wife waiting there. Jarrett was holding a handkerchief to his face.

'You all right, Mate?' asked the catering officer.

'Okay,' Jarrett breathed heavily. He took the blood-stained handkerchief from his mouth and examined it. 'Serves me right. Should have seen it coming. Especially from a drunken man.'

'You're not all right,' said Sandy firmly. 'That's a most awful gash on your lip.'

'Come on,' Foley said irritably. He was in the lift, his finger on the 'Open Door' button. 'Let's get moving. It's late.'

His wife gave him a withering look as they got in. 'You must let me look at it, Freeman,' she said. 'We'll bathe it with disinfectant. Put something on. You may need stitches.'

'Well, if it does, you can't do them for him. That's for sure.' Foley grinned with satisfaction.

'I'll see to it,' said the catering officer. 'No problem.'

'It's nothing,' said Jarrett quietly. 'Just a split lip.'

When she got down to the cabin Foley was already in bed. He turned on his side, looked at his watch with affected concentration. 'Well, well,' he said. 'So you're back at last.'

'What exactly does that mean?' she challenged.

'You've been in Freeman Jarrett's cabin for more than half an hour.' He paused, glared at her. 'Why did you have to make all that fuss about his lip? If it needed attention the catering officer could have done it. He's got a first aid certificate, which is more than you have.'

She began to undress. 'For your information the catering officer did do it. I happened to be helping him. Any objection?'

'Yes, plenty. A lot of fuss about nothing. The average kid gets a thick lip at least once a term without all that bother.'

She turned on him with angry eyes. 'It was not a thick lip. It was a badly cut one, but you're such a jealous bastard you can't admit it. If it hadn't been for Freeman Jarrett we'd have been stuck at the top of the gangway watching those drink-crazed wretches tearing each other to pieces. Just because you and the

40

others didn't have the guts to stop it, isn't a reason for being unpleasant about the man who did.'

Foley propped himself up on his elbow. 'Couldn't you see that your friend was showing off as usual? Officers aren't supposed to become involved in fights between drunken crewmen. It's asking for trouble and it's bad for discipline.'

'I see,' she said with heavy sarcasm. 'He should have stood there watching them murder each other, like you other brave lads.' She kicked off her shoes. 'If you really want to know what I think, I think it was extremely brave of him.'

'Brave my foot. They were both drunk. Anybody could have laid them out.'

'Well, anybody didn't and he did.' She took off her bra, sat on the edge of the bed peeling off her tights. 'You loathe Jarrett, don't you . . . and you're madly jealous because . . .' She checked herself.

'Because what?' insisted Foley. 'Come on, let's have it. Feel free to speak your mind.'

She looked at him with narrowed eyes, hating him at that moment, wondering how far she could go. 'Because he likes me and I like him. And because he can do things you can't. Like knocking out those two men and preventing God knows what.'

Foley's face was tense and drawn as he pulled the sheet over his shoulder and turned his back on her. 'I hope the bloody lip goes septic,' he muttered.

'That's exactly the rotten sort of thing you would hope,' she said. 'You're all mixed up, aren't you?'

'Oh, for God's sake shut up and turn out the light. I want to go to sleep.'

She got into the bed, turned off the light and lay there thinking. She had remained in the chief officer's cabin after the catering officer had gone. She re-lived those minutes, the things Jarrett had said, the way he'd held her, his cheek against hers because, as he'd explained, 'I can't kiss you with this bloody lip.'

So she had kissed him, given him a final hug, and left the cabin.

It was the breakthrough, and it had been very exciting.

Chapter 6

Nico Kostadis took the dinner bill from the waiter and went on talking while he checked it with the detached air of a man well able to distribute his attention. 'Thank you,' he said replacing it on the salver. 'We'll have coffee and brandies on the terrace. Don't be long.'

'I'll be there, sir.' Kostadis was a generous tipper. A man, the waiter decided, with a large expense account.

Foley followed his host on to the terrace. They sat at a table above the swimming pool, a discreet comfortable place, dimly lit, where the sound of the sea breaking on the rocks below masked conversation. It was a warm night, dark with no moon, and from the lighthouse which stood like a giant sentinel in front of the Oyster Box, a long finger of light swept the sea at regular intervals.

The waiter brought coffee and brandies, Kostadis signed the chit and told him to come again before too long. The two men talked inconsequentially of many things, laughing at times, silent at others. The waiter reappeared occasionally to replenish the brandies and coffee and, inevitably, conversation became more personal as the night wore on.

'If I'm to hold her I've got to leave the sea,' said Foley. 'Make real money. God knows how. And why the hell? Tanker life suits me. The company pays well . . .' He shook his head. 'But . . . I don't know . . .' He left the sentence unfinished, looking into his brandy as if it was in some way involved in his perplexities.

'She doesn't like being left on her own?' Kostadis decided privately that this was probably the misstatement of the year.

'I don't know. I think it's more than that. Her ambitions are way ahead of wife of the second mate of a tanker. She's very status conscious. You know – wants a big house, two cars – Jag for me, Lotus for herself – sort of thing. Holidays at Cannes.' Foley drained the goblet. 'And clothes, my goodness, how she goes for clothes. Expensive ones. No wonder we struggle.'

Kostadis examined the end of his cigar with studied care, sighed audibly. 'You know, George, behind most successful men

42

there's a woman like Sandy. Ambitious, pushing, determined to make her man exploit his potential. It's not a bad thing. It happened to me. I didn't get to where I am without that sort of prodding. Kate wasn't going to end her days as the wife of a tanker engineer and she let me know it.'

'We quarrel a lot,' said Foley gloomily. 'She gets steamed up at the drop of a hat.'

'Sounds like married life,' Kostadis observed dryly. 'Look, George, as marine-superintendent I'm the last person to suggest that you should leave the sea. But you've got a problem. Hell . . . I can see that. At twenty-six you've a lot of life ahead of you. You've already got an Extra Master's Certificate. That's pretty good. Unusual. Shows drive. If you're convinced the only way to hold her is to make good ashore, get on with it. I've no doubt you've got the necessary qualities.' Kostadis leant forward, his voice all the more deliberate. 'Let's be honest. Prospects at sea are worse than they've been for a long time. Bottom's dropped out of the tanker market. Ships are being laid up. *Ocean Mammoth* will probably be one of them soon. We're waiting for a decision. Don't repeat that. It's highly confidential but it's a fact.'

'Christ.' Foley sounded startled. 'That's great, isn't it. Especially with things the way they are ashore. Economy in a mess. Record unemployment. Not much chance of my landing anything.' He grimaced, shrugged his shoulders in a hopeless sort of way. 'Join the dole queue, I suppose.'

Kostadis drank more brandy, drew on this cigar. 'Let me tell you something, George. Pessimism is a coward's philosophy. You never know what's round the corner. Every man is confronted at least once in a lifetime with an exceptional opportunity. It usually comes when least expected and it's not always recognized. The reason why some men succeed where others fail is just *that*. They see the opportunity – and, equally important – ' he paused, looking out to sea, describing an explanatory circle with his cigar, 'they have the courage, the guts if you like, to seize it. To take the risks almost always involved if something big is to be achieved.'

Foley was silent, thoughtful, chin in hand, looking down to the pool where splashing and laughter came from late night bathers. Two men daring a bikini-clad woman to join them. Foley was wondering whether he should tell Kostadis what was on his mind. Make it clear that he hadn't just sat idle, let opportunity slide by.

He decided he would. 'Opportunity's not so easily come by,' he said. 'I don't mind telling you now. Because of Sandy, I've applied for three shore jobs in the last twelve months. One was in the Australian harbour service – another as marine-super to a North Sea oil outfit – and the third for a post with a navigation school in Southampton. In each case an Extra Master's ticket was an essential qualification. In each case my application was turned down.'

Kostadis turned to him, smiled sympathetically. 'There's fierce competition for that sort of job nowadays, George. Always a lot of well-qualified applicants, many with experience of command at sea. But don't give up hope. You never know when opportunity will come knocking at the door.'

'I suppose so,' Foley conceded, lost in private thought.

Kostadis changed the subject. 'You don't like Jarrett. What's the trouble?'

Foley showed surprise. It was the first time Kostadis had mentioned the chief officer, and the question was irrelevant to what they were discussing. 'You know that, do you?' He paused, frowning at the older man. 'Chemistry, I suppose. We're allergic to each other.'

'Nothing else?' The marine-superintendent watched him through half-closed eyes. Foley fidgeted with the stem of the brandy goblet. 'He fancies Sandy. Makes passes at her.'

'She's an attractive woman, George. Of course men are going to notice her.'

'It's more than that. She thinks he is,' he mimicked his wife's accent, *'quite outstanding.'*

Kostadis knocked ash from his cigar. 'He's a very capable man, I'd say. But that's no reason for you to do the jealous husband bit.' He was silent for a moment. 'Would you say he's a dependable man? One who could be relied on?'

Before Foley could answer a man came from the darkness at the lower end of the terrace, walked past their table, turned and came back. 'Nico Kostadis, isn't it?' He held out a hand.

Kostadis stood up, stared at the newcomer doubtfully, then with a sudden laugh took his hand. 'Stefan! What the hell are you doing here?' They shook hands warmly. Kostadis introduced the two men. 'Stefan Suvic – George Foley. Stefan and I haven't seen each other for years. He's from Nicosia. Or used to be. Sit down, Stefan. Have a drink.'

44

A waiter came up, took the order and disappeared. For some time Kostadis and the newcomer monopolized the conversation, exchanging news, enquiring after mutual acquaintances and generally bringing each other up to date. Kostadis explained what had brought him to Durban – that he was staying at the Oyster Box and likely to be there another week. Suvic, it appeared, had flown in the day before on behalf of Iranian principals. 'To sort out a tangled sugar contract,' he said. 'I'm staying at the pub next door.' With a thumb he indicated the massive tower block of the Beverly Hills Hotel. 'I'll be flying back to Teheran shortly. Report to the people there. Then back to Nicosia.'

The waiter came to the table. 'Excuse me, sir,' he said to Kostadis. 'You're wanted on the phone. It's urgent, the caller says.'

Kostadis apologized and hurried off.

'Probably a woman,' suggested Suvic. 'It's always urgent with them.' He was a dark man with a low hairline and an expressive simian face, its seams and folds constantly changing. The mid-European accent suggested Czech or Yugoslav. Foley wasn't sure which, but he decided there was something very likeable about the stranger, whatever the country of origin.

While they waited for Kostadis they exchanged the small talk of men who had just met. Suvic asked Foley what he did and where he was from. He expressed surprise when he learnt that he was second officer of a supertanker. 'Which one?' he enquired.

'*Ocean Mammoth*. The ship Nico Kostadis has been talking about.'

'Is that so? How d'you like the job?'

'Not too bad. Has its snags like everything else.'

The conversation turned to the forthcoming OPEC price increase, the state of the tanker market, the North Sea oil bonanza, and efforts in the West to develop alternative power sources.

Suvic was an interesting, well-informed man and Foley was disappointed when Kostadis came back. It meant he had to take a back seat again.

'Sorry,' said the marine-superintendent. 'It was Hoffman of Marinreparat. The new rotor will be delivered to the ship tomorrow morning.'

'Thank God for that,' said Foley. 'It's been a long time coming.'

For Suvic's benefit Kostadis explained briefly the repair

45

problem, more drinks were ordered, and the three men sat talking to a late hour. Before they parted Suvic had invited them to dinner at Beverly Hills on the following night.

'I'd like that,' said Foley. 'But I'll have to clear it with my wife.' He grinned apologetically. 'Two consecutive nights out on my own, you know.'

'Of course,' said Suvic. 'I understand.' He looked at his watch. 'And now if you'll excuse me, gentlemen, I must go. I have much work tomorrow.'

When he'd gone Foley said, 'Nice chap. What does he do for a living?'

'Visiting fireman,' said Kostadis.

'What's that?'

'Trouble-shooter, fixer. When the big boys have a problem they send for him. He fixes it. That's how he made his money.'

'What's his nationality?'

'Czech. But he's lived in Cyprus for years.'

It was close to one o'clock when Kostadis saw Foley to the car which he'd organized for the second officer's journey back into Durban. 'You'll find the Marinreparat launch waiting for you at the Point Ferry Jetty. I fixed it with them this afternoon.'

'Thanks very much, Nico. And thanks for the dinner. It was great.'

'Glad you enjoyed it,' said Kostadis. 'See you tomorrow.'

A tug towing a lighter arrived alongside *Ocean Mammoth* early in the afternoon of the following day. It made fast abreast the after superstructure on the port side, the ship's gantry crane was run out to plumb the lighter, and the HP rotor was lifted clear. Sandy Foley, watching the operation with two other wives, was surprised how relatively small this much discussed and important piece of machinery was. About three and a half feet in diameter, she estimated, and four or five feet long. But it was heavy and had to be handled carefully. From the top of the gantry it was hauled inboard along the overhead transverse crane which travelled across the beam of the ship through the superstructure housing at maindeck level. Once amidships the rotor was transferred to the fore-and-aft overhead crane which traversed the length of the engineroom. When it was immediately above the HP turbine casing it was lowered gently into position and the contractors began the work of fitting.

The arrival of the new rotor had a remarkable and tonic effect on morale. There was cheerful chatter, laughter and an air of happy expectation throughout the ship. It was as if a great weight had been lifted from the shoulders of those on board. It was, in fact, no more than the old truth that delays in harbour make for restless sailors and a longing for the sea, for getting on with the voyage which must at its end bring them home.

Kostadis had arranged to meet George Foley on the verandah of the Royal Hotel to drive him out to Umhlanga Rocks where they were to dine with Stefan Suvic.

When Kostadis arrived he was full of apologies. 'Sorry, old chap. I can't make it tonight. Have to attend a conference with the Marinreparat people and the marine surveyors. We've a problem to sort out. My driver will take you to the Beverly Hills. Tell Stefan I'll come along after dinner if we finish early enough.'

They evidently didn't finish early enough, because Kostadis hadn't turned up by eleven o'clock when Foley bade Suvic good-night and got into the car which was to take him to the Ferry Jetty in time for the eleven-thirty launch.

Not that Kostadis's absence had in any way detracted from a memorable evening. On the contrary, the dinner had been unusually good and Stefan Suvic had proved to be an entertaining host with interesting and important things to say. Afterwards, on the journey back into Durban, Foley realized how fortunate it was that the marine-superintendent had been otherwise engaged.

Chapter 7

Two days after the new turbine rotor had been delivered to *Ocean Mammoth*, Captain Crutchley, Kostadis and Lars Hammarsen were discussing ship's business in the Master's dayroom.

'We're now two assistant stewards short,' said the Captain. 'Transferred one to the bulk carrier with Middleton last week. We've managed without him, but this morning we discharged Alvarez to hospital. Acute duodenal ulcer. Bad, they say. We'll need a replacement before sailing.'

Kostadis said, 'Can you manage that, Lars?'

'Yes. I'll see to it.' Hammarsen made an entry in his notebook. 'I've a man in mind.'

'Who's that?' enquired the Captain.

'Remember Beau Rivage? Where we lunched on Sunday.'

'Yes. Up on the ridge.'

'The waiter who looked after us. Piet Pieterse. He's the man.'

Captain Crutchley appeared doubtful, but said nothing.

'I've been using Beau Rivage for several years,' went on Hammarsen. 'He's always looked after me well. For the last few months he's been begging me to find him a ship. Wants to get to Europe. Comes from the Cape. His brother got into some sort of political trouble and is in prison. That was the last straw for Pieterse. He wants to get out.'

Kostadis looked up from under bushy eyebrows. 'Will the authorities let him go?'

'Yes. I know the people here. There won't be any problem. He has a clean sheet. No trade union snags either, with the ship Cypriot-registered.'

'I see.' Captain Crutchley was thoughtful. 'When will he join?'

'The day before sailing,' said Hammarsen. 'In say three or four days. Can you manage until then?'

'We'll have to,' said the Captain.

Kostadis looked at his watch, stood up. 'Don't move, gentlemen. I've an appointment with the marine surveyor and the contractors at eleven-thirty. Must go now.'

'Very well,' said Captain Crutchley. 'There's not much left to discuss.'

When Kostadis had gone, Hammarsen said, 'There's a hardworking go-getter for you. No wonder he's so highly thought of in Zurich.'

'A busy man.' The Captain said it with studious indifference. 'What about the other half?'

'Thank you. Gin and tonic.' Hammarsen handed over his glass. Crutchley refilled it from the silver salver on the coffee table between the armchairs and passed it back.

'Not having another, Captain?'

Crutchley held up his half-finished drink. 'Still going strong.'

Hammarsen looked at him curiously, wondering what was going on behind the dark glasses. He had long ago decided that this was a strange, unpredictable man – a loner if ever there was one. 'So McLintoch is happy with the progress of the repair work,' he prompted.

'Satisfied. Not happy.'

'Any doubts about keeping to the provisional sailing date? The twenty-sixth?'

'No,' said Crutchley.

Hammarsen raised his glass. 'Cheers then, Captain. That's good. I'll confirm with the port authorities this afternoon. If that meets with your approval.' He took a printed form from his briefcase, unfolded it and inserted the date. 'Provisional notification of departure,' he said. 'Doesn't commit us and we don't have to indicate a time until the day before sailing. Even then it's subject to final confirmation. Has to be signed by the Master. I wonder if you'd mind?'

Captain Crutchley took the form, pulled himself out of the armchair. 'I'll get my pen,' he said.

Hammarsen took one from his pocket. 'Use mine, Captain.'

'Thank you. I'll get my own.' The Captain went through to the bedroom, took off his dark glasses and studied the form with a magnifying glass. Satisfied, he signed it.

He went back to the dayroom, handed it to Hammarsen. 'Our future movements. Still no news?'

'None, I'm afraid.' Hammarsen nodded sympathetically. 'Kostadis says London and Zurich are making every effort to find a charter. I'm afraid these are difficult times.'

Through his sun-glasses Captain Crutchley tried to read the

blurred image of the agent's face but he could find no clue there to the truth he suspected. No subtlety of expression came through but perhaps that was because of the blurring.

'The agents in the Gulf are trying, too,' Hammarsen was saying. 'Without success it seems.' Over the Captain's shoulder he could see through a window to the blue waters of the Bay. 'Even if there's no charter by sailing date, you can always be diverted at sea.'

'Yes,' said Captain Crutchley. 'We can.'

Hammarsen held up his drink. 'Anyway. Let's drink to a successful voyage.'

The Captain nodded as if that were toast enough, drained his glass and replaced it somewhat noisily on the salver. He hoped the gesture would encourage Hammarsen to leave. Only when he had could Crutchley go to the bathroom, attend to his eyes and take something for the headache which had grown more severe as the morning proceeded.

A breeze came through the open windows of Beau Rivage high on the ridge above the Umgeni River, and table candles flickered discreetly on the faces of the diners. To the south the lights of the city shone anonymously, their glittering pattern ruled off abruptly in the east by the dark flank of the Indian Ocean.

'Marvellous view.' Suvic pointed with his cheroot to the south.

'Absolutely marvellous,' agreed Jarrett. 'And poor old *Ocean Mammoth* somewhere down there in that sea of light.'

'Surely not old and poor. New and worth fifty million dollars I gather.' Suvic coughed, half choked, frowned at the cheroot. 'That's a lot of money,' he finished hoarsely.

Behind the dissonant voices and sudden bursts of laughter, taped music wove a thin pattern of sound. Suvic looked at the cut on Jarrett's lip. 'Still worrying you?'

Jarrett touched it with a finger. 'Not really.'

'What happened to the man?'

'He was logged and fined.'

A waiter appeared from behind the folds of a drawn curtain, took the wine from the ice-bucket and refilled their glasses. 'Coffee, gentlemen?'

'Please.' Suvic looked at Jarrett. 'Port or brandy?'

'Brandy,' said Jarrett.

50

'Make it two,' said Suvic. The waiter returned the wine bottle to the ice-bucket and disappeared.

Suvic said, 'Good man. Always around when you want him. Never says an unnecessary word, gets on with the job and knows when to smile.'

Jarrett smiled. 'You sound like a restaurateur.'

'I know quite a lot about waiters,' said Suvic. 'Most of it not to their credit.'

'I'll tell you something,' said Jarrett. 'He's a Cape coloured. The only waiter I've seen here tonight who isn't Indian.'

'What's a Cape coloured?'

'Half-caste. Mostly from the Cape. The remnants of colonization.' Jarrett lit the cheroot Suvic offered him, drew on it. 'How did you find this place, Stefan?'

'Nico Kostadis told me of it. His agent Hammarsen put him on to it. Don't you remember the discussion? The other night when I bumped into you and Nico at the Oyster Box. That chat about Durban's alleged night life?'

Jarrett shook his head. 'I don't remember that, I'm afraid. Haven't found the night life, anyway.'

Suvic watched him through a haze of blue smoke. 'You'd gone off to pee perhaps.'

'Maybe.'

The waiter came back with the coffee and brandies. 'Black or white, sir?'

'Black for me,' said Suvic.

'Fifty-fifty,' said Jarrett. 'I like it coloured.' He winked at the waiter who smiled but said nothing.

In the boardroom off the Seefeldstrasse a meeting had just concluded. It had been a difficult, gloomy affair. Among other things, Kurt Raustadt had reported on his telephone conversation with Kostadis in Durban that morning. Repair work in *Ocean Mammoth*'s engineroom was well in hand, and should be completed within the next few days. But that was the only good news, if indeed it was good news since there was no employment for the ship.

As for the rest, it was anything but good: the Liechtenstein banks, said the chairman, had proved as unco-operative as the Zurich consortium. Urgent attempts to raise finance in Paris,

51

London, Frankfurt, New York, Tel Aviv and Bahrain had all met with the same chilly response. Bankers were in no mood to rescue tanker owners in a faltering economic climate and with so much tonnage unemployed.

'It seems,' said the chairman despondently, 'that we have come to the end of the road. Short of a miracle we face the unpleasant reality of liquidation.'

Le Febre, having expressed his customary concern that the caution he'd so long advocated had been flouted, finished with, 'The disastrous results of that disregard are now plain for all to see.' He sat back with the injured dignity of a prophet without honour in his own country.

The chairman forced an astringent smile. 'No one likes liquidation, my dear le Febre, but it is not the end of the world. Your personal shareholding is no more than nominal, if I remember correctly?'

'The holdings of those I represent are anything but nominal,' rasped the Frenchman. 'And much of the institutional money comes from the savings of small investors.'

'Then I suggest you leave the grief to them.' The chairman gathered his mobile features into the affected smile of a man who knows he's made a quick kill. 'And now,' he said, 'I would like to get on with the business of the meeting.'

That business was fairly quickly dealt with: one, *Ocean Mammoth* was to return to the United Kingdom in ballast for laying-up in a Scottish loch, her crew to be paid off on arrival in the Clyde and informed that there were no prospects of re-employment in the foreseeable future. Two, there was to be another meeting in a week's time when the Board would consider the liquidation report to be drawn up by Raustadt in consultation with the company's auditors and legal advisers.

On this gloomy note they had broken up, the chairman and deputy-chairman remaining in the boardroom after the others, including the staff, had left.

'Shall we go through to my office?' suggested the managing-director.

'Of course, Kurt,' said the chairman. 'Let us do that.'

In a bay window on the south side of the managing-director's office, the three men sat in leather easy chairs, their faces pallid in the light from green shaded lamps on tall stands behind them.

The chairman leant forward, hands grasping the arms of the chair, his lined features troubled. 'Is he sure he's picked the right man, Kurt?'

'Yes. Quite sure.'

The deputy-chairman, bald, hunched, came upright with the sudden jerk of a glove puppet. 'I dare say. But are *we* sure?'

Kurt Raustadt smoothed his thick black hair with what was intended as a reassuring gesture but which his listeners took to be nervousness – it was in fact both. 'How can *we* be sure? We have to be guided by those on the spot.'

'You are absolutely certain we cannot be involved?' The chairman's gathered brow and narrowed eyes reflected a concern which went to the marrow of his being.

'Yes. Absolutely. Only he knows who has been selected. No one else. Not us. Not even Kostadis. The matter will be handled by three different Swiss banks. He will send instructions to them as from three different clients. From Cairo, Barcelona and Algiers. In no way can they be traced to us.'

The chairman drew on his cigar, expelled the blue-grey smoke and watched it absent-mindedly on its slow climb to the ceiling.

'The deposit,' he said. 'Is that in hand?'

'Yes. He has a bearer receipt with him. To be completed and handed over on acceptance.'

'That's no guarantee of fulfilment.' The deputy-chairman's tone was belligerent.

'True enough,' conceded Raustadt. 'But it buys confidence. That's an important ingredient.'

'A great deal of money is involved,' said the chairman. 'He must be successful.' He unclasped his hands, sat upright, drumming on his knees with his fingers. 'Now let's change the subject. Something more pleasant. A drink for example, Kurt?'

'Of course, Chairman.' The managing-director walked over to the Louis XV rosewood corner cupboard, unlocked and opened its curved door. 'What would you like?'

'Scotch-on-the-rocks, Kurt.'

'Me, too,' said the deputy-chairman.

The managing-director sighed audibly. 'At least that problem is capable of solution.'

Chapter 8

Monday, 25 October, promised to be an important day for *Ocean Mammoth*. The engineroom repairs had been completed and the day was devoted to testing the new turbine rotor and shaft coupling while the ship was still alongside. All being well she would sail from Durban at five-thirty that afternoon. To what destination was as yet unknown.

The atmosphere of expectation and excitement which these events inspired was at its height when Captain Crutchley spoke over the ship's broadcast at 0930.

'Attention all hands. This is the Captain speaking. As you know the ship is due to sail at five-thirty this afternoon. Until half an hour ago I did not know our destination. At nine o'clock I received a message from the agents ashore repeating one received from London. Here it is: On leaving Durban *Ocean Mammoth* is to proceed at three-quarters speed to the Clyde to be laid up until such time as the charter market for crude oil carriers has recovered. The crew will be paid off on arrival at the Clyde. The management regrets there is no prospect of their re-employment in the foreseeable future. Those who are on contract will be dealt with on a redundancy basis.

'That,' said Captain Crutchley, 'is the end of the message. I can only say how deeply I regret having to convey such news to you.'

The broadcast shed gloom throughout the ship and confirmed for Crutchley his original foreboding that nothing good would come of the Durban visit.

The day of sailing is always a busy one for a ship's master, and there was a steady stream of people to see Captain Crutchley, most of them with documents to be signed: port and health officials, representatives of the contractors, Lloyds agents, the marine surveyors, ship's chandlers, the media and many others. Somehow he managed to cope with them, to sign where he was required to sign, to offer a drink where custom demanded he should, to be as businesslike yet courteous as befitted the Master.

At times, between the arrival and departure of one official visitor and another, he would go to the bathroom and attend to his eyes. Yet despite this, they became more inflamed and the accompanying headaches more persistent as the day proceeded.

Somehow, too, he found time in the course of this busy day to write to his wife for he felt it was important she should learn from him and not from rumour what lay in store for *Ocean Mammoth* and those who served in her.

He did not, however, tell her the result of his visit to the ophthalmic surgeon two days earlier. The news he had sent her was, he felt, bad enough without that.

During the afternoon the chief engineer and the contractor's representative informed the Captain that tests of the new turbine rotor and shaft coupling had shown that certain adjustments were necessary. It was expected these would be completed by midnight. Captain Crutchley telephoned Lars Hammarsen and the port authorities and the time of sailing was put back to 0530 the following morning. The Captain decided to adhere to his decision that there should be no further shore leave before sailing.

Later that day *Ocean Mammoth*'s refilled swimming pool, discreetly sited against the engineroom housing on the port side aft, was once again in use. It was a hot day and the sun shone down from a cloudless sky. There were only two bathers at the pool. Both were women, and they lay on li-los at opposite ends as if they had gone to some pains to get as far as possible from each other, which was indeed the case. Around them lay bathing towels, caps, sun-tan oils, periodicals, paperbacks and transistors.

Sandy lay on her back, a straw hat over her eyes, a cassette recorder at her side purring Abba music. She was almost asleep when Jarrett, who'd been inspecting mooring lines and winches in the stern, arrived silently. He put his hard hat and R/T set on the bench, took out a handkerchief, mopped his face and considered the almost nude figure at his feet.

'Hi,' he said.

She started, pushed the sun-hat away from her eyes and saw him. 'Hi, Freeman. Come to swim?' She turned down the volume on the recorder.

'Not bloody likely. Too busy, love. Heard the buzz about sailing?'

'Yes. It was broadcast. Five-thirty tomorrow morning.'

He looked towards where Doris Benson lay at the far end. 'She may be asleep,' he said, 'but turn up that volume again in case she isn't.'

The volume went up and Abba delivered their message of love more loudly. 'That's better,' he said. 'Now I can tell you what's on my mind.'

'What is it?'

He dropped his voice. 'A very important message. You've got a beautiful body. It's a challenge. It does things to me.'

She laughed happily. 'Thank you, sir. You do things to me.'

He leant closer. 'How about doing them now?'

'Freeman! How can you suggest such a thing to a respectable married woman.' She folded her hands on her breasts in a gesture of modesty. He looked at her with half-closed eyes, speculating, trying to read her thoughts. 'Has George any clue about our lunches?'

She shook her head. 'Definitely not. And let's keep it like that.'

'A room with a view,' he said. 'Remember?'

'Can I ever forget? Fabulous view over the sea.'

'I didn't see much of that. There was a lot else to look at.'

'Don't be so basic, Freeman. Anyway, stop it. You're turning me on.' She sat up, put on her sun-hat, clasped her hands round her knees. 'What are you going to do when we get back to the UK?'

'I'm not worrying. You know I'm fed up with this life. I've wanted to make the break for a long time. Now the decision's made for me. On balance I like that.'

She looked at him with concerned, affectionate eyes. 'It's a terribly bad time to be looking for a job.'

He stood up, stretched and yawned. 'I'll be okay, Sandy. Something worthwhile will turn up. It always does. I was born under a lucky star.'

'I hope it does, Freeman. I hope you were.'

The R/T set on the bench came alive. It was the Captain requesting the chief officer to report at once to his office.

'Bloody hell,' said Jarrett. 'Man can't even chat up a girl friend.' He put on the hard hat, picked up the R/T, put the leather strap round his neck.

''Bye now, Sandy. Look after the body beautiful.'

'Don't you ever think of anything else?'

'Not often where you're concerned.' He smiled, blew her a discreet kiss and made for the accommodation housing.

The atmosphere in *Ocean Mammoth*'s bar-lounge that evening was a mixture of gloom and gaiety. There was relief that the long stay in Durban was about to end, that uncertainty about the ship's destination and the crew's employment had gone, and some comfort that they were homeward bound. But those thoughts were overshadowed by the realities of their situation, the knowledge that at the journey's end the ship would be laid up and they would have to face the problem of unemployment.

Kostadis and Lars Hammarsen, only too well aware of these feelings among the ship's officers, did their best to instil some sort of optimism as they made their farewells.

'Look,' said Kostadis, facing those nearest him at the bar. 'Tanker markets recover as quickly as they collapse. We've seen it before and we'll see it again.'

'Not much comfort when you're out of a job,' said Foley.

'You'll have your redundancy hand-out,' Kostadis reminded him. 'That should see you through the worst of it.'

'Three months' pay? You must be joking. And my wife expecting,' declared Jerry Whitelot recklessly, his voice thick with whisky. 'That's a fine bloody prospect.'

'We're a small company and a young one.' Kostadis's eyes narrowed. He didn't like criticism of the company, implied or otherwise. 'We do our best for you but we don't control the world's tanker market.'

'Some of the circulars from Head Office give the impression you try to.' Freeman Jarrett smiled sardonically, looked into his tankard. 'But let's cheer up. Things are never as bad as they seem.'

'A damn sight worse, usually,' suggested George Foley.

'They are if you care to make them that way.'

'Meaning what?' challenged Foley.

'Anything you like to think.' Jarrett turned his back on the second officer, slid his tankard across the counter. 'I'll have the same again.'

The steward filled it, passed it back.

Lars Hammarsen, sensing the tension, lifted his glass. 'Here's to you, gentlemen. And to you, ladies,' he added as Sandy Foley and Doris Benson joined them. '*Bon voyage*, and may the future not be as black as it looks.'

'Hear, hear!' Kostadis raised the tankard and his long nose almost disappeared into it.

At a nearby table Abu Seku, a young Ghanaian, one of several fifth engineers on board – the 'fivers' – raised his tankard to his Welsh colleague. 'Balls,' he said, 'to all agents, ship owners, oil sheiks and other exploiters of the working classes.'

'A fine sentiment, Abu,' said Gareth Lloyd, who was also a 'fiver'. 'I'll drink to that. Balls to the lot of them.' He drained the tankard in two mighty gulps. 'Thank Christ I'll be home soon and along to Cardiff Arms to see the Welsh massacre the bloody English.'

'Another fine sentiment,' said the Ghanaian. 'Racist bastards. Let's have the next pint.'

At the bar Jarrett was ordering a gin and tonic. He took it over to Sandy Foley. 'Have a good swim?' he asked in a low voice.

'Marvellous,' she whispered.

'Meet any interesting people?'

'Yes. A handsome stranger.'

'Nice guy?'

She eyed him mischievously over the edge of her glass. 'Dishy,' she said. 'In spite of a cut lip.'

'Watch it. Men like that are dangerous.'

'That's what makes them attractive.'

He dropped his voice. 'See you. Here comes George.' He went over to Kostadis and Hammarsen.

'Enjoying his drink?' George Foley came up and looked at his wife with studious calm.

'Yes. I always enjoy G and T.'

'Especially when our *friend* pays for it.'

'Oh, for Christ's sake, George! Grow up. Can't he buy me a drink without you being unpleasant?'

'I was up on the bridge this afternoon.'

'Were you? Doing what?'

'Watching you and him chatting each other up beside the pool.'

'So that's a crime, is it?'

'What were you talking about?'

'The future. What he proposes to do when we get back. Anything else you'd like to know?'

58

'Yes. Whether you're telling the truth.'

She turned her back on him and joined Doris Benson. It was just about the most provocative thing she could do because he knew she couldn't stand the second engineer's wife.

Hammarsen and Kostadis, having said their goodbyes, left the bar-lounge and made their way to the Master's suite for a formal leavetaking and farewell drink. They found the chief engineer with the Captain.

The four men discussed briefly the final stages of the repair work, McLintoch assuring them that there would be no further delays. They got on to the ship's departure the next morning. 'The Port Captain's providing three harbour tugs,' said Captain Crutchley. 'Pilot's boarding at 0515.'

'Good.' Kostadis raised his glass, his deep-set eyes fixed on the Captain. 'Here's to a successful voyage.'

'I'll second that,' said Hammarsen, raising his. McLintoch did the same, but Crutchley left his glass on the salver. '*Safe* would be more appropriate than successful,' he said.

Kostadis searched the weathered features for some indication of what lay behind the remark but the dark glasses baffled him and he knew Crutchley too well to ask for an explanation. He had long sensed the Captain's reservations about him and put them down to a seaman's disapproval of an engineer filling the post of marine-superintendent.

'Well.' Hammarsen looked at his watch, stood up. 'We must be going, I'm afraid. Did Pieterse report aboard this morning?'

'Yes,' said Crutchley. 'I've signed him on.'

Hammarsen nodded approval. 'No doubt you made it clear he'll be out of a job when you reach the other side?'

'I did.'

'It suits him,' explained Hammarsen. 'He wants to get out.'

'Yes.' Captain Crutchley stared at the agent. 'I know.'

The chief officer escorted the departing visitors down to the maindeck and along the pipe-lined catwalk towards the gangway. He thanked them for all they had done to help the ship and make the stay in Durban an agreeable one. Kostadis assured him it had been a pleasure. 'I only wish,' he said with a lugubrious expression, 'that we were saying goodbye under happier circumstances. But we'll be seeing you again before long. As soon as the market recovers *Ocean Mammoth* will be brought back into service and you'll be hearing from us. In the meantime the best of luck to you.'

Hammarsen endorsed these sentiments, there were warm handshakes, and the two men went down the gangway to the waiting launch.

Jarrett, busy with his thoughts, watched it for some time as it made its way towards the Point. 'I'm going to *need* the best of luck,' he muttered. 'All very well for you lot. Nice cushy jobs ashore.'

He thought once again about the letter he'd seen Foley hand Kostadis a few minutes earlier. They'd been waiting for the lift on Deck One and he'd heard the second officer say, 'Would you mind posting this? It's to do with what we discussed recently.'

Kostadis had smiled understandingly. 'Of course,' he'd said, and put it in his briefcase.

Chapter 9

To seaward, across the sweep of dark water, the rim of the sun showed pink above the cloudbank and along the seafront shorelights winked in the haze of early morning. A dawn breeze ruffled the sea and the supertanker, caught in the rhythm of the swell, rolled ponderously as befitted her great size.

Out on the wing of the bridge Captain Crutchley looked astern to where the pilot cutter was making its way into Durban harbour. 'Thank God,' he said to himself, 'that we're at sea at last.'

Crutchley was a rational, well-balanced man, but years of confrontation with the elements had left him with that respect for superstition which is common among those who spend their lives at sea and it was woven deeply into the fabric of his world.

It had long worried him that the great ship he was so proud to command had been launched from the builder's yards on a Friday the 13th – and on the outward voyage, in the South Atlantic, a dead albatross had been found on the maindeck at dawn one morning. These were ominous portents and indeed it had proved an unlucky voyage: the breakdown, Price's accident, the loss of the charter, the decision to recall and lay-up the ship, the exacerbation of his personal problem. He wondered what the voyage homeward held in store.

In the meantime the vibrations of the hull, the creaking of the huge superstructure, the hum of machinery, the clicking of gyro-repeaters, were to him welcome reminders that *Ocean Mammoth*, so long inanimate, was once again alive. These things, the sounds, the smells, the feelings, the fresh sea air he breathed, were the parameters of his environment. For the first time since the breakdown he began to feel secure, at peace notwithstanding what might lie ahead.

He left the bridge and went into the wheelhouse, to the front windows, without so much as a glance at the officers and quartermasters there. He had an enormous capacity for not noticing people. For some time he stood, large and silent, his head raised as if listening, his attention focused it seemed on something far beyond the forward sweep of the maindeck.

Aware of the Captain's habits, his men waited patiently knowing he would speak when necessary, that he disapproved of small talk on the bridge while the ship was manoeuvring.

At last he broke the silence. 'Ship's head now, Mr Jarrett?'

'One-three-five, sir.'

'Starboard easy, then. Bring her round to one-five-zero.' His deep voice had the assurance of long experience in command.

The chief officer repeated the order, the quartermaster turned the small horseshoe wheel – more appropriate to the cockpit of an airliner than the wheelhouse of a supertanker – and the gyro-repeater on the steering stand ticked off the degrees. Later the quartermaster checked the swing of the ship's head, waited, then reported. 'Steady on one-five-zero, sir.'

The chief officer acknowledged the report. Captain Crutchley continued to look straight ahead. 'Time, Mr Foley?'

The second officer glanced at his wristwatch, checked with the clock on the console. 'Six-thirty-two, sir.'

'Bearing and distance of Coopers?'

Foley went over to the TM radar, switched to the six-mile range, checked the speed and gyro input, looked into the display. 'Bearing two-five-eight, distance three point four miles, sir.'

'Check that by gyro compass, Mr Foley.'

Foley went to the starboard wing, trained the bearing plate and prism of the gyro-repeater on Coopers, then on the South Breakwater. In the chartroom he plotted the bearings, drew a neat circle at their point of intersection, noted the time against it. With dividers he measured the distance. Allowing for the movement of the ship it more or less confirmed the radar position.

Next, with the assistance of the standby quartermaster, he got on with the departure routine: gyro-repeaters had to be checked against the master-gyro, gyro and magnetic compass readings compared, engine data on the wheelhouse console checked with the engineroom, state of ship and fire warning systems checked, bridge movements and deck logbooks written up and much else attended to.

The engines were still on manoeuvring speed, the steering on manual. Foley, who'd laid off the courses for the journey down the South African coast, knew those states would be maintained until Coopers was abeam, approximately five miles distant.

Not long after half past six Coopers came abeam, distant 5·4 miles, course was altered to 206 degrees and at 0640 Captain

Crutchley gave the long awaited order 'Full-away', adding, 'Confirm with the engineroom that we want only three-quarters speed. Bring her up to sixty revs – see how that goes.'

Foley phoned the engine control-room, started the electric log and set the figures on the course-to-steer indicator. He went to the Decca Navigator, took the lane co-ordinates from the digital display and plotted the position on the chart. He phoned the radio office, gave Tim Feeny the ship's position and a time check. He got back to the wheelhouse just as Captain Crutchley ordered, 'Engage auto-steering.'

The quartermaster shifted the switch on the steering stand from manual to auto. 'Auto-steering engaged, sir. Course two-zero-six.'

The chief officer ordered the lowering of the flags flown on departure, leaving only the Cypriot ensign aloft: the flag-of-convenience, the full extent of which convenience was known only to those in Zurich who controlled the destiny of *Ocean Mammoth*.

Jarrett handed over the bridge watch to the third officer at eight o'clock that morning, but one way and another he didn't reach the saloon for breakfast until after eight-thirty. Although the table to which he went was the Master's, used by senior staff, Captain Crutchley was not there. He seldom took his meals in the saloon, preferring the solace of his dayroom. On this occasion only McLintoch and Doris Benson were at the table. The radio officer, the catering officer and his wife, and a sprinkling of junior engineers were at one or other of the remaining tables.

'Morning, Chief. Morning, Doris.' Jarrett pulled out a chair, sat down, rubbing his hands. 'Burrh! Cold in here,' he complained. 'Fine and warm outside.'

Without looking up McLintoch muttered a subdued 'good morning'. The air-conditioning temperature, for which he was responsible, was the subject of a running battle between him and the chief officer.

Jarrett turned to Doris Benson. 'Where's Ben then?'

'In the engineroom.'

'Not his watch,' said Jarrett. 'Hope that's not a bad omen.'

McLintoch's eyes continued to focus on his bacon and eggs, and Jarrett, correctly and with some pleasure, interpreted this

63

and the momentary frown as 'why don't you mind your own business'.

'Talking of bad omens,' McLintoch munched away, glaring at his plate, 'have we managed to miss the Aliwal Shoal?'

'Yes,' said Jarrett. 'I went to a lot of trouble about that.'

'Like keeping to the course laid off by the second mate.' There was a note of triumph in the chief engineer's voice. He knew of the feud.

A steward arrived with a menu. 'Good morning, sir.' The voice was unfamiliar. Jarrett looked up. 'Hullo. When did you join?'

'Yesterday afternoon, sir.'

'So you've taken Alvarez's place.' The chief officer studied the man's face. 'Seen you before, haven't I?'

'Yes, sir. At Beau Rivage.'

'Of course. That's it. You waited on us. What's your name?'

'Piet Pieterse, sir.'

Jarrett studied the menu. 'Right, Piet. I'll have some porridge, bacon and eggs. Two eggs. I like them turned. Toast and coffee.'

Pieterse repeated the order. Jarrett leaned back in his chair, looked at the coloured man quizzically. 'What makes you want to exchange a job like that for steward in a tanker on its way to be laid up?'

'I want to get overseas. Better opportunities there.'

'What! With a million and a half unemployed, and you . . .' Jarrett hesitated.

The steward smiled. 'And me coloured you mean, sir?'

'Yes. It doesn't help, you know.'

'I know that, sir.' The steward went off to the pantry.

'Must be daft,' Jarrett observed to the table in general.

In the pantry adjoining his dayroom Captain Crutchley was steaming open the flap of a sealed envelope. When he'd finished he switched off the kettle, went into the dayroom, took a magnifying glass from the drawer of the writing table and sat himself down in an easy chair under a window. Slowly and with some difficulty he read the letter. Given to him a few days earlier by Grundewald, the ophthalmic surgeon in Durban, it was addressed to a consultant in Harley Street. Its terms were personal though professional. The consultants were evidently well known to each other.

64

For Crutchley its contents were profoundly disturbing: . . . *an unhappy instance of incorrect diagnosis by a country GP . . . failure to refer the patient to a consultant . . . the condition has evidently been acute for some time . . . evidence of permanent visual damage and secondary glaucoma.*

Crutchley put down the letter, closed his eyes, thought once again of the interview in Durban.

'Yes, I see. The eyeballs are inflamed. The eyes water badly, do they? . . . Yes. Are they tender and painful? . . . Yes. Do you suffer from frequent blurring of vision? . . . Yes, worse sometimes than others. How do you sleep? Any difficulty? . . . Yes. The pain keeps me awake. I get severe headaches. Does the light hurt your eyes? . . . Yes. Very much so. Any difficulty in opening the lids? In the morning for example? . . . Yes. Difficult. Bathing them with hot water and boracic helps.'

Grundewald had stood back from the surgical chair, looked at him sympathetically. 'Well I think that will do. Now come over here and let us have a chat.' He'd gone back to his desk and Crutchley, fumbling with his spectacles, had sat down opposite him. Embarrassed, fearful, he'd felt like a prisoner awaiting sentence.

Grundewald had asked how long he'd be in Durban. Leaving for London by air in a few days, Crutchley had lied, just as he had about his name. This man must not know he was a master mariner, let alone Captain of *Ocean Mammoth*. The name of the Captain of the biggest ship ever to visit Durban had been mentioned in the local media too often. So he was Mr Creightley, the London businessman passing through Durban.

'How long before you get back to London?' asked the consultant.

'Have to stop off in Nairobi for a few days . . . then again in Rome. Shouldn't be long before I'm back.' Crutchley disliked the recollection. Lying didn't come easily to him.

The ophthalmic surgeon had looked uncertain, tapped with a ballpoint on a prescription pad, his eyes averted from the rugged face opposite. 'The trouble is not conjunctivitis, I'm afraid. It's iritis in a somewhat acute form. Treatment under supervision is necessary. It is essential that you see a consultant as soon as you reach London. The sooner the better.'

'Will it take long to restore my eyesight to normal?' Crutchley had stared at the man on the other side of the desk, wondering what the brain behind the blurred face knew and was possibly withholding.

'With proper treatment your vision should improve considerably. It will not, I'm afraid, be as good as it was, but it should be adequate. After the treatment your eyes will be tested for new lenses. They will help.'

Grundewald had told him how to treat his eyes until he got back to London: ointment to be applied at two-hourly intervals, eye drops three times a day. Since heat relieved pain and reduced inflammation, he was to wrap a bandage round cotton wool on a wooden spoon, dip it in boiling water and hold it as close to the eyes as possible.

He'd given Crutchley a prescription for these things, including capsules to be taken at night on retiring.

'They'll relieve pain and help you sleep.' Finally he'd given him the letter to the man in Harley Street.

Back in his ship that afternoon, Crutchley had put the letter in the drawer of the writing table. The envelope was sealed and that had worried him. In the days that followed he'd carried out faithfully the treatment prescribed. There had been some relief from pain, and he thought the eyes had shown improvement. The capsules induced deep sleep. The letter, however, had remained at the centre of his thoughts, and what it might contain had become an obsession. Those contents concerned him and his future, his wife and children and no one else. Why then should they be kept from him? He was a man of honour but on this, his first day at sea, the temptation to open the letter had proved overwhelming.

For some time he sat thinking, the words *evidence of permanent visual damage and secondary glaucoma* constantly passing before his closed eyes. Looking into what seemed a stark future the only comfort he could find lay in his personal insurances. It was fortunate, he reflected, that he had always been prudent in that regard.

Chapter 10

Throughout that day *Ocean Mammoth* made steady progress down the South African coast and towards midnight East London, no more than a thin shimmer of distant light, was abeam. With the aid of the Agulhas Current speed had averaged fourteen knots. The weather remained fine and warm, the sea moderate as the great ship drove steadily through the southern night, rolling slowly to a beam swell. But for this, the distant hum of the turbines, and the unceasing vibrations, those on board might not have known they were at sea. As it was, with the ship in ballast, the vibrations were so pronounced that every fitting which could rattle did so, plates and glasses on smooth surfaces hummed as they slithered and cups clattered noisily in their saucers.

Down in the dayroom of her husband's suite, Sandy lay on a settee propped up by cushions, her hands clasped behind her head, her handsome body more revealed than concealed by the wrap she wore. George Foley, changing, getting himself ready for the bridge where he would relieve the third officer at midnight, looked at her with a mixture of affection and admiration. 'Well, the future may seem dismal but I'm glad we've got the next few weeks together at sea. That's some consolation.'

'Yes, of course,' she said casually, as if passing the topic in review.

In the bar-lounge after supper they'd seen a film, Dirk Bogarde and Charlotte Rampling in *The Night Porter*, and stayed on afterwards for a chat and drinks. It had not been a happy occasion. Conversation kept returning to what was uppermost in the minds of them all. What would happen at the end of the voyage? What did the future hold for them? The speculation was predictably gloomy. Back in their cabin, the Foleys had continued the discussion on a more personal level.

Disenchanted though she was with the role of tanker officer's wife, Sandy knew what a blow the laying up of *Ocean Mammoth* was to her husband, and she felt for him. He liked the sea, was content with his life in tankers, and she had no doubt that, but for her, he would have soldiered happily on until he got command of his own ship. These feelings of sympathy were sharpened by her conscience. It had been worrying her a good deal lately. In the early hours of the morning she would lie awake thinking of her disloyalty, trying to excuse it to herself and failing and with feelings of guilt and unhappiness she would fall into a deep sleep. Then, with daylight and the beginning of the new day, her mood would change; she'd see Freeman Jarrett at breakfast and the fears and misgivings of the night would vanish.

'Did you hear what I said?' Foley looked at her reproachfully.

'Yes. I'm sorry, George. Really sorry because I know what it means to you.'

'Can't be helped. Nobody's fault. Maybe it's a good thing.'

'How d'you mean?'

'Now I'll *have* to find a job ashore. You'll like that, won't you?'

She looked at him, nodded slowly. 'Yes. From a selfish point of view I will. I know I'm a bitch about it, but I do honestly believe there's not much future for us if you stay at sea. I want more than you can give me with things the way they are. And it's no good leaving me on my own. I can't help it, George. That's the way I'm made. I know you're not keen on a shore job. It's not what you really want, and for you this couldn't have come at a worse time.' She leant forward and with both hands threw her hair back over her shoulders. 'Terrific unemployment. Redundancies all over the place. It's a grotty outlook. I really am terribly sorry.'

He seemed embarrassed, deprecatory. 'Never know what's round the corner, Sandy. Opportunity knocks at surprising times. Something fabulous may turn up. I might get into real money ashore. Who knows?'

'How, George? Tell me how.' She watched him uncertainly.

He shrugged his shoulders, looked at her in a strange way. 'It's just a thought.'

She smiled the sad but affectionate smile of a mother listening to a wayward child. 'Poor George. I'm afraid that's all it's likely to be.'

'Perhaps you're in for a surprise.'

'Wish I was, darling.'

The phone rang. Foley picked it up. 'Two-Oh here. Yes. Thanks, Alan. No, I haven't gone to bloody sleep. Won't keep you waiting. Don't worry.' He put the handset back on its cradle. 'That was Alan with my five-minute call.'

'D'you mean to say it's nearly midnight?'

He pointed to the clock on the bulkhead. 'Five minutes to. Time you were in bed, Sandy.'

'I suppose so. I'm not really tired.' She yawned. 'Or am I?'

'Only you know. I reckon bed's a good place. I'll join you there at four.' He winked and kissed her. 'I'm off. Mustn't keep Alan waiting. I was a Three-Oh myself once. 'Bye now.'

He buttoned on a uniform jacket, slipped the strap of the R/T set over his head and left the dayroom.

Not long after he'd gone to the bridge she heard a discreet knock.

She put down the paperback, pulled her wrap more firmly about her and went to the door. An envelope had been pushed under it. On it her name had been scrawled in a large angular hand. She thought of looking into the passageway to see if there were any signs of the deliverer, but thought better of it, went back to the settee and opened the envelope. It was a hastily scribbled note from Jarrett: *Please come along to my office. Have something important for you. L of L – F.J.*

She read it with mixed feelings. It was fifteen minutes past midnight. It would not do to be seen going into his cabin at such a late hour. On the other hand it was extremely unlikely that she *would* be seen. Jarrett was evidently not worried or he wouldn't have made the suggestion. She wondered what it was all about. Was there really something so important that it couldn't wait for morning, or was it simply a ruse to get her there? That, she decided, was more likely. She laughed nervously.

The more she thought about the invitation the more excited she became. The note was a challenge and she wasn't the woman to refuse that sort of challenge. She could feel her heart beating faster, almost thumping, and her legs felt like jelly. 'How stupid,' she muttered to herself. 'I'm behaving like a sixteen-year-old.'

Of course she'd go. One only lived once. She wouldn't stay long and she felt sure – well, almost sure – she could handle him. It was the element of doubt that made it all the more exciting. She tore the note into small pieces, went into the bathroom, flushed the pieces away, came out, put on her bra and pants, slipped a caftan over her head, did her face and hair, sprayed

69

herself generously with *Madame Rochas* and went to the long mirror. She thought the result wasn't bad. The white caftan with gold embroidered sleeves and collar went well with sun-tan, dark hair and brown eyes.

She slipped into the alleyway. The entrance to Jarrett's accommodation, the door of his office, was on the opposite side, two up from theirs. She had reached it, was about to open it, when she thought she heard someone coming at the far end of the alleyway. She hesitated, nobody appeared, so she turned the handle and went in, closing the door gently behind her. The lights were on but he was not there, so she went through to the dayroom. A shaded lamp was burning and in its dim light she saw him slumped in an armchair. She went closer and saw him smile through half-closed eyes.

He got up slowly, yawning and stretching. 'Marvellous, Sandy. Thought you'd never come.'

'Sorry. I thought I'd done rather well. Ten minutes to dress, put on a face and do my hair.' She spoke quickly, nervously, little more than a whisper.

He put his hands on her shoulders, bent down and kissed her. 'You're a clever girl.'

'I'm a woman, not a girl.'

'Yes. I had noticed that.'

She pushed him away with both hands. 'What's it that's so important?'

'Hold on a moment and I'll tell you.' He went through to the office and came back soon afterwards with a small, gift-wrapped package. 'This,' he said, and gave it to her.

She looked at him, then at the package, puzzled, amused. 'It won't blow up, will it?'

'Probably. Try.'

She unwrapped it carefully and neatly as women do, until the brown and gold plastic box was revealed. She opened it and took out the small bottle of Rochas's *Audace*. 'Oh, Freeman. It's fabulous. You know I adore it. How marvellous. You are a nice man.' Still holding the perfume she put her arms round his neck and kissed him. He tried to make more of it, but she pushed him away again. 'No. For God's sake not now, Freeman.' She was suddenly serious, her dark eyes wide under the frown. 'This is quite crazy. Anybody could come in.'

'Anybody couldn't,' he said. 'I've locked the door. There's

70

nobody about. If anybody wants me, which is highly unlikely at this hour, they'll phone or use R/T.'

'What happens if George phones from the bridge and I'm not in my cabin?'

'You'd gone up on deck for a breath of fresh air. Gone to the pool. Anywhere. This is a bloody great ship. There's no law that says you can't leave your cabin.' He went to the corner cupboard beside the refrigerator. 'Calm down. Let's have a drink. Then you can go back to bed.'

'You must sleep, Freeman. You go on watch at four.'

'No problem. I had a good kip this afternoon and I've been asleep in that chair for the last hour or so.'

She looked at him doubtfully. 'Are you sure it's all right?'

'Of course. What'll you have? G and T?'

'After midnight?' She made a face. 'What else can you suggest?'

'Chartreuse.'

'Super.' She smiled affectionately, sat on the settee. 'I still think we're crazy.'

He ignored the remark, went on pouring the drinks. When he'd finished he put the glasses on top of the coffee table and joined her. 'Now I'll tell you a bedtime story.'

'You'd better do that, Freeman.' Her eyes were mischievous. 'There's not going to be anything else.'

By thirty minutes past midnight Foley had settled down to the routine of the watch. The third officer on handing over had made the customary reports of course and speed, ship's position, distance off shore, traffic approaching, ETA for the next alter-ation of course – 0250 off Great Fish Point – the engineroom state, manned on this occasion, and he'd handed over the traditional cup of coffee the quartermaster had prepared. He'd stayed chatting with Foley for a few minutes, then made his way below.

When Simpson had gone, Foley carried out a quick radar check, after which he established the ship's position by Decca Navigator, took a radar bearing of the light at the mouth of the Buffalo River, and checked it with a gyro compass bearing. He compared the echo-sounder reading with the depth of water shown on the chart, compared the gyro and magnetic compass readings, checked gyro-repeaters, determined the error of the magnetic compass by means of a star azimuth and finished with a

71

brief chat by phone with Jonathan Malim, the engineer on watch in the engine control-room. It was a subdued humourless exchange. Since his wife's death the third engineer had become more morose and withdrawn than ever, rarely leaving his cabin except to go on watch.

Despite its grim name, 'The Graveyard Watch', Foley enjoyed the middle-watch at night and was grateful that by long standing tradition it was his. In the small hours of morning, between midnight and four o'clock, life in a ship at sea was at its lowest ebb. But for the bridge and engineroom watchkeepers, the crew were asleep. Those quiet undisturbed hours suited him admirably. The middle-watch at night was perhaps that part of life in tankers which he relished most.

Now he had the bridge to himself but for Gomez the quarter-master who was on standby, the ship being on auto-steering. It was a fine warm night with no moon, the southern sky was brilliant with stars and out on the starboard wing of the bridge a light breeze fanned his face. Bracing himself against the roll of the ship he leant over the gyro, turned up the brilliance and took bearings of two ships bound up the coast. They were inshore and well clear of *Ocean Mammoth*. There were three other ships in sight, all to port. Two were coming up astern and the third, having overtaken in the first watch, showed no more than a dim sternlight fine on the port bow. He judged her to be ten miles ahead. He went to the AC radar, selected the twelve-mile range, and read off the ranges and bearings of the ships in sight. Though there was no risk of collision, he placed relative motion markers on the echoes of the two ships coming up the coast. He did this because he enjoyed using the technique and it helped pass the time. He left the radar and went out to the port wing. Shortly afterwards Gomez came out to tell him the Captain was in the wheelhouse.

Coming back from the starlit sky to the dark of the wheel-house, he saw nothing at first but the subdued light of neon dials and displays along the console. Soon he made out the dim shape of the Captain standing at the radar sets. He joined him. 'Good morning, sir.'

There was a longish pause before the Captain answered. 'Much traffic about, Mr Foley?'

One of the Old Man's ploys, thought Foley. He's looked at the displays and wants to see if I know what's going on. 'Three ships to port, sir. Bound down the coast. Two astern, overtaking but well clear. One fine on the bow which overtook in the first watch. There are two ships northbound, both out on the starboard bow and well inshore.' Anxious to show that he had the situation under control he added, 'I put relative motion markers on them. I'll check again.' He bent over the hood of the AC radar and checked the display. The echoes had as he'd expected moved away from the collision courses indicated by the markers. 'They're on parallel courses, sir. They'll pass several miles inshore of us.'

Captain Crutchley said, 'Good.' He moved along the console until he reached the midships gyro-repeater. Foley checked the time – 0053. The Captain usually stayed for twenty minutes. It was his custom to do this before going to sleep. As a rule he came up between half past twelve and one o'clock. Foley's thoughts were interrupted by the ring of a telephone on the console where a light glowed red. He lifted the handset. 'Two-Oh here.'

A hoarse voice he did not recognize answered. 'Your wife needs you urgently in your cabin, sir.' Before he could ask any questions he heard the click of the caller's phone being put down. He wondered what on earth could have happened. She wouldn't have sent for him unless it was really important. But why hadn't she phoned herself? God, he thought, she must have had an accident. He turned in the darkness towards the Captain. 'That was my wife, sir. There's been some trouble. She wants me urgently. I think she may have had an accident.'

'Then go to her at once, Mr Foley. I'll look after the bridge with Gomez. I trust it is nothing serious.'

'Thank you, sir. I won't be long.'

Foley raced through the chartroom, down the stairs to Deck One and along the passageway to the door of his cabin. Stuck to it with sellotape was a crudely pencilled note: *Your wife is in the chief officer's cabin.*

73

Chapter 11

Foley was sure the unidentified voice on the bridge phone and the writer of the note were the same person. Who he was and his motive, he could not imagine. Perhaps a hoax aimed at hurting him and Sandy? Foley knew that Jarrett's weakness for her was no secret. Was that it? An attempt to make trouble? To show her up? These jumbled thoughts were in his mind as he tore off the scrap of paper, stuck it in his pocket and opened the door.

The lights were on but she was not in the dayroom. He went through to the bedroom. That, too, was empty. Next he tried the bathroom, but drew a blank there. The wrap she'd been wearing when he left was on the bed together with a small hand towel. The sheets had not been turned back, the bed had not been slept in, and the room reeked of *Madame Rochas.*

By now he knew that the phone call and the note on the door were no hoax. His anxiety changed abruptly to suspicion and anger. So she *was* with the chief officer.

He went down the passageway to Jarrett's office, opened the door and went in as quietly as he could. The lights were on but the office was empty. He listened at the door of the dayroom. All he could hear was the thumping of his own heart and his laboured breathing. The door was locked. That confirmed his worst suspicions. He knocked but there was no response, so he banged with his fists but still nothing happened. 'I know she's in there,' he called. 'Open up.' Although he had almost lost control, he did not shout. He had no wish to advertise his wife's indiscretions.

Moments later Jarrett called out, 'What the devil's going on there?' There was the sound of a key turning, the door swung open and the chief officer appeared. 'What the hell d'you think you're doing?' he demanded.

Blinded by rage and jealousy, Foley forced his way past him and made for the bedroom door. It, too, was locked. He banged on it. 'Come out, Sandy. I know you're there.' His voice was hoarse with emotion. Before he could get an answer Jarrett was hauling him off the door. Foley wrenched free, got an arm round the chief officer's neck, took a wide stance and threw him to the

74

deck. 'Get up, you bastard, and I'll give you what you deserve.' It was a hoarse, threatening growl.

Jarrett scrambled to his feet, raised his fists and made for the second officer. 'Come on, do that,' he said in a voice thick with anger.

Foley waded in with flailing fists and wild swinging punches. What he lacked in skill he made up in sheer rage and animal strength. Both men were strong, there was little between them in height and weight, but Jarrett was the cooler fighter and he held Foley off with solid lefts and rights to the head. Had the fight gone on one or the other would probably have been knocked out. As it was the bedroom door swung open and Sandy emerged in the white caftan, her eyes wild, her hair untidy.

'Stop it, you maniacs,' she shrilled, clawing at them. 'Stop it, for God's sake. You'll kill each other.'

That brought them to their senses and they stood, bruised and dishevelled, their arms at their sides, breathing heavily. Blood trickling from Jarrett's nose and from a cut on his eyebrow left crimson stains on his white shirt and shorts. Foley's lower lip was swollen and bleeding, and he had bruises on his forehead.

'For God's sake try and behave like civilized human beings,' she implored looking from one to the other, her eyes alternately threatening and pleading. 'All right? Now let's go.' She went out of the dayroom. Foley followed her to the door, stopped and looked back. 'Keep your hands off my wife, Jarrett, or I'll kill you.'

Jarrett gestured angrily, turned away. 'Oh, get to hell out of it,' he muttered.

They got back to their accommodation and Foley shut the door. She turned to him, her face white and drawn. 'I'm sorry, George. Terribly sorry. I know I've let you down.'

He gave her a long hard look, shook his head, but said nothing. He went into the bathroom, took off the blood-stained shirt and filled the hand basin with water. She came in a few minutes later. 'Can I help?' she asked in a low voice.

'No. Don't touch me. Go to bed. You've done enough damage already.'

She went into the bedroom and he heard her sobbing but he was in no way moved. It was too late for tears. He got on with dabbing the swollen lip and the bruise on his forehead, using

75

water as hot as he could bear. After he'd dried his hands and face he put on a clean shirt. He felt a grim satisfaction that most of the blood on the one he'd taken off was Jarrett's.

The phone in the dayroom rang. He looked at his watch. It was eleven minutes since he'd left the bridge. He picked up the phone. 'Two-Oh here.'

'Captain here, Foley. How's your wife?'

He was ready for this. He'd been rehearsing it as he bathed his bruises. 'All right, sir. I'll be up in a moment. There was a short on the bedside lamp. The lead started smouldering. Sandy woke up, smelt burning and was frightened. I've fixed it. I would have been back sooner but I slipped on the stairs coming down. Got a few bruises but everything's okay now.'

'Good,' said Captain Crutchley with characteristic brevity, and rang off.

Foley hoped that his voice had not given him away. He was in a highly emotional state. Once again he wondered who had phoned the bridge and put the note on the door.

Something else which Foley had rehearsed was handing over the watch to Jarrett at four o'clock that morning. He was determined to keep it cool, not to refer to what had happened. If Jarrett chose to do so that was his responsibility. In the hours he'd had to himself since the Captain left the bridge, Foley had done some hard thinking. While he put the greater part of the blame on the chief officer, he knew that it took two to create a situation of that sort. Others would say that Sandy was just as much to blame and maybe they'd be right. She was old enough and experienced enough to know what she was doing. While this in no way diminished his hatred for the chief officer, he was too intelligent to believe that a further row could repair the damage. The least said now the better. Fortunately it had happened in the middle of the night, behind closed doors, and it was unlikely that anyone had heard. Jarrett would be the last person to talk about it.

In the event, the chief officer had come up at four o'clock as was his custom. They'd not greeted each other and in the sheltering darkness of the wheelhouse neither could see the damage done to the other, which was just as well. Foley had handed over in monosyllabic and more cryptic terms than usual. Jarrett had acknowledged curtly, asked no questions, and by four o'clock the handover had been completed. Foley went to the chartroom, spent a few minutes there writing up the logbooks and then went below.

There had been one notable departure from normal routine. He'd not handed over the traditional cup of coffee.

Chapter 12

Throughout the following day *Ocean Mammoth* made steady progress down the South African coast. Cape Recife, guarding the southern flank of Algoa Bay, was abeam soon after eight o'clock in the morning. At 1153, Cape St Francis was abeam to starboard, distant 15 miles, and course was set for Cape Agulhas, the most southerly point of Africa. With the aid of the Agulhas current the supertanker, though steaming at only 12 knots, had by noon that day averaged 14·3 since leaving Durban.

The weather remained fine with a light southerly breeze, a long swell from the south-east and a calm sea. Both sea and air temperatures had dropped but the barometer remained steady. Along the coast to starboard banks of cloud lay on the distant ranges of the Outeniqua Mountains, but for the greater part the sky was clear.

From the bridge, high above the sea, Alan Simpson, the third officer, looked down on the diminutive figures of crewmen at work along the great expanse of the maindeck. Far away in the bows, so far that they seemed antlike on that huge scale, men were working on the windlasses and cables; others were painting the tripod mast, set well forward, which carried running lights and the foremast siren; further aft again crewmen were busy on the steam winches.

Simpson, young and new to supertankers, had never ceased to be amazed at the enormous size of *Ocean Mammoth*. He often thought she was too big, too remote from the sea, a giant floating tank of frightening proportions. Yet he took boyish pride in being officer-of-the-watch in a ship of 320,000 tons. More than four times the tonnage of QE2, he used to remind himself.

For the greater part of that day Captain Crutchley, whether on the bridge or in his stateroom, tussled with his personal problem.

Withdrawn and reserved by nature, aloof from his officers as befitted the Master of a big ship, he had not confided in anyone on board, nor had he reported what he believed to be a temporary disability to London. The dark optical glasses which concealed his eyes had not attracted attention for he had worn them for several years to counter the effects of bright light. Even Middleton had not known his secret.

Grundewald's letter to the Harley Street consultant had come as a profound shock, for it enormously complicated his problem. Should he report to London by radio telephone now that he knew what it was, or say nothing? If he reported, London would probably instruct him to hand over command to the chief officer for the return voyage. In that event he would almost certainly be landed by shore-based helicopter at Cape Town to fly home.

Crutchley did not believe that his eye trouble endangered the ship. He had every confidence in his officers, *Ocean Mammoth* was equipped with highly sophisticated navigational aids, his judgement and experience were unimpaired, and the ship would be back in the United Kingdom in a few weeks. In the meantime, with Grundewald's treatment, the eyes should improve. He wished, however, that Middleton was still on board. He had been a great help.

A man of strong character, Crutchley was honest enough to admit to himself that in this matter he had been influenced by personal considerations. Having married a second time he had a young wife and family to support, school fees to pay, a large mortgage, a pension scheme and other personal insurances to finance. Inter-Ocean Crude and Bulk Carriers Ltd. – small, impersonal, speculative and a late starter in the ship-owning world – had no pension scheme for its officers. Its policy was to pay well and leave it to them to make their own arrangements. This Crutchley did, but he had to remain at sea for a least another five years if he was to meet his commitments.

Two other factors complicated his problem. One was that the ship was about to be laid up, the other that the redundancy clause in his contract would be void if he were medically unfit for command at sea. It was essential that he should complete the voyage and continue to guard the secret of his eyes, if he were to take advantage of that redundancy clause. It would give him as Master a year on full pay. In that time, he argued, treatment should have restored his vision, the tanker market would have recovered, and he would be able to seek re-employment. There would be little chance of doing that if the record showed he had been relieved of command because of defective eyesight.

79

After a long fight with his conscience, Crutchley decided against informing the company. He was not happy about the decision but felt it had been forced upon him.

Jarrett and Foley were at considerable pains that day to avoid each other. At four o'clock in the afternoon when Foley handed over the bridge watch, it was once again done quickly, curtly and impersonally. By custom they had always sat at different tables in the saloon and while at sea had meals at different times, so no problem arose there. It was known that they had long disliked each other, and the absence of communication and bonhomie, more pronounced that day than others, might have passed unnoticed had that been all. But it was not.

At breakfast Jarrett had explained away his puffy nose and cut eyebrow as the result of walking into a wheelhouse doorframe in the dark hours of the morning. As a rule Foley did not breakfast in the saloon; instead he would have coffee and an apple in his dayroom. To those who saw him that day he ascribed the swollen lip and bruised forehead to a fall on the stairs leading down from the chartroom to Deck One when he came off watch.

As the day progressed tongues began to wag. By late afternoon it was rumoured that there had been a fight and there was much speculation. Doris Benson thought she'd heard shouting and banging in the early hours but could not be sure. 'You know what a heavy sleeper I am,' she added apologetically.

The catering officer's wife said, 'Well, I'm not on that deck so I wouldn't know. But you'd think the Chief or the Captain would have heard. After all they're in adjoining accommodation.'

Doris Benson shook her head. 'The Chief was down in the engineroom with Ben, and though the Old Man's suite adjoins Jarrett's their bedrooms are four away from each other's. Not that I'm suggesting that anything happened in the *bedroom*. Maybe it was in Jarrett's office or dayroom.'

'Of course you're opposite, aren't you, Doris?'

'Yes. Our bedroom is right opposite his dayroom.'

'Well. I don't know.' The catering officer's wife wrinkled her nose and forehead. 'What on earth could they have been fighting about?'

'Don't be so naïve, love.' Doris Benson tidied her hair with one hand. 'Everybody knows Sandy and Jarrett fancy each other. And the men hate each other's guts.'

'But George was on watch between midnight and four this morning.'

'That was it, wasn't it, dear?' Doris Benson chuckled. 'Maybe he went down to get a clean hanky.'

The catering officer's wife looked at her with wide eyes. 'You don't mean to say he could have found . . . ?'

'I don't mean anything, love. But I did hear peculiar noises.'

'It could have been George falling downstairs, like he said. Both being bruised could be a coincidence. I mean, their stories may be true.'

Doris Benson shook her head. 'That's being a bit unrealistic, isn't it, sweet?'

'Well, she doesn't look as if anything unpleasant's happened. Cool as a cucumber,' said the catering officer's wife.

And indeed Sandy was. She had looked and behaved quite normally throughout the day, laughing and chatting, swimming and sunbathing, as if nothing had happened.

Down in the Foleys' cabin, however, things were somewhat different. The tension was acute and they did not speak to each other. She had tried hard but it had been impossible to break his stubborn silence. For his part he behaved as if she were not there.

When Foley relieved the third officer at midnight the ship was off Still Bay. The coastline, some twenty-five miles to starboard, now ran more or less east and west across the bottom of the African continent. It was a fine clear night, the southerly breeze had died away, the sea was calm, the barometer high, but the long swell from the south-east persisted. The temperature had dropped and Foley wore a jersey over his denim shirt and slacks. Captain Crutchley did not object to informal dress during the night watches as long as it was, in his words, 'clean and well scrubbed'.

The second officer had not been on the bridge long when a phone rang. He picked it up. 'Two-Oh here.'

'Midnight met report ready, George.' It was Tim Feeny speaking from the radio office.

'Fine. I'll send for it. Any problems?'

'Not really. Maybe fog later.'

'Much later I hope.'

Feeny laughed. 'Like after four o'clock.'

'You said it, Sparks.' Foley replaced the handset and summoned the quartermaster who was on bridge lookout.

Gomez came into the wheelhouse. 'Sir?'

'The met report's ready, Jorge.'

'Okay, sir. I fetch it.' The quartermaster disappeared into the darkness. He was soon back with the report. Foley went into the chartroom and read it in the light of an angle-poise lamp. The forecast indicated fairly settled conditions over the ensuing twenty-four hours with calm sea and light winds. It concluded with a warning that in the vicinity of Cape Agulhas and the area immediately westwards there was a possibility of fog. In accordance with Standing Orders the second officer at once informed the Captain by phone.

Crutchley said, 'Good. I'll be up shortly,' and rang off.

The second officer clipped the report on to the forecast board over the chart-table and returned to the wheelhouse.

Cape Agulhas was the focal point for shipping around the southern extremity of Africa and there was a fair amount of traffic about. It was this which Foley now examined with binoculars from the starboard wing. Later he returned the night glasses to their box in the wheelhouse, went to the AC radar, adjusted the display hood and pressed his face into the rubber eyepiece. He turned up the brilliance and for some time watched the sweep circling the screen, switching through the range scales and identifying the echoes of the ships he'd observed visually. He put relative motion markers on two of them and noted the time, 0017.

He was at the steering stand comparing the ship's head by gyro compass with the magnetic compass reading in the periscope above, when he heard the Captain's heavy tread in the chartroom. Five minutes later he heard a chart-table lamp click off and the Captain came into the wheelhouse. 'You there, Mr Foley?'

'Aye, sir.'

The Captain said no more but took up his usual position at the console, to starboard of the steering position. Foley could just see the solid shape of the Master in the darkness, standing squarely, braced against the slow roll of the ship, looking ahead. On the bridge, high above the water, the roll was exaggerated by the pendulum effect.

'No sign of fog yet, sir,' ventured Foley after a long silence.

There was the customary pause as if the Captain was weighing every word said, before he answered. 'It's unseasonal. But I've experienced it here before at this time of year.' It was a long sentence for him.

82

Foley said, 'Yes, sir. I imagine with this high glass it must be due to radiation.'

There was another long silence, broken at last by the Captain's. 'I'll take a walk on the bridge, Mr Foley.'

'You'll find the temperature's dropped a bit, sir.'

The Captain went out of the port door. It was some time before he returned. As he passed through the wheelhouse he said. 'Keep a sharp eye on the traffic, Mr Foley.'

Through the glass panels along the top of the screen between wheelhouse and chartroom, Foley saw the reflection of a chart-table lamp as it was switched on.

It must have been fully ten minutes before the light went out and he heard the Captain making his way to the head of the stairs. He knew he'd been writing up his night order book.

Crutchley changed into pyjamas and went through to the bath-room. There he boiled water in an electric kettle, poured it into a jug, worked cotton wool round the head of a wooden spoon, secured it with a bandage and dipped it into the hot water. For a minute or so he held the pad as close to his eyes as he could bear, repeating the operation several times. Next he put in the eye drops, applied the ointment to the lids and massaged them gently with his fingertips. When he'd finished and put things away he went through to the bedroom.

It was the end of a tiring day and he had used his eyes too much. Strained them, he supposed, for the pain and irritation were severe. The eyes soon began to feel better but his head continued to throb. Worrying too much about his personal problems. But it was impossible to escape them and, as he lay waiting for sleep to come, they paraded through his mind in an endless procession. The family dominated because they were his main concern . . . Emma, sad, wistful, so much younger than he, so considerate and sympathetic, a fine wife and mother . . . the boys: Andrew, intelligent, diligent, thoughtful in his adolescence but somehow distant and unapproachable: Bobby, still at preparatory school, full of good-natured fun, unperturbed by indifferent school reports. It was a splendid little family and every fibre of Crutchley was determined to defend it . . . Kostadis, lean, sharp-faced, long-nosed, appeared in a vaguely threatening role and Crutchley rejected him, only to find that a picture of *Ocean Mammoth*, red with rust and neglect in some Scottish loch, had taken his place . . . the service contract joined the procession, clause after clause of it passing before his eyes like a cue-sheet until it stopped on the redundancy clause: *unless the employee shall be declared unfit for service at sea for medical or other reasons or by virtue of loss of certificate/s of competency* . . . Grundewald came next; calm, grave, sympathetic, pronouncing sentence: *your vision should improve . . . it will not, I'm afraid, be as good as it was . . . new spectacles, these should help.*

Why 'should' and not 'will'? . . . the picture of a dole queue presented itself, and Crutchley recognized the man in a ragged overcoat waiting despondently at its tail as himself . . .

The headache was intolerable. He switched on the light, leant over, took two of Grundewald's capsules from a small bottle in the drawer of the bedside table and washed them down with water. He switched off the light and lay in the dark thinking about the meteorological forecast. The possibility of fog did not worry him unduly. The ship had every conceivable aid to safe navigation and he had full confidence in his officers; they had much experience of fog in northern waters – waters more confined and heavily trafficked than those off Cape Agulhas. He had, however, written in his night order book, 'I am to be called at once in the event of fog, and in any case before alteration of course off Cape Agulhas.'

With any luck he would get in four hours of sleep before then. Comforted by the thought he dozed off.

At 0240 the second officer consulted the Decca Navigator, noted the lane co-ordinates from the digital read-out, identified them on the Decca chart, plotted the ship's position and transferred it to the Admiralty chart. He found that over the last hour current had set the ship 1·3 miles to the north-west, that was towards the land. For some time he worked on the chart with parallel rulers and dividers. On the assumption that the north-westerly set would continue throughout the rest of the watch, he determined the new course to steer to reach the 0530 ETA position ten miles off Cape Agulhas.

He switched off the lamp, went through to the wheelhouse and checked the auto-pilot gyro. The ship's head was steady on 264°. He turned the handwheel, counting the clicks and watching the gyro-repeater until the ship had settled on the new course which he then set on the course-to-steer indicator. He noted the time,

0246, and recorded the alteration in the deck logbook and on the chart.

Jarrett came to the bridge to take over the watch at five minutes to four that morning; five minutes earlier than usual. Foley would normally have commented on this, perhaps even been flippant about it, but their relationship was under intense strain. Instead he got on with the handover as quickly and impersonally as he could. He rattled through course and speed, ship's position, ETA 0530 for the alteration of course off Agulhas, distance off shore, details of traffic approaching and the engineroom manning state. He finished with a terse reference to the meteorological forecast, the possibility of fog and the Captain's night order book. Then, having once again deliberately defaulted on the preparation of coffee, he went to the chartroom where he wrote up the deck logbook and recorded and charted the 0400 position by Decca Navigator.

In his desire to hand over with almost indecent speed he failed to mention the north-westerly set of the current, but succeeded in going below a good deal earlier than usual – a fact noticed by Gomez the quartermaster whose relief, much to his disgust, had not yet arrived.

A few minutes later Jarrett asked where Fernandez was.

'Not come yet,' said Gomez. 'I call him ten minutes already. He say he fall asleep.' The quartermaster expressed his disapproval with a sharp hiss.

'Okay, Gomez. She's on auto-pilot. You go below now. Tell Fernandez to shake it up or he'll be in trouble.'

'Thank you, sir. I kick his backside then he come quick.'

'Watch it.' Jarrett laughed. 'He's bigger than you.'

Gomez slipped round the screen into the chartroom and went down the stairway.

Not long afterwards Fernandez arrived, breathing heavily. 'Sorry, sir, I sleep too much.'

'Not good, Jorge. You keep Gomez waiting.'

The quartermaster made apologetic noises.

'Right,' said Jarrett. 'Now you can do something for me. Slip down below and get my blue jersey. Third drawer down, right-hand side of the wardrobe cupboard. It's colder up here than I reckoned.'

The relationship between the chief officer and Fernandez the

85

senior quartermaster was a good one and they would often chat to each other while on watch. Fernandez never took advantage of this and always treated Jarrett with respect.

'Okay, sir.'

When the quartermaster came back with the jersey Jarrett told him to go to the bridge wing. 'Keep a sharp lookout. There's a fair amount of traffic about.'

Fernandez left the wheelhouse and Jarrett went to the chartroom. He stayed there for some minutes before returning to the wheelhouse, when he called Fernandez in to make coffee.

While the quartermaster was doing this, Jarrett went back to the AC radar.

Chapter 13

The chief officer took binoculars from the rack and searched the horizon. The radar display had shown three ship echoes ahead in the twelve-mile range. Of these one, an echo fine on the starboard bow at eight miles, was approaching. The others on the port bow, at five and nine miles, were on parallel courses and drawing ahead.

He was focusing on the running lights of the ship approaching when they began to fade. They showed again momentarily then blurred and faded slowly until they had disappeared.

The fog had come.

On the radar display he identified the echo again, pressed the key switch and aligned the range and bearing markers. The target ship was seven miles ahead now, relative bearing 003°. A mile in two minutes, thirty knots. Fernandez broke into the chief officer's mental arithmetic. 'Coffee's ready, sir.'

'Leave it there, Jorge. We've a fogbank ahead and a ship coming down in it. Take the wheel.'

'Aye, sir.'

Fernandez went to the steering stand and moved the switch from 'auto' to 'manual'. He grasped the small horseshoe wheel, looked into the gyro and checked that the ship's head agreed with the figures on the course-to-steer indicator on the console. 'Steering two-six-seven, sir.'

'Very good.' Jarrett consulted the radar again. The range on the target ship had dropped to six miles. Combined speed of approach still thirty knots, a mile every two minutes, twelve minutes to close the distance. The mental arithmetic was instinctive, force of habit. He put a relative motion marker on the echo and noted the time, 0421.

'Starboard easy, bring her round slowly to two-nine-five,' he ordered.

'Starboard easy, sir.'

The gyro clicked off the degrees as the ship's head moved slowly to starboard. Jarrett watched the echoes on the display as they wheeled to port like well-drilled troops, their after-glow describing little arcs like the tails of comets descending. It was a long slow turn and it was some time before Fernandez reported 'Steady on two-nine-five, sir.'

'Very good.'

The chief officer went to the centre of the wheelhouse, picked up the binoculars and again examined the horizon. But sea and sky had merged into an opaque wall of darkness and he could see no lights. The fogbank was still some distance ahead. He went back to the radar. The target ship was now twenty-five degrees on the port bow and the relative motion marker showed that her course would take her well clear. He switched the range to twenty-four miles and the sweep threw up the coastline in bright relief. He examined it carefully, picked out Cape Agulhas, seventeen miles ahead, and from the Cape followed the glowing neon line round Struys Bay and away to the north and east. He switched back to the six-mile range, and stood at the front windows searching the darkness ahead.

'We're not up with the fog yet,' he said. 'But it can't be far now.'

'Fog no good for big ship,' observed Fernandez.

'You're right, Jorge. It's nobody's friend.'

'I don't know.' Fernandez was hesitant. 'Sometimes good for fish.'

Jarrett could just see the face of the quartermaster in the dim light of the steering gyro. Jorge's thoughts were back in the Cape Verdes, he decided. The islanders had all been fishermen in their time.

It was not long before the first tenuous swirls of fog appeared and Jarrett went to a bridge wing where he looked over the side and saw the reflection of the port steaming light, red against the smoke-like whorls. Forward he could see a halo round the foremost running light. The mast which supported it, and the bows, were almost hidden by the streaming smoke-like mantle. It poured over him, wet and clinging, condensing in his hair and eyebrows. The silence had grown deeper, his awareness of sounds, amplified by the fog, more acute so that those he would not normally have noticed, the slap and gurgle of water passing down the side far beneath him, the distant hum of machinery from the engineroom, had become unusually loud.

The ship was now without any point of reference, a huge steel structure, most of it invisible to him, floating in a limbo of fog, its forward motion no longer apparent because there was nothing to which it could be related.

Away to port he heard the faint thrum of a siren and was able to place it broad on the bow. It was the ship for which he'd altered course. The radar echo had shown that it was a big ship. The deep note of the siren confirmed this.

The fog grew denser, swirling across the bridge, shutting out the wheelhouse, isolating him on the port wing. He went back to the wheelhouse, switched on the clearview screen and the automatic wipers on the big front windows.

'Now for that coffee,' he said. 'If it isn't too cold.'

Fernandez didn't like fog, but most of all he disliked supertankers in fog. Too big to stop, too slow to turn, no quick way of getting out of trouble. Not like fishing boats. Very small, easy to turn, easy to stop, easy to escape from trouble. Unless your nets were out and a big ship came blundering through the fog and ran you down. He had lost friends and relatives that way.

With these giants, he asked himself, what can a man do? Three hundred and twenty thousand tons pushing through the fog at twelve knots, or sixteen when they were in a hurry. All right, he conceded, they have the scientific instruments on the bridge; radar, electronic position and direction finders, autopilots, depth finders, press-button engine controls. They have these things but the ships are too big. They are not for sailors. For technicians if they want them and if . . .

His thoughts were interrupted by the chief officer. 'Who's on standby below?'

'Cavalho, sir.'

Jarrett picked up a phone and dialled the recreation room. A sleepy voice answered. 'Is Cavalho here.'

'Chief officer here. We've got fog. Come up to the bridge for lookout. Make it snappy.'

Next Jarrett phoned the engine control-room. Benson answered.

'We've got some fog, Ben. Won't need to reduce speed. We're on three-quarters already but I'm going to put her on "manoeuvring". Keep the revs at sixty. Okay?'

'Right, Mate. Now?'

'In two minutes. I'll log it at 0430.'

'Okay. 0430. Don't use that bloody steam whistle though. There's a lot of people aft trying to sleep.' The steam whistle was on the funnel close to the accommodation and the disturbance caused by its shrill blast was much resented.

'Do I ever? It'll be the foremost siren. Pneumatic, auto, marvel of modern science, nearly a thousand feet from the accommodation.'

'Why use a siren? Everybody's got radar. You're all peering at each other on your comic little screens. See each other bloody miles away. What's the use of a sound signal? Right old relic of the past.'

'You're right, Two-E. I agree. But the Old Man doesn't. 'Bye now.'

The chief officer removed the Perspex safety cover from the engine-control buttons, put his thumb on 'manoeuvring speed', a light glowed in response and he replaced the cover. He pressed the switch to activate the pneumatic auto-siren on the tripod mast in the bows. Once on 'auto' the siren would give a six-second blast every two minutes. On this occasion it did nothing. He pressed the switch again, tried several times, but the siren remained silent.

'Bloody thing's on the blink. Would pack up when it's wanted,' he complained aloud.

He phoned the engineroom. Benson answered again. 'What's it now, Mate? Want me up there to take over?'

'The auto-siren's gone on the blink.'

'Tried pressing the auto-switch?'

'Several times. Like to come and try yourself?'

'Expect you pressed the wrong tit. I'll send up one of my high technology boys.'

'Great. Tell him to wipe off the grease and bring a ten-pound hammer.'

'Listen, Mate. Don't use this as an excuse for that bloody steam whistle. We'll soon fix the auto. Right?'

'Right. Remember to speak up for me.'

'Okay. Jackson will be along to check the circuit. We'll have to call the poor sod, so don't get impatient.'

The chief officer went to the radar, pressed his face into the rubber-lined aperture of the hood and studied the display. Soon afterwards he picked up a phone and dialled. Fernandez heard him report the onset of the fog to the Captain, explaining that he'd informed the engineroom, put the engines on 'manoeuvring speed' and stationed a fog lookout on the bridge. He had added that the pneumatic siren was temporarily out of order, but the engineroom was sending up an electrician to attend to it. Fernandez heard him say, 'It won't take long to fix, sir. If you've no objection I'd rather not use the steam whistle. Disturbs too many people.'

In response to something the Captain must have said the chief officer replied, 'Yes. There are a few ships on the display. Mostly on parallel courses. I've had to alter for a big ship approaching on a reciprocal course. She's well clear now. About four points on the port bow. There are two small echoes on the starboard bow at six and ten miles. Trawlers, I'd say, from their course and speed. I'll keep a close eye on them.'

The Captain must have asked about the weather. The chief officer said, 'Fog's fairly dense, sir. Probably just a bank that's come off the land. There's a light north-westerly breeze, calm sea, south-easterly swell.'

There was a longish pause before the chief officer made sympathetic noises and said, 'Sorry to hear that, Captain. It's probably nothing a good sleep won't put right.'

Later Fernandez heard him say, 'Don't worry, sir. I'll keep a sharp lookout. We should be out of it before the end of the watch.' The chief officer then returned the handset to its cradle and went back to the display hood.

Jarrett compared the displays on the AC and TM sets. Satisfied, he left the TM radar and concentrated on the AC display. The TM set was intended for coastal navigation, but *Ocean Mammoth*'s officers preferred the AC radar with its anti-collision facilities. With the use of markers it could do the work of both sets, giving true motion and relative motion simultaneously.

Jarrett left the radar and went out to the starboard wing. Cavalho was standing on the wooden grating around the gyro compass. 'Cheer up, Cavalho,' he said. 'It's sunrise soon after five. Seen anything?'

'Nothing, sir. Fog too thick. I hear ship on port side.' As he spoke the faint boom of a siren sounded on the port beam.

'She's less than two miles away, Cavalho. A couple of points ahead of the beam.'

'It seem more than two miles, sir.'

'Fog does funny things to sound.'

'Yes. I know this.'

91

Jarrett said, 'There's a couple of small vessels ahead four points on the starboard bow. Trawlers, I think.'

'I hear nothing on starboard, sir.'

'Too far still, but we're closing them. Keep a sharp lookout.'

It was the old liturgy of the sea, 'keep a sharp lookout', said ever since man had sailed the waters. Even with radar it had a special urgency in bad visibility. The fog was thicker now, a moist opaque blanket which Jarrett could taste and feel. He stayed on a little longer, the two men silent with their thoughts. Back in the wheelhouse he spoke to Fernandez. 'We'll be altering course to port soon. Must get back on our course.'

'I think so, sir.'

'There are a couple of trawlers ahead to starboard. Soon as the nearest is clear we'll alter.' Jarrett went to the AC set and studied the display for some time, switching through the range scales, then returned to the six-mile scale and placed a relative motion marker on the nearest echo. With a white plotting pencil he wrote the time against it. He went to the coffee shelf at the back of the wheelhouse, switched on the kettle and made a cup of fresh coffee. The one Fernandez had given him had long since gone cold. He tasted the coffee. 'That's better,' he said. 'Scalds the tongue.' He took it with him into the chartroom.

When Jarrett came back a few minutes later Fernandez greeted him with, 'Ship's head still on two-nine-five, sir.'

'That's right. That's what it should be on.'

Fernandez realized from Jarrett's tone that he had resented the reminder. The quartermaster was hurt because he'd tried to be helpful. He saw the dim shape move across to the radar units. Soon afterwards he heard him complain, 'This chap's a sodding nuisance. On a collision course now. Has to be a trawler the way he's behaving.' A moment later he ordered, 'Starboard easy. Bring her round quietly to three-two-zero. Five degrees of wheel will do.'

Fernandez repeated the order, put on five degrees of wheel and watched the gyro as the ship's head began its slow swing to starboard. What seemed to him a long time later he checked it with port wheel, steadied the ship on the new course and reported, 'Three-two-zero, sir.'

'Steer three-two-zero.' The chief officer consulted the radar again.

92

'I'd better pass well astern of him. Must have his trawl out.'

Fernandez said, 'Yes, sir.' His sympathies were all with the trawler. Fishing was a hard enough life without having to get out of the way of supertankers. He wasn't pleased when the chief officer added, 'That's the trouble with the Agulhas Bank. Lousy with trawlers. You never know what the silly sods'll do next.'

Fernandez made an ambiguous noise. It could have been agreement or disapproval. 'Must go to where fish is,' he added in an undertone, a truth which seemed to him beyond dispute. The chief officer may or may not have heard for he said nothing as he went through to the chartroom.

Jarrett recorded the change of course and the time – 0438 – in the deck logbook and on the Admiralty chart. Before returning to the wheelhouse he consulted the note on the board above the chart-table which gave the times of sunrise and sunset in Foley's neat script. He saw that sunrise was just after five o'clock.

He'd not been in the wheelhouse long when the electrician arrived. Jarrett looked at the clock on the console – 0445. It was more than a quarter of an hour since he'd asked Benson to send someone up to look at the auto-switch. 'Hullo, Jackson,' he said. 'You certainly haven't wasted time.' The sarcasm didn't amuse Jackson. A taciturn, humourless man, he was bowed down by the multiplicity of electrical faults in a new ship with many circuits still unfamiliar to him. 'Did my best,' he said sourly. 'What's the trouble?'

'The circuit on the foremost siren is dead. Nothing happens if I press the auto-switch.'

'Could use the steam whistle aft, couldn't you?'

'I know I could, Jackson, but the higher echelons who sleep under it seem agreed that I shouldn't.'

The electrician shook his head. 'Don't seem much point in having a steam whistle then.'

'It has other uses,' Jarrett reminded him.

The electrician was about to say something but changed his mind. He sighed noisily, put down the tool carrier and set about dismantling the auto-switch by the light of a torch. 'Like as not the trouble's somewhere else but I'd better make a start on this.'

93

Chapter 14

Inside the wheelhouse it was dark but for the subdued glow from gyro-repeaters and the dials and indicators along the bridge console. To Fernandez the chief officer was a dark shape, sometimes identified by the faint reflections of neon light which illuminated his face.

The windows were shut to keep out the fog, and the atmosphere was pungent with the mustiness of charts and books, the stale smell of deck polish, of coffee and of human bodies, and the indefinable yet unmistakable odour of electronic instruments. The background noises in that enclosed space were always the same: the clicking of gyro-repeaters, the hum of radar sets, and the faint sounds of machinery from the engineroom, shut off though it was from the bridge.

While one part of Fernandez's mind concentrated on keeping the ship on its course, the other was occupied with his thoughts. They were mostly about the fog. Why was it, he asked himself, that in fog with the sense of direction gone he always had the feeling that the ship was turning slowly to port? Although the compass told him she was not, the sensation was irresistible. It happened to him whether he was in the northern or southern hemisphere. Always the ship seemed to be turning to port. Was it because the earth revolved in one direction or because of the direction in which the propeller turned, or . . . he gave up. It was too complicated.

Fernandez was unhappy in fog, especially in the wheelhouse where nothing could be heard if the windows were shut. He looked at them now, those in front and the others to port and starboard. But for the windows where the clearview screen spun and the two wipers clicked to and fro like giant metronomes, they were blanked off by fog. Beads of condensation kept forming on them, grew too large, collapsed and ran down, leaving spidery trails.

Somewhere out there, he thought, beyond the opaque windows, hidden by fog, were other ships: trawlers, big ships, container ships, tankers, all making for Cape Agulhas because it was the only way round the southern tip of Africa. And here he was at the wheel of this vast ship, moving blind but for its instruments, its crew – other than the handful on watch – asleep below; warm, secure, unaware of what was happening. But he had a sense of disquiet for notwithstanding the telephone conversation he'd overheard he was puzzled by the Captain's absence from the bridge. It was unusual.

He shivered involuntarily. He always felt insecure and helpless in fog, aware that he was being carried along by forces and events over which he had no control.

At 0453 the radar display revealed that the trawler had crossed ahead of *Ocean Mammoth* at a range of 1·5 miles, the relative bearing shifting from starboard to port and opening steadily. Cavalho phoned in from the starboard wing to report that he'd heard the siren of a ship ahead. 'It make one long blast, then two shorts,' he said.

'Good,' said Jarrett. 'That's the trawler. It's crossed ahead of us. Moving away now on the port bow.' He replaced the phone on the console. 'She had her trawl out,' he said to Fernandez. 'Cavalho heard a long and two shorts.'

'I hope trawler catch plenty fish.'

Jarrett could see the white of Fernandez's teeth in the reflected light of the steering gyro. The quartermaster was grinning with vicarious pleasure.

'We'll have to let her get well clear. Don't want to foul up that trawl.'

Fernandez, very much in agreement with the decision, nodded his head. 'That is good, sir.'

'Glad you approve.' Jarrett sounded cheerful. Soon afterwards he ordered five degrees of port wheel and *Ocean Mammoth* began to move in a long slow turn to port. It was some time before he ordered Fernandez to steady the ship's head on 258°.

Fernandez applied starboard wheel, checked the swing to port and steadied on the new course. 'Two-five-eight, sir,' he reported.

'Steer two-five-eight,' said Jarrett. 'That puts us on course for the position off Cape Agulhas.' When he'd adjusted the course-to-steer indicator to show 258°, he went out to the starboard wing to speak to Cavalho again. From far away on the port quarter came the sound of a siren. It was answered soon afterwards by a deeper, more compelling note. 'That's a couple of optimists trying to dodge each other,' he said. 'The best of British luck to them.'

Cavalho said, 'Yes, sir. I report one already. First time now I hear the other.'

The silence which followed was broken only by the ripple and splash of the ship's passage through the water and the subdued hum of her turbines. Before he left Jarrett heard the long blast followed by two shorts of the trawler's siren. The sound came now from abaft *Ocean Mammoth*'s port beam.

The chief officer stood in the entrance to the chartroom and in its dim light watched the electrician busy at the junction box on the after bulkhead.

'Any joy, Jackson?' he enquired.

The electrician started, almost dropped the screwdriver he was using. 'Gave me quite a turn you did, sir. Didn't hear you come in.'

Jarrett pointed to his feet. 'Plimsolls, Jackson. They don't disturb those asleep below. Like not using the steam whistle. Found anything yet?'

Jackson nodded. 'Yes. It's in the junction box. The supply to the auto-switch comes through it.'

'What's the trouble then?'

'The leads have been clipped off short and the terminal panel removed.'

'Christ! Who'd do a thing like that?'

'Anyone, I'd say. We've been swarming with shore workmen for weeks.'

'But what would they want it for?'

'Don't ask me, sir. They'll scrounge anything, that lot. Probably to use at home.'

'How long will it take to fix?'

'I'll have to dismantle the junction box to get at the leads and extend them. First I'll have to get a new panel, leads and fuses from stores. Thirty – forty minutes I'd say.'

'Thank the Lord for radar.'

Jackson shook his head gloomily. 'I thought the deck officers tested the sirens before leaving harbour.'

'You're right. It's the second mate's job. He used to get Middleton to do it. I expect it was overlooked.'

'Not like Mr Foley to forget.' The electrician straightened his

96

back, put his tools in a corner and went down the stairway to Deck One.

Fernandez looked at the shadowy figure of the chief officer bent over the radar and wondered what a man with his knowledge and training thought about fog. Was he worried, did he feel insecure? His thoughts were interrupted by Jarrett. 'That's all we're short of. The silly sod to starboard has altered course for Cape Agulhas. Now we're on converging courses. Damn his eyes. If he'd stayed on his southerly course we'd have been well clear.'

He looked into the display again. 'He's coming up from the direction of Struys Bay. Another trawler. Making for Cape Town to land his catch, I suppose.'

Fernandez was used to the chief officer's running commentaries and liked them. They helped pass the time on watch and on occasions like this kept him in the picture. Not that he had to be kept in the picture, but it wasn't very pleasant on the wheel in thick fog, blind, not knowing what was going on, just standing there keeping the ship's head on a compass course. He believed the chief officer liked having someone to talk to, particularly when things were happening. Before Price's accident Jarrett used to have the cadet on watch with him. There was plenty of talk then.

'You think he's finished trawling, sir?' Fernandez knew when to make conversation. The chief officer liked a lead now and then.

'Yes, he's doing twelve/thirteen knots. Must have recovered his gear.'

There was a long silence after that broken at last by Jarrett's, 'Bloody hell! He *is* on a collision course. The sod *must* have radar, and we *must* be the biggest ship echo he's ever seen. Surely to God he can keep clear.'

He looked ahead through the wiper-windows. 'Still thick as a wall.' He hesitated and Fernandez heard the nervous tap of his finger nails on the console. 'Right. There's nothing for it. We'll have to give way. Come round to starboard again and pass astern of him. The sooner the better. Starboard very easy, Fernandez. Bring her round slowly to three-two-zero.'

Fernandez put on five degrees of wheel and the long slow turn began.

When the ship's head was steady on the new course Jarrett altered the figures on the course-to-steer indicator to 320° and

97

noted the time – 0512. Having checked the reading on the gyro-repeater he went to the chartroom.

Later he came back into the wheelhouse, picked up a phone and dialled the radio officer's cabin. There was a short delay before a sleepy voice answered, 'Feeny here.'

'Chief officer here. Sorry, Sparks, but we've got problems. The Decca Navigator's gone on the blink. Can't get anything from it. No signal *at all*. Can you come up?'

'Jesus, Mate. What a time to call a man.'

'Come on. You've had plenty of kip. We're in fog. Make it snappy.'

There was a pause. Jarrett could hear the radio officer's heavy breathing.

'Fog. Haven't heard a whistle.'

'Some twit has fiddled with the auto-siren circuit. Jackson's trying to fix it.'

'Blimey, you *are* in trouble then.'

'We certainly are. Now get off your backside and come and join in the fun.'

'Okay.' There was the sound of an exaggerated sustained yawn. 'I'll be up in a few minutes. Cor, the things I do for England.'

'For the Swiss, Sparks. Strictly for the Swiss.'

Jarrett replaced the phone and went out to the starboard wing. Halfway along the bridge he stopped and listened. The sound of distant sirens came from the port side; one, very deep, answering another with a high frequency. He reached the end of the bridge and spoke to Cavalho. 'There's another trawler on our starboard bow. We've altered course so that he can pass ahead. Heard him?'

'No, sir. If I hear I report.'

'Okay. I wasn't getting at you. I've been listening myself. Heard nothing to starboard. Probably one of these sensible blokes who can't be bothered. He's got radar, we've got radar. So why steam about the ocean making a bloody awful noise.'

'Yes, sir,' Cavalho said respectfully, adding for good measure, 'I'm sure.'

Jarrett made for the wheelhouse. He was tense, nervous; it was wet and cold out on the bridge and he was glad to leave it. He switched on the direction finder in the chartroom and took a bearing of the radio beacon on Cape Agulhas. Next he switched on the echo-sounder and read off the depth recorded – 34 fathoms. He had compared the reading with the depth on the chart, plotted the DF bearing, ringed the estimated position and noted against it the time – 0515 – when Feeny arrived, a jersey over his pyjamas, eyes puffed with sleep.

'Hullo, Sparks,' said Jarrett. 'Sorry to bother you but this is no time to be without the Decca Nav.'

'What's the trouble?'

'Don't ask me. That's your job. Dead. No response. Kaput. Savvy?'

'Right. I get the point. Just leave me to it, Mate.'

'I intend to. We're in thick fog and I'm bloody busy.' As he left he heard Feeny muttering something about why does it have to happen now.

Not long afterwards the radio officer came into the wheelhouse. 'I've had a look at it. Haven't a clue yet what the bother is. I'm going down for some bits and pieces – and the manual.'

'The Lord forgive you,' said Jarrett. 'Talk about plumbers.' He looked at his watch. It was 0519.

The chief officer straightened up from the display hood. 'We've passed astern of him now. Better get back on course for Agulhas.' He ordered easy port wheel and before long the ship's head began its slow turn to port. It was some time before he told Fernandez to steady on 250°.

When Fernandez had reported the ship steady on the new course, Jarrett set the figures on the course-to-steer indicator, went through to the chartroom and recorded the alteration and time – 0527 – in the deck logbook.

'How goes it, Sparks?' he asked Feeny who was working on the Decca Navigator immediately to the right of the chart-table.

'Tell you later, Mate.' Feeny was abrupt, rattled, clearly in no mood to communicate.

As Jarrett left he heard the radio officer addressing no one in particular to the effect that he couldn't take bloody electronics anyway, particularly in the early hours of a sodding foggy day.

The eastern sky was growing lighter in spite of the fog which continued dense and impenetrable; so dense that no more than a hundred or so of the nine hundred feet of maindeck forward of

99

the bridge were visible through its swirls.

'Maybe this fog will disperse when the sun gets up,' suggested Jarrett.

Fernandez said, 'When the wind comes the fog will go. We have no wind, sir.'

'You're right. Only a light whiff from the nor'west.' Jarrett picked up a phone and spoke to Cavalho. 'Heard that trawler yet?'

'No, sir. If I hear I tell you.'

'Good. Thought you might have dozed off.'

'I not doze, sir.' Cavalho sounded resentful.

Jarrett moved along the console, restless, worried, full of tension now. He looked into the AC radar and switched through the ranges. 'Bloody hell,' he exclaimed. 'Now this lot's on the blink. What's going on with our electronics?' He turned his attention to the TM set, fiddled with the controls, but the display remained blank. 'My God. This one too. I can't believe it. *Had* to happen now.'

'What's the trouble, sir?' Fernandez was apprehensive.

'No radar. That's the trouble.'

The quartermaster felt very insecure then. Something in the chief officer's manner told him that he, too, was worried.

'Very bad, sir. Can be many ships around Agulhas.'

'You're bloody right there can.' Jarrett pounced on a phone and dialled the engineroom.

Benson answered. 'Two-E here.'

'Radar's on the blink, Ben,' said Jarrett. 'Better go to standby. But remain on present revs.'

'Right. What time?'

'Now – now, 0529.'

'0529 it is.'

Jarrett put down the phone and pressed the 'standby' button on the ER control panel. A neon light glowed in response. That's one essential done, he said to himself as he went into the chartroom. I'll log that. Now for another.

'More problems, Sparks.' The radio officer's back was towards him. 'Both radar sets are on the blink.'

Feeny spun round, his mouth wide open. 'For God's sake! What's it now? Turned up the brilliance too much? Burnt the bleeding tubes?'

'Watch it, Sparks,' warned Jarrett. His voice had hardened. He

100

didn't like flippant criticism, particularly when he was on edge. He gave the radio officer a long hard look. 'Both units are U/S. You'd better get cracking. We're not far off Cape Agulhas and there's traffic around. We can't afford to be blind.'

Feeny stared back aggressively. 'What d'you want? Decca Nav or radar? I can't do both.'

'For Christ's sake, radar of course. We're in bloody fog and there's traffic about. Fix the radar first – either set – then the Navigator.'

Feeny tightened his lips, shook his head, turned his back on the chief officer and went into the wheelhouse. Jarrett followed.

The radio officer got to work on both sets, checking through the controls first then, having removed the inspection panels, he examined the complicated circuits by torchlight.

He stood up, scratched his tousled hair and began thinking aloud, rather pointedly neither speaking to Jarrett directly, nor looking at him, yet keeping him informed. 'It'll take time,' he mumbled. 'Got to check through these circuits, that's for sure. Nothing coming through from the transceivers to the displays. Could be the inter-switching unit. Might well be. I'll have a look there first. If that doesn't work, then I'll check out the circuits.'

Feeny went through to the chartroom and began to examine the inter-switch unit which was on the after bulkhead.

In the wheelhouse Jarrett stood at the wiper-windows looking ahead, tapping uncertainly on the console. Increasingly he felt himself to be losing touch with reality, he and the ship lost in a limbo of wet and clinging fog, all points of reference gone, the swiftly flowing stream of events beyond his control. A gnawing doubt nagged at the pit of his stomach. It was almost as if a fire were burning there.

101

Chapter 15

A phone rang on the console. Jarrett picked it up. It was Cavalho. 'I hear noise like motor car hooter, sir. Ahead to starboard. Three, maybe four shorts. Far away.'

'Probably a fishing boat, Cavalho.'

'You see on radar, sir?'

'Radar's packed up,' said Jarrett. 'Didn't see anything there when last I looked. Keep a sharp lookout. We need your eyes and ears now if ever we did.' He put down the phone and made for the chartroom. There was no sign of the radio operator but Foley was at the chart-table, his back towards him. The second officer had evidently not heard him come in, and for some moments Jarrett watched in silence.

Wearing a navy polo neck, blue denims and white plimsolls, Foley was in the act of sliding parallel rulers over the chart. When he realized he was not alone he stopped, switched round and looked at the chief officer with startled eyes.

Jarrett's stare was belligerent. 'What do you think you're doing here . . . in my watch?'

Foley pushed the parallel rulers aside. 'Something funny's going on. This course I mean . . .' His voice was hoarse. 'The Decca Nav's dead. There's no siren sounding? What the . . . what's happening?'

'And I dare say you sabotaged the Decca,' Jarrett snapped back. For a moment it looked as if he was about to use violence. 'What are you doing creeping around here when you're supposed to be off watch? Why didn't you report to me when you came on the bridge?' He darted an angry, suspicious glance round the chart-room. 'Where's Feeny?'

'Went down below as I came in.' Foley said it mechanically as he turned back to the chart-table and pointed to the chart. 'These aren't the figures I wrote against the course before you took over. I wrote two-five-seven, not two-six-seven degrees. Who changed that?' The words trailed away as if it were all too much for him. He moved over to the far side of the chart-table, switched on the echo-sounder. 'For Christ's sake,' his voice was suddenly strident.

'Look at this . . . we're in eight fathoms! . . . look! It's shoaling . . . my God, it's shoaling.'

For a moment Jarrett watched the flickering neon figures with staring eyes. 'Christ!' He ran into the wheelhouse shouting, 'Hard-a-port! Hard-a-port!'

Fernandez repeated the order, put the wheel hard over and the helm indicator travelled slowly across its red arc. He knew from experience that it would take fifteen seconds to complete the movement to hard-over. They seemed to him to be fifteen very long seconds.

Jarrett depressed the 'Full Ahead' button on the control console and phoned the engineroom. Benson answered.

'Mate here, Ben. I'm going to sound emergency stations. We could run aground. Keep her full ahead. We've gone hard-a-port. May get clear.' There was a shocked 'Jesus!' from Benson. Jarrett rang off and thumbed the siren button for 'emergency stations'. The comparative quiet of early morning was shattered by ear-splitting roars from the steam whistle on the funnel abaft the bridge. In the sudden silence which followed, the water noises along the hull and the rising note of the turbines sounded unusually loud.

Jarrett pressed the speak-button on the handmike of the broadcast system. 'Emergency stations, land close ahead,' he warned. 'Emergency stations. Land close ahead.'

Foley, who'd dashed into the wheelhouse on the heels of the chief officer, went to a radar set and began fingering the controls. Jarrett shouted, 'No good. They're on the blink.'

The second officer joined him. The two men, their animosity forgotten in the face of sudden disaster, stood at the front windows, their bodies rigid, their eyes straining to see through the fog.

From somewhere ahead came a series of two short blasts followed by a long blast – the 'U' of the International Code – 'you are standing into danger'. An agitated voice with a strong Afrikaans accent came over the VHF loudspeaker on the bridge. 'Ship bearing due east. You are standing into danger. Repeat, you are standing into danger . . . this is Agulhas lighthouse.'

Somebody touched his elbow. It was Jackson the electrician. 'Sorry for the delay, sir. Storekeeper's fault. I've got the parts for the auto-switch.'

Jarrett waved him away. 'For God's sake, Jackson. You heard

the alarm. Forget the bloody switch.'

The turn to port was only half completed when the ship shuddered, seemed to check, moved on only to shudder again, this time more severely. There followed violent deceleration, accompanied by the muffled sound of rending metal. From forward came the sharp hiss of vent valves discharging from the gas line. The men on the bridge knew then that deep down in the ship seawater must be rushing into empty oil tanks through torn plating, compressing the inert gas in the tanks which was exhausting through the PV-breakers, blowing oil slush and water over the fog-shrouded maindeck. Above these harsh sounds came the thin shrill of a woman's scream and the shouts of men, followed by the piercing shriek of steam exhausting from the funnel, a sound which drowned all others.

Quite suddenly *Ocean Mammoth* came to a lurching stop, the force of the impact throwing those on the bridge forward, spread-eagling Foley and Jarrett over the consoles and winding Fernandez who was forced against the steering standard.

The moment Jarrett recovered his balance he pressed the 'emergency full astern' button. It was an automatic response, a conditioned reflex, but even as he did it he knew it was futile. Another of his automatic responses was to note the time – 0539. It was little less than two minutes since he'd found Foley in the chartroom.

Cavalho slid open the door from the bridge-wing. 'It *was* motor car I hear before, sir,' he said triumphantly. 'Now I hear him again. Also dog barking. Now you see we hit the rocks.'

A stern authoritative voice interrupted. 'Sound the fire alarm, Mr Foley.' It was Captain Crutchley. He had come from the chartroom into the dark wheelhouse, the sound of his footsteps drowned by the noise of escaping steam and the rattling of windows and other loose fittings as the ship's emergency astern movement built up. The harsh jangle of fire-bells now added to the din, competing with the shrill of escaping steam and the high-pitched hiss of gas venting through the safety valves. The Captain spoke into the ship's broadcast system. 'Captain speaking. Take up stations for fire forward. This is a precaution, but get there smartly. I want the pumpman on the bridge.' The even voice sounded absurdly formal in the turmoil.

Jarrett called out, 'I've already sounded emergency stations, sir.'

104

'I know that, Mr Jarrett. But you were wrong. Fire is the greater risk. Go at once to your fire station.' There was a sharpness in the Captain's voice which brooked no opposition.

The chief officer said, 'Aye, sir,' and left the wheelhouse.

Soon afterwards the pumpman arrived on the bridge. 'Captain, sir?'

'Chapman. I want you to sound the deep tanks and lower holds right away. Work from forward aft and report to me as soon as possible.'

The pumpman said, 'Yes, sir,' and disappeared at the double.

Captain Crutchley, wearing a uniform coat over his pyjamas, remained at the forward windows staring ahead into the fog. He had considered illuminating the maindeck but decided against it because floodlights would be largely ineffective in fog, and a fire risk if power lines were damaged.

The sound of escaping steam stopped as the emergency astern movement relieved pressure on the boiler's safety valves. From time to time the ship shuddered and ominous noises came from strained plating and frames as *Ocean Mammoth* took the full impact of the south-easterly swells which rolled in on her port beam, their powerful undulations surging up against the high steel wall of the hull.

The jangle of fire-bells ceased suddenly. In the unfamiliar silence which followed, men moving about the deck and occasional shouted orders could be heard; and the new and chilling sound of breakers as the swell spent itself on the rocky headland.

'Mr Foley.' Captain Crutchley continued to stare ahead. 'Where has the ship grounded?'

'Cape Agulhas, sir. The light-keeper spoke to us on VHF a moment ago. Gave our bearing as east of the lighthouse.'

'Get Decca Nav and radar fixes at once, Mr Foley.'

'They're unserviceable, sir. The Navigator and both radar units.'

'My God! What has been going on in this ship?' The Captain paused, and in the half light of early morning Foley regarded the broad-shouldered back with anxious eyes. Believing that he understood what was in Crutchley's mind, he began to speak in an uncertain, apologetic tone. 'I was off watch, sir. I went to the chartroom only a few minutes ago. Before emergency stations was sounded. I found the Decca Nav dead. I couldn't understand the course we were steering. The chief officer came in. Then . . .'

105

He hesitated as if he were trying to recall the sequence of events. 'Then I switched on the echo-sounder . . . and told him we were in eight fathoms, with the water shoaling. He rushed into the wheel-house, ordered hard-a-port and emergency-full-ahead, and we struck soon after that. It was . . .'

'That will do, Mr Foley. This is no time for explanations. Go at once to the chartroom and give me a DF bearing of the radio beacon at Agulhas lighthouse.'

A bell rang on the communications console. It was Tim Feeny. 'Radio Office here.'

'Captain here,' replied Crutchley.

'Anything for transmission, sir?'

'No, Mr Feeny. But stand by.' He rang off, picked up the ship's broadcast mike. 'This is the Captain speaking. We have run aground near Cape Agulhas lighthouse. There is no immediate danger. Keep calm. Remain at fire stations for the time being.' He paused and his deep breathing could be heard over the loudspeakers. 'The third officer is to report to me in the wheel-house at once. That is all.' He released the 'speak' button and replaced the mike on the console.

Foley came back from the chartroom. 'Agulhas lighthouse bears two-six-eight, sir.'

'How is the ship's head, Mr Foley?'

The second officer went to the steering gyro on the console. 'Two-two-seven, sir. We're lying on a sou'westerly–nor'easterly axis. Beam on to the swell.'

Captain Crutchley was silent for almost thirty seconds. To the second officer it seemed a great deal longer. Then he said, 'Stop engines.'

Foley pressed the 'stop engines' button and moments later the rattling and shaking of the bridge superstructure died away.

The deep voice with the Afrikaans accent sounded again on the VHF speaker. 'This is Cape Agulhas lighthouse. What ship is that east of the lighthouse?'

The Captain picked up the VHF handmike. 'VLCC *Ocean Mammoth* bound for the United Kingdom in ballast. Captain speaking. We are aground. We have the bearing of your beacon. Two-six-eight degrees. Can you give me a distance?'

'No, sir. We can't see you. The fog is very thick. Visibility under a hundred metres. We haven't got radar. I reckoned from your siren and the sound of steam blowing off that you must be about

106

due east of the lighthouse. Very close inshore.'

'Thank you, Agulhas.'

'I will report your stranding to Cape Town, sir. Is there any message I can pass on for you?'

'No, thank you. As soon as matters here are clarified I'll be speaking to them by radiophone. We'll come back to you if necessary.' The light-keeper acknowledged and Captain Crutchley replaced the handmike. 'Now, Mr Foley. Have soundings taken immediately, right round the ship. And give me the times of high and low water.'

The third officer arrived on the bridge as Foley left. The Captain said, 'Look after things here for a moment, Mr Simpson. I'm going through to the chartroom.'

When he got there he switched on the angle-poise lamps, removed his dark glasses and cleaned them, took the magnifying glass from its bracket above the chart-table and examined the chart. With parallel rules he checked the pencilled course line to the position ten miles off Cape Agulhas. It was 257°, but written against it in pencil in Foley's neat small figures was 267°. No alterations of course since 0400 were shown on the chart, but a line of bearing from the radio beacon had been plotted and a position circled on it over the 34-fathom mark with the time – 0505 – against it.

Next he turned to the deck logbook. Under 'Course' at 0400, the end of the middle-watch, '267°' had been entered in ink; again the figures were Foley's. Since that entry the chief officer had recorded in his bold angular hand, several alterations of course and the times at which they'd been made. The checking of that data would have to wait, decided Crutchley – there was no time now. He moved across to the starboard side of the chart-table, leant forward and peered into the rectangular face of the course-recorder. It was an instrument which plotted the courses steered and the times of alteration by means of a stylus on moving trace paper.

'My God,' he muttered, repeating what he'd said to the second officer. 'What has been going on in this ship?'

The broken edges of the trace paper were visible at the top of the frame where the moving sheet had been torn off. The record of courses steered since 0200 had been removed.

Chapter 16

As the morning wore on the sky grew brighter with the rising sun but the fog, changed now from charcoal grey to smoky white, remained dense, moist and clinging. Nothing could be seen of the shore from *Ocean Mammoth* and only occasionally were her foremast cranes visible from the bridge less than a hundred metres away.

The crew had been ordered to stand down from fire stations when it was evident that the danger of fire had receded. Now men were busy with hoses sluicing away oil slush splattered about the maindeck by PV-valves on tank tops, while others turned out lifeboats and made them ready for lowering.

Foley's report on the times of high and low water did nothing to reassure Captain Crutchley. High water was at 0527, low water at 1132. The ship could not, he reflected, have struck at a worse time – close to high water on a falling Spring tide. Not only did this bode ill for salvage but as time passed and the tide fell the weight of the ship would bear more heavily on the rocks; already fractured steel structures could be heard straining and breaking, for the stresses to which the hull was subjected were compounded by the formidable swell. Under its impact *Ocean Mammoth* from time to time shuddered and ground in protest.

Soundings taken round the ship showed that she was firmly aground on a rocky bottom for two-thirds of her length. From the bulkhead between numbers 5 and 6 tanks, aft to the stern transom, she was still afloat but with little water beneath her.

The pumpman's report on tank soundings confirmed Captain Crutchley's worst fears. From the forepeak aft to number 6 tank, every lower compartment was flooded. It could only mean that for more than half her length the bottom plating had been torn away or otherwise critically damaged. To the Captain that was not surprising. The momentum of a 320,000 ton supertanker at thirteen knots represented forces of enormous magnitude.

The slop and splash of thousands of tons of seawater moving about in the tanks could be heard on the maindeck and it soon became evident that the ship's prodigious pumping capacity –

10,000 tons an hour – could make no impression on the flooding since much of the bottom was open to the sea.

In the course of an urgent conference between Captain Crutchley and Mr McLintoch, with Jarrett and Benson present, it had been decided that notwithstanding this setback the ship should be lightened as far as possible before the next high tide at 1731. Consequent upon this decision the emptying of some intact ballast tanks was begun, anchors were lowered on to the bottom and their chain cables run out to bare ends. Fortunately there was no list, the ship for the greater part of her length resting squarely on the bottom. The fore and aft level was, however, tilted so that seen from aft the maindeck rose gradually towards the bow.

During the morning Captain Crutchley spoke by radiophone to Nicolas Kostadis in London. The marine-superintendent – who had already received a cryptic report from the agents in Cape Town – appeared to be deeply shocked by Crutchley's account of the stranding and the extent of the damage. He expressed dismay that *Ocean Mammoth* with her highly sophisticated navigation aids should have run aground.

'What on earth was the ship doing so close inshore in fog?' he asked, his voice rising in plaintive disapproval.

'That is a question I cannot at this stage answer,' replied Captain Crutchley, adding with some asperity, 'Nor would it help the ship if I could.'

'Nevertheless it's a shocking occurrence,' insisted Kostadis, whose ill-concealed anger had sounded clearly over the six thousand miles between them.

They went on to discuss the steps to be taken to deal with the situation. Captain Crutchley would, it was agreed, at once get through to the company's agents in Cape Town to ask for the despatch to the site of a marine surveyor and a salvage expert, and to request that salvage tugs be put on short notice. 'I'll confirm this to them by phone as soon as I can get through,' said Kostadis. 'But in the meantime you must get on with it. They should be able to reach you by the afternoon. They are to phone me direct from the ship as soon as they're ready to report. We can then decide what has to be done. How is the weather out there?'

'Dense fog. Calm sea. Heavy swell. Glass steady.'

'Well, that's something to be thankful for,' said Kostadis.

'Cape Agulhas is no place to be in a storm.'

Captain Crutchley, who felt that he did not need to be told this by an engineer, made no comment and the conversation ended soon afterwards.

The reaction of those on board to disaster had been fairly predictable. The officers and engineers had remained calm, doing all that was required of them quietly and efficiently whatever their private feelings. The Cape Verdians, used to battling with the elements in the frail fishing craft of their islands, had responded well: rather better than the Goanese stewards whose nervous at times noisy excitement was noticeable. It was only among the passengers – the officers' wives – that any real emotion had been displayed. Woken from sleep by the raucous blasts of the steam siren they had jumped up frightened and confused, hurriedly pulling on whatever garments were handy, grabbing lifejackets and making for their lifeboat stations. Only one husband was in his cabin when the alarm sounded and that was the catering officer.

Before the women had time to reach their stations and put on their lifejackets they'd felt the shuddering and jarring of the ship, followed by violent deceleration as she struck. Soon afterwards the fire-bells had jangled and it was then that Jean Simpson burst into tears and Doris Benson, who lived in a permanent state of terror of a tanker explosion, had become hysterical. Sandy Foley had rescued her from that by first slapping her face – something she had long wanted to do – and then, largely by the coolness of her own demeanour, pacifying her fears. That done, she'd turned her attention to Jean Simpson and succeeded in calming her too. Sandy was in fact very frightened, particularly as her husband had been missing from the cabin when the alarm sounded. She couldn't understand how it was that he'd gone before the alarm. It was most unlike him to have left her in the lurch if there were danger in the offing. But she had no intention of showing her fear and to some extent it had been allayed by Freeman Jarrett's reassuring words a few minutes earlier.

Piet Pieterse the new steward, on his first voyage in any ship, had been in a state of mystified apprehension, but once it had become apparent that *Ocean Mammoth* was neither about to sink nor explode, his ebullience and natural good humour asserted themselves and he got on with his duties as if the stranding of a super-tanker in fog was an everyday occurrence. He did, however, incur the displeasure of Figureido, the second steward, by whistling in the serving pantry. 'You must not make whistling,' said the Goanese. 'Unlucky for the ship, especially at this time.' Pieterse had felt that the ship couldn't have been much unluckier at that time but, anxious as always to please, he stopped whistling and apologized.

While the fire alarm was still sounding, Jarrett, on his way down the stairway to Deck One, had met Sandy coming up. She'd clutched his arm and with troubled eyes pleaded, 'What's happened, Freeman?'

He had stopped for a moment, smiled sympathetically and given her arm a reassuring squeeze. 'We've run aground, Sandy. No danger. Nothing to worry about. Just go along to your station quietly and try to calm the others.'

Then, strong, handsome and purposeful, he'd raced on down the stairway.

The Cape Town agents phoned the ship at eleven o'clock to inform Captain Crutchley that the marine surveyor and a salvage expert would leave for Cape Agulhas by helicopter that afternoon. Their ETA at the ship was 1430, provided the fog had by then lifted; if it had not the helicopter would land its passengers at Bredasdorp and they would do the remaining sixty-five kilometres by road. The light-keeper at Cape Agulhas would in that event arrange for a boat to take them off to the ship from St Mungo Bay, the small indentation off which the ship was stranded. Salvage tugs had been alerted, as had the National Sea Rescue station at Gordons Bay, 150 kilometres away. Newspapers and the SABC had already tried to get through to the ship, but the radio officer had informed the GPO Cape Town that *Ocean Mammoth* could not accept such calls at the present time.

The Captain had been on the bridge continuously since the ship struck but now, having done all that was possible, he went down to his stateroom, leaving the third officer in charge of the bridge. With the fog persisting there was nothing for Alan Simpson to do but monitor the alarm systems and keep a general lookout. This, he decided wryly, meant looking hopefully into the blanket of fog which encompassed the ship. With the coming of

111

low water and the exposure of greater areas of rock, the sound of the breakers had grown in volume. Other sounds which could be heard were those made by auxiliary machinery, by crewmen working on deck, and occasionally the distant blare of fog-horns.

Once down below Captain Crutchley went to the bathroom and bathed his eyes, changed into uniform and went through to his dayroom where he sat down to toast and coffee brought him by Figureido. The simple meal finished, he decided he could no longer delay tackling a problem which had been on his mind ever since the ship struck.

He switched on the R/T, made contact with the chief officer in the cargo control-room, and told him to report to his office at once. Jarrett arrived soon afterwards.

'You sent for me, sir?'

'Yes. Shut that door and take a seat, Mr Jarrett.'

The younger man shut the door and sat down facing the Captain, his hard hat on his lap, his R/T on the deck beside him. For some time Captain Crutchley stared at him in silence, his eyes anonymous behind the dark glasses. At last he spoke. 'Mr Jarrett. The marine surveyor and the salvage expert are due on board at two-thirty if this fog has lifted. Otherwise they'll come from Bredasdorp by road. Either way they should be here within two or three hours.'

'Yes, sir. I'm afraid the ship is in a bad way. This low water has done her no good.'

'I am aware of that, Mr Jarrett.' The Captain paused, the concealed stare never wavering. 'I want you within the next hour to hand me a written account of how the ship came to run aground during your watch this morning.'

'Certainly, sir. I'll get on with that right away.'

'There is one question to which I must have your answer now, Mr Jarrett.'

The chief officer looked puzzled. 'And that is, sir?'

'Did you read my night order book before taking over the watch from Mr Foley at four o'clock this morning?'

'Yes, I did. And I signed it.'

'My orders required you to call me in the event of fog, and in any case before the alteration of course off Agulhas, did they not?'

112

'Yes, sir. That is correct.'

'Why then did you not call me?'

The chief officer's face was a picture of surprise. 'I did call you, sir. I reported the fog by phone. Told you of ships in the vicinity. That I'd placed an extra lookout. I explained why we couldn't use the pneumatic siren. The defective auto-switch. You agreed we shouldn't use the steam whistle aft because of the disturbance it creates. You told me you had a bad headache. That you'd taken some pain-killers – so that you could sleep – and wouldn't be coming up. You asked me to keep a sharp eye on things. To let you know if I wanted you to come up at any time.' The sentences came tumbling out in puzzled protest.

Captain Crutchley rose to his feet, a large formidable figure. 'You did no such thing, Mr Jarrett. At no time did you report to me.' His voice was firm, emotionless. 'That is entirely a figment of your imagination.'

By now the chief officer, too, had risen. His expression as he regarded the Captain was a mixture of sympathy and surprise. 'I expect the sleeping pills were more effective than you realize, sir.' He hesitated. 'I have a witness to our telephone conversation.'

'A witness,' said Captain Crutchley grimly. 'You must be out of your mind.'

'No, sir. Fernandez was on the wheel. He must have heard the conversation.'

'I don't believe for a moment that such a conversation took place, Mr Jarrett. You have been negligent and you are trying to cover yourself.'

Jarrett's eyes narrowed and his voice took on a hardness which had not been there before. 'I must decline to discuss this any further, sir. The court of enquiry will no doubt satisfy itself as to the truth.'

'How dare you threaten me like that.' Crutchley's voice rose in unfamiliar anger.

Shaking his head as if mystified, the chief officer left the Captain's office. For some time after he had gone Crutchley sat at the desk, head in hands. As he brooded over what Jarrett had said a small but insidious doubt took shape in his mind.

Could the sleeping capsules have so dulled his mind that the phone conversation was beyond recall?

Chapter 17

The chief officer was back five minutes later to report to the Captain that chart No. 2083 – covering the approach to Cape Agulhas – was missing and that the day's pages of the deck and Decca logbooks had been torn out. That was not all, he said; the course-recorder trace had been torn off and there was no record of the courses steered since 0200. He had last consulted the instrument at 0525, soon after altering course for a trawler. The trace was writing normally then.

'All this has been done since I was on the bridge at 0540, sir,' he added in a resentful, suspicious way.

Captain Crutchley, still simmering from their recent clash, looked at him for some time before answering brusquely, 'Who do you suggest did this?'

The chief officer shook his head. 'I don't know, sir,' he said hesitantly, lowering his voice, and watching the Captain carefully. 'It would be in the second officer's interests that those records should not be available, wouldn't it? He handed over an incorrect course at four o'clock. Just before we went aground he was in the chartroom.' Jarrett's voice was all the more deliberate now. '*In his watch below.* He was also there a few minutes ago, and as far as I know he's still there.'

The Captain's anonymous stare continued to be focused on the chief officer. After what seemed a long time he said, 'Would it not be more in *your* interests, Mr Jarrett? You were officer-of-the-watch when the ship ran aground.'

'I take strong exception to that, sir.'

'Take what you damn well please, Mr Jarrett. Now go back to your quarters and get on with that report.' The Captain turned away, and the set of his mouth and jaw made it clear that the interview was over.

The chief officer seemed undecided for a moment. He picked up his hard hat and R/T, moved slowly to the door, looked at Crutchley once more with disbelief, and left the office.

No sooner had he gone than the Captain dialled the second officer's cabin. Sandy answered. Her husband, she said, was on the bridge. In the chartroom she thought.

Next Crutchley dialled the wheelhouse. The third officer answered.

'Captain speaking. Is Mr Foley there?'

'He's in the chartroom, sir.'

'Tell him to report to me right away, Mr Simpson.'

'Aye, aye, sir.'

The Captain replaced the phone. It was not long before the second officer arrived, his face drawn, his eyes red-rimmed over dark pouches. He had not slept for twenty-four hours.

The Captain pointed to a chair. 'Now, Mr Foley. I want you to let me have, within the hour, a written account of the events leading up to the stranding of this ship. Only in so far as you know them personally. I want no hearsay. In particular I want to know the ship's position as plotted and logged by you at the end of your watch, the course and speed you then handed over to Mr Jarrett, and an explanation of how you came to be in the chartroom during his watch shortly before the ship ran aground.'

The second officer turned away from the Captain's disconcerting stare and concentrated on a picture which hung on the foremost bulkhead. It was a full-rigged ship under sail, the original *Ocean Mammoth*.

'I will do that, sir. But it's going to be very difficult.'

'Explain yourself, Mr Foley.'

'I've just come from the chartroom, sir. The chart we used for the approach to Cape Agulhas has disappeared. So have today's pages of the deck and Decca logbooks. They've been torn out. The course-recorder trace from two o'clock onwards is missing. Torn from the frame.'

Captain Crutchley's mouth tightened. 'When did you discover this, Mr Foley?'

'About ten minutes ago, sir. It was the first opportunity I'd had of going to the chartroom. Because of something the chief officer said, I wanted to check the courses steered since I'd handed over to him at four o'clock.'

'What did the chief officer say?'

'When he came into the chartroom just before we ran aground I told him that someone had altered the figures I'd pencilled in against the course line. The two-five-seven I'd written had been changed to two-six-seven. He said I'd given him the course verbally as two-six-seven when handing over. He also said those

115

were the figures shown on the course-to-steer indicator.'

'Well, Mr Foley?'

'That was untrue, sir. I don't make those sorts of mistakes. I'd drawn a course line of two-five-seven on the chart and written two-five-seven against it and in the deck logbook. Those were the figures I'd set on the course indicator and given him verbally.'

Captain Crutchley sighed audibly as he recalled what he had seen when he examined the chart and deck logbook in the chart-room soon after the stranding. His mouth tightened and he pushed the frame of the dark glasses further up the bridge of his nose. 'Something very strange has been going on in this ship, Mr Foley.'

'That's exactly what I said to the chief officer in the chartroom before we ran aground, sir.'

'Who do you think removed that chart, tore those pages from the logbook and the trace from the course-recorder?'

The second officer hesitated. 'I don't like to say, sir. But no one would have a stronger motive than the officer-of-the-watch at the time of stranding.'

'You mean the chief officer?'

'Yes, sir. For obvious reasons.' A nervous smile flickered across the second officer's face.

'I see you smile, Mr Foley. Some might say the *obvious reasons* could equally well apply to you.'

The second officer shook his head vigorously. 'No, sir. That is not correct.'

As soon as Foley had gone, Captain Crutchley went up to the chartroom. He took possession of the deck and Decca logbooks, and the paper trace from the course-recorder for the period since leaving Durban up to 0200 that morning.

For those on board *Ocean Mammoth* the most worrying time had been that between the stranding early in the morning and the order to stand down from fire stations which had come two hours later. By then it was evident that there was no immediate danger and though the fog persisted both crew and passengers began to adapt themselves to the new conditions. They had been reassured by the Captain's broadcast and by Jarrett and Benson who were at pains to tell those they met as they went about their duties that there was no cause for alarm. Sandy continued to be a pillar of

116

strength among the wives to whom her calm and cheerfulness proved a steadying influence. She had now emerged as their undisputed leader.

Diaz, the bosun, a big-boned man with many years in tankers, feared and respected by his men, had had no difficulty in maintaining the morale of the islanders, and in this he'd been ably assisted by the pumpman and the storekeeper. Oddly enough it was Piet Pieterse, the newcomer and a stranger to ships, whose good-natured humour had done most to calm the worried Goanese stewards.

It was known that the ship was in touch with the authorities ashore, that when the fog lifted salvage experts would appear on the scene, and there was general belief that though *Ocean Mammoth* was in serious trouble her great size was in itself a guarantee of personal safety for those on board. Even so there was a natural tendency for people to keep together; few remained in their cabins for company was comforting, and though every effort was made to keep crewmen busy there were not many tasks on which they could be usefully employed once the emergency measures had been seen to. Thus small groups of men gathered in different parts of the ship to discuss the disaster, often laughing and joking with forced gaiety.

After fire stations it had been announced that breakfast would be served as usual and it was not long before places in the saloon began to fill. The wives having dressed hurriedly and otherwise made themselves presentable, lost no time in getting there. But once the meal was over they moved into the bar-lounge and as the morning progressed it became the focus, the place where there was always someone to talk to. From time to time officers and engineers, free for the moment from their duties or passing that way, would join the women or form their own small groups in the lounge. The stranding was the sole topic of conversation: their thoughts when the ship struck; what the fog would reveal when it lifted; how had the ship gone on the rocks; who was to blame; what would happen next, and how and when would they be taken off the ship; would they be flown back to the United Kingdom or given passage in one of the company's ships – and if so how long would they have to wait in Cape Town?

And of course there was humour. The catering officer's wife told of how she had gone to her emergency station in a Japanese

117

kimono, barefooted, lifejacket in one hand and bra in the other; and having put on the lifejacket first had been confronted with the problem of the bra.

In a corner of the bar-lounge Gareth Lloyd and Abu Seku discussed some of the more esoteric aspects of the stranding over mugs of hot coffee.

'Indeed, and it would be bloody Africa that gets in the way,' complained the Welshman.

'A great continent,' pronounced the Ghanaian. 'Puts out a rocky finger and stops three hundred and twenty thousand tons of Western technological bullshit from fourteen knots in seven seconds. Wham! Bang! Wham! Like Ali, you know. That's Africa, man.'

The suggestion of the catering officer's wife that they watch a Morecambe and Wise show on closed-circuit television was turned down.

'We can always see them,' pleaded Sandy. 'We've got a real shipwreck on our hands now. That's much more exciting.'

'Couldn't agree more,' said Jean Simpson.

'Sorry, dear. I was only trying to be helpful,' said the catering officer's wife.

Sandy put her arms round her shoulders. 'Of course you were. Perhaps later when we get bored with being shipwrecked.'

The atmosphere of comparative calm and acceptance in *Ocean Mammoth* was rudely shaken when the meteorological broadcast to shipping was received at midday. It forecast dispersal of the fog but warned of the imminence of a south-westerly gale in the area which included Cape Agulhas. It required all the calm assurance of the Captain's broadcast, reinforced by Sandy's morale-boosting among the wives, to restore some confidence. But that confidence was, they all suspected, no more than a front.

Everyone capable of intelligent thought was fearful of what was to come.

Chapter 18

By early afternoon the fog had dispersed. A falling barometer and rising wind from the north-west brought scudding clouds and frequent squalls of rain.

As the fog drifted away colour drained back into the landscape and the rocky projection that was Cape Agulhas slowly revealed itself, its tall red-and-white-ringed lighthouse tower standing up boldly against the undulations of the land behind.

With his binoculars the second officer could see a small village from which a scatter of seaside cottages stretched out towards Northumberland Point, a promontory some miles to the north-east. Closer at hand he saw groups of people and parked cars along the high ground beyond the rocks and realized they were sightseers. He took bearings of the lighthouse and Northumberland Point to fix *Ocean Mammoth*'s position, and found she was aground just on a mile off Cape Agulhas, bows heading to the south-west. The long swells, swollen by the rising tide, were breaking heavily on the foreshore. With the wind increasing in force and backing to the south-west the sea, broken and confused, came rolling in at right angles to the swell.

Earlier the light-keeper had called *Ocean Mammoth* on VHF to report the gale warning. Captain Crutchley had acknowledged the message with thanks, adding that the ship had already received the meteorological forecast. The light-keeper had then asked if there was anything he could do to assist. Captain Crutchley again thanked him but said he was in direct touch with the authorities concerned. He added that steps were being taken to assess the salvage problem. Once that had been done the necessary assistance would be requested.

At two-thirty the helicopter en route from Cape Town contacted *Ocean Mammoth* by voice radio. In the ensuing exchange it was agreed that it should land at Bredasdorp until the weather moderated. Its passengers would travel down to Cape Agulhas by road to view the situation from the shore, Captain Crutchley having made it clear that the weather precluded any possibility of their coming off to the ship by boat from St Mungo Bay.

By mid-afternoon the south-westerly wind was gusting at gale force. Rain squalls so reduced visibility at times that the light-house became difficult to see. At a conference between Captain Crutchley and Mr McLintoch, with Jarrett and the second engineer present, the situation posed by the weather was discussed. It was agreed there was little that could be done in the ship. The chief engineer reported that boilers and machinery were so far intact. He saw no danger of losing power unless condenser intakes were damaged.

It was decided that there was no point in asking for salvage tugs to stand by during the gale, since they would be unable to do anything until it had blown itself out.

'If it should be necessary to take off the crew, what then?' enquired Mr McLintoch whose thoughts, reinforced by un-pleasant recollections of an earlier experience, were travelling ahead of the discussion.

Speaking with calm assurance Captain Crutchley said, 'I trust it will not come to that, Chief. But if it should, the job will probably be done by helicopters.'

The chief engineer agreed and it was decided to ask the Cape Town agents to alert Court Helicopters Ltd. – the company which specialized in supplying the offshore needs of shipping round the South African coast, including the operation of a highly efficient sea rescue service. In talking to Cape Town the Captain stressed that assistance should be available at short notice.

In Zurich, in the old house off the Seefeldstrasse, an urgent meeting was taking place in the managing-director's office.

'Raustadt has important news.' The parchment folds of the chairman's seamed face were grave. 'I thought we should lose no time in discussing it.'

'You've certainly chosen an awkward time.' Neumann, the deputy-chairman, a fussy elderly man with a rasping voice, looked at his watch. 'I have a luncheon appointment in five minutes.'

'You'll be late,' said the chairman. 'But you won't mind. Now, Raustadt, tell us the news.'

'The Cape Town agents phoned shortly before noon today ...' Raustadt paused, enjoying the drama. 'Early this morning *Ocean Mammoth* ran aground in thick fog.'

The deputy-chairman's hunched shoulders opened and shut

120

like the wings of a large bird. He leant forward. 'My God! Where?'

'On Cape Agulhas.' Raustadt looked very stern.

'Good heavens! Well, I never.' Neumann ran a hand across his bald head. 'Can they get her off?'

The chairman looked up from the pad on which he was drawing geometrical shapes with a gold pencil. 'We don't know.'

'The agents say she is badly holed,' continued Raustadt. 'She was apparently travelling at speed when she ran aground. On a rocky bottom, they say.'

'Good heavens. But how extraordinary.' Neumann frowned in bewilderment. 'That huge ship – all that expensive technology. What on earth can Captain Crutchley have been doing to let such a thing happen? He has an excellent record, has he not?'

'He has,' said the chairman. 'But ships do run aground in fog. Even modern ones.'

'We have no details yet,' said Raustadt. 'No way of knowing how it happened.'

The deputy-chairman blinked through thick lenses. 'What a disaster. Incredible. Can you imagine it. A three hundred and twenty thousand ton VLCC running on to the rocks at speed.' He took a cigar from the box on the table with a wrinkled, bony hand.

Raustadt looked at the chairman, who nodded affirmatively. 'The Cape Town agents say the meteorological broadcast to shipping at noon today warned of a gale in the Agulhas area.'

'How would they know that if you spoke to them *before* noon?' challenged Neumann.

'Cape Town's time is two hours ahead of ours.'

'Of course, I'd forgotten that.' He lit a match and drew on the cigar. 'But my God! Now a gale. What a disaster. That fine . . .' He coughed noisily, took out a handkerchief and wiped his eyes. 'Sorry. The cigar. As I was saying . . . that fine ship. All that money. The insurers won't like it, will they? Fifty-five million dollars. That should ease our loan problems.'

'The thought had occurred to me.' The chairman looked at Raustadt speculatively. 'Has the ship been posted as a casualty at Lloyds?'

'Yes, Chairman. I spoke to London – to Kostadis – immediately after the Cape Town call. He is in touch with the brokers. They will be keeping a close watch on things.'

121

'Good. There isn't much else we can do now. Just wait and hope for the best.'

The deputy-chairman stood up. 'Well, I must be off to lunch. Thank you for bringing me in on this so soon.' He hesitated, a hand on the door. 'The crew? I mean, I hope they're going to be all right. The gale, you know.'

The chairman looked up from under bushy eyebrows. 'Of course, my dear Neumann. We all hope that.'

Jarrett and Foley had succeeded in avoiding each other most of the morning but soon after eleven o'clock, while the second officer was working at the chart-table, Jarrett came into the chartroom.

The chief officer looked at him with suspicion. 'What's that chart you're working on?'

Foley went on with what he was doing. 'Two-oh-nine-five,' he said without turning his head. 'Durban to Table Bay.'

'I suppose *you* wouldn't know where two-oh-eight-three was?'

'I thought you might know that, Jarrett. *You* used it last.'

The chief officer stiffened and his mouth set in a tight line. It was a double insult. The second officer had never before addressed him as 'Jarrett'. 'Better watch it, Foley,' he warned. 'I'm not taking any lip from you.'

The second officer pushed the parallel rulers aside, turned slowly and stared at him. 'Aren't you really,' he said. 'You know what you can do.'

Jarrett moved closer, thought better of it and stopped. 'If the situation wasn't so serious I'd knock your bloody teeth down your throat.'

'Oh, get stuffed,' said Foley, turning his back on him.

Chapter 19

Captain Crutchley finished reading the reports by the chief and second officers, laid them on the desk, took off his glasses and dabbed his eyes with cotton wool. He had demanded that they be written immediately because he wanted Jarrett and Foley to commit themselves while matters were still fresh in their minds. He knew from experience that given time, the benefit of hindsight and the advice of third parties, such accounts could be highly coloured.

His interviews with the two men earlier that morning had led him to expect the reports to be contradictory, but nothing like to the extent they were; each man seemed now to be striving to saddle the other with responsibility for the disaster; each was implying negligence on the part of the other; each was denying responsibility for the missing chart and other records. Captain Crutchley read the reports a second time before locking them in his safe with the logbooks and the course-recorder trace. The reports had sown grave doubts in his mind and he was much disturbed. Though he had heard rumours that these men disliked each other their behaviour was a blow to him for they had always stood high in his estimation. One of them, possibly both, had been negligent, or at least responsible for grave errors of judgement, but that charts and logbooks should be removed and that brother officers should turn on each other at such a time was to him indefensible. It was not in accord with the traditions of the sea; traditions which had served generations of British seamen and to which Captain Crutchley attached much importance. In the absence of the chart and other missing documents it was going to be difficult either to reconstruct an accurate picture of what had happened or apportion blame. Not that he had any doubt that as Master he was ultimately responsible in spite of the negligence of others. That, too, was a tradition of the sea.

There was much that needed explanation. The failure of the siren switch and the navigation aids. Electronic devices did fail from time to time, often through improper use, but the failures on this occasion exceeded anything in his experience, and taken together with the missing records might be thought to suggest something more than coincidence.

His thoughts went on: there would be a preliminary enquiry followed by a court of enquiry. Since the stranding had taken place on the South African coast the proceedings would be under South African jurisdiction.

A question to which the court would certainly address itself was why the Master had not been on the bridge once the ship encountered fog. He would draw attention to his night order book and explain that the chief officer had failed to call him. But Jarrett would deny that and give the court his own account.

The more Crutchley thought about this the more worried he became. The chief officer had said, 'You told me you had a bad headache. That you'd taken some pain-killers so that you could sleep – that you wouldn't be coming up.'

Some time after midnight, when the headache had become unbearable and he couldn't sleep, he had taken two of Grundewald's black and red capsules. But unless the conversation *had* taken place, how did the chief officer know about the sleeping pills? The only man in the ship who might know was Figureido who could have seen the bottle in the bedside cupboard and read the injunction 'Take two before retiring'. Could the steward have told Jarrett?

Once again the nagging doubt took hold of him. Though he had no recollection of the phone conversation was it not possible that he'd forgotten it, that drug-induced sleep had obliterated the memory? Jarrett had been so positive, insisting that Fernandez must have overheard the conversation. The chief officer would not have done that unless his story could be corroborated. Was he doing the man an injustice in disbelieving him? The more he thought about it the more uncertain and confused he became. Yet, with the ship in fog, Crutchley could not believe that he as Master would have said, 'I'm not coming up.'

He had never lacked courage and now he faced resolutely the fact that he was in for an extremely difficult time at the enquiry. With his thoughts much on his young wife and family in Farnham he got up from the desk, went to a window and looked out on the grey wind-swept sea. The dayroom, double glazed for air-conditioning, insulated him from sounds of the rising storm but the ship was shuddering as seas broke against the hull, and leaping sheets of spray, blown by the wind, swept across the deck.

124

To starboard, exposed to wind and sea, Cape Agulhas and the rocky coastline west of it frothed with white water and high-thrown spray. The light was fading and fast-moving clouds chased each other to the north-east, shedding their load as they passed. He could just make out the ringed tower of the light-house, a forlorn barber's pole poking into the darkened sky.

As he watched, a ball of fire flashed from its summit and he realized that the light had just been switched on. Instinctively he counted the seconds: one and – two and – three and – four and – five and – before the light flashed again. Five-second intervals. That was correct.

He looked once more along the immense sweep of the main-deck, thought of a whale stranded and dying, and felt an intolerable burden pressing upon him.

Darkness fell and shut out the land, leaving only a thin scatter of shore lights and the stabbing beam of the lighthouse. Earlier the light-keeper had called the ship by VHF and asked the Captain to speak to the marine surveyor and salvage expert who'd flown from Cape Town and were now in the signal station.

Crutchley got through and discussed with them the situation of *Ocean Mammoth*, the tank and sea bottom soundings, the apparent damage, and the steps already taken to lighten the ship. They talked about the latest weather report with its forecast of gale force winds and high seas on the Agulhas Bank, and agreed that if conditions worsened fuel oil from the ship's bunkers could be pumped overboard, forward on the windward side, to break the force of the seas.

The men ashore confirmed that nothing could be done by way of assessing the damage and considering the salvage problem until the gale had blown itself out and they were able to come on board. They expressed their sympathy with Captain Crutchley, adding rather forlornly, 'You may rest assured, Captain, that everything possible will be done for your ship.' Having explained that they would be back in the morning, they bade him good-night. Not long afterwards he saw headlights probing the darkness ashore, sweeping round in a wide arc and travelling inland.

The gale mounted as the night wore on and by ten o'clock the ship's anemometer was recording gusts close on ninety miles an hour. The wind, blowing now from west-south-west, was driving mountainous seas before it. Little affected by the fuel oil which was swept away by wind and sea as quickly as it was discharged, they broke against the stranded ship with increasing violence. The wind brought with it squalls of rain accompanied by thunder and lightning which revealed momentarily the wildness of the storm. In the intervals of darkness, only its sound and fury remained.

Captain Crutchley stood at the wheelhouse windows staring ahead, hypnotized by the swinging arms of the wipers, the powerful flash of the lighthouse, and the thud and drum of seas striking the ship.

It was the after superstructure, the tower of steel rising more than a hundred feet above the water, which took the full force of the gale, the wheelhouse shaking and shuddering to its buffeting.

By midnight the storm appeared to be reaching its zenith. The stern of the ship – still afloat and bearing the burden of the after superstructure and engineroom – strained against the stranded hull and despite the clamour of wind and sea the sound of metal groaning could be heard on deck. Mr McLintoch was soon on the bridge to report to the Captain.

'The welds on the maindeck above the transverse bulkhead between seven and eight starboard wing tanks are beginning to fracture.' His voice, hoarse with anxiety, was raised against the noise of the storm.

Captain Crutchley received the news in silence. 'You heard what I said, Captain?' prompted the chief engineer.

The Captain nodded. McLintoch must not know his thoughts; that he believed the ship to be dying; that the gale had sealed her fate. Instead he said, 'That is grave news, Chief. I take it nothing can be done.'

'Nothing, Captain. The free floating part of the ship is being forced by wind and sea to strain against the stranded hull. The stresses are enormous.' He stopped to shake the water from his oilskins and wipe his face.

There was no need to say more. Both men knew that VLCCs were designed as floating entities, to flex and whip in a seaway. With the forward two-thirds of the ship flooded and fast aground that was not possible.

'What can you see on deck, Chief?'

'It's no more than a slight buckling on the starboard side with

126

hairline fractures just now, Captain, but it's extending all the time. We can see and hear what's happening on the maindeck, but God knows what's going on down below. It's there the real trouble will be brewing.'

The Captain looked at the clock on the console. 'It's just gone low water, Chief. A few minutes ago.'

Mr McLintoch made a sucking noise through his teeth. 'Aye,' he said and stared through the window. There was a flash of lightning, the sound of thunder, and he saw the seas bearing down on the ship. The lee door of the wheelhouse slid open and they heard in all its rawness the scream of the wind rising and falling as it gusted. The crewman who'd come in slid the door to. Mr McLintoch shivered. 'If this gale continues the stresses will increase as the tide floods. God help her then,' he said.

'If the stern breaks away, Chief. How do you see things then?' It was a rhetorical question, for Captain Crutchley had only too clear a picture of how he saw things then.

For a while Mr McLintoch was lost in thought. 'Depends,' he began cautiously. 'Depends on the weather and the damage done when the bulkheads collapse . . .' He corrected himself. '*If* they collapse. If the transverse bulkheads between seven and eight wing tanks go, then eight will flood. If it does the bulkheads aft of that will probably go. The fore and aft bulkheads may go. Then the centreline bulkheads. One thing leads to another. One stress compounds another. In this gale . . .' he hesitated again. 'No use bluffing ourselves, Captain. In this gale I don't see much hope for any part of the ship if she breaks.'

'We shall see. She may not break. We must help her by assuming she will not break. The weather may moderate. We must believe it will. That, too, can help.' Captain Crutchley spoke with almost religious fervour. 'It is possible that we are near the end of the storm.' He paused but when he went on the fervour had gone. Now he was matter of fact, businesslike. 'There is one thing, Chief, which we both know. If she shows real signs of breaking we must flood the engineroom. There's not much water under the ship aft. A fathom or two depending on the tide. We must get the stern settled on the bottom as quickly as possible if it breaks away. If it still has positive buoyance it'll drift. God knows what would happen to it in this gale.'

Mr McLintoch's voice took on a deep melancholy. 'Aye, Captain. But it's a desperate remedy. I had it in mind but didn't care to say so. It's an awful thing to flood the power out of a ship.'

The Captain's mouth tightened. 'I know. It's as bad as murder, Chief. But it may have to be done. We must be ready to do it at short notice.'

McLintoch sighed noisily. 'Aye. I'll tell Benson to prepare for that. We'll blackout the main boiler right away and switch to the auxiliary. Make ready for getting the inspection covers off the condenser doors . . . aye, and slacken alternate nuts on the sea-water circulating pump casing. It's quite a job, it is.' He shook his head in the darkness, went through the chartroom and down the stairway to the lift.

On the Captain's orders the signal lamp on the starboard wing was trained on deck to illuminate the area where the fractures were reported. Nothing could be seen from the bridge but the light would help the men keeping watch down there.

The wheelhouse shook, the ship shuddered as if suffering from ague and the wind screamed as Captain Crutchley slid open the port door and went out on to the bridge. It required all his strength to stand against the gale. Driving rain, cutting into his face, obscured the dark glasses so he took them off and faced the storm, waiting for the lightning. When it came he saw as a blurred picture the huge stretch of maindeck, wet and glistening, reaching out ahead of him. Walls of spray leapt into the air to starboard and were driven by the wind across the ship, foaming as they sluiced away under the long lines of piping beside the catwalk. He raised a clenched fist in the darkness. 'For Christ's sake stop it,' he shouted against the storm. 'You are killing her.' Then he was silent, suddenly ashamed of the display of emotion, of the futility of the gesture.

'She is dying,' he told himself soberly as he struggled towards the wheelhouse. 'Nothing can save her.'

Chapter 20

The chief engineer had been gone for more than ten minutes when he called the wheelhouse by R/T. 'The fractures and buckling along the welds are opening and extending, Captain.' McLintoch's urgent voice was almost drowned by the sounds of the storm, but someone near him could be heard to say, 'Christ! Look at that.'

'Flood then, Chief. Flood right away.'

'Aye, Captain. I'll do that.'

The Captain called out, 'Mr Foley, tell the radio officer to inform Cape Town and the sea rescue station at Gordons Bay that the after part of the ship threatens to break away from the hull. We are flooding the engineroom in order to anchor the stern section if the break occurs.' The Captain hesitated. 'Tell them we require immediate assistance. A tug or rescue craft to stand by. We know there's little they can do in this weather so close inshore, but we'd appreciate the moral support and – ' The Captain hesitated again. 'That's enough. They'll know what I mean.'

'Yes, sir.' Foley, whose pulse rate had risen appreciably, passed the message. Feeny repeated it, adding, 'I'll get that off right away.' By the time Foley had replaced the handset the Captain was talking into the ship's broadcast system.

'Pay attention. This is the Captain speaking. Pay attention. It is possible that a break will occur in the hull between numbers seven and eight tanks. Small fractures have appeared there.' The Captain's voice was calm and measured; no trace of anxiety, no hastening of speech, no slurring of words. 'We are flooding the engineroom as a precautionary measure and to ensure stability if the after part of the ship breaks away. The flooding should make it possible for the stern to settle on a more or less even keel with the after superstructure well above water. The auxiliary diesel will supply power for lighting and communications once flooding shuts off our main supply.' The Captain paused. 'There is no cause for alarm. Passengers and stewards are to assemble in the bar-lounge and remain there until further notice. Crewmen not already assigned to special duties must assemble in the recreation room and remain there until further notice.' The Captain stopped, cleared his throat, then began to speak again, very slowly and deliberately. 'We are in touch with the authorities ashore. They will no doubt be taking action to assist us. I will see that you are kept fully informed. You can help me – and your-selves – by keeping calm and in this way setting an example to others. That is all.'

The Captain did not tell them that the barometer showed no signs of rising, that the force of the wind was, if anything, increasing. Nor had he explained that there was no point in sending them to emergency stations since no boat could be lowered in that weather. And he had not told them of his grave doubts about the after part remaining stable if it broke away. The flooding would take time and he doubted if they had much time available. Finally he had not told them that rescue services, sea or air, could not possibly operate under the conditions prevailing. Negative information could not help morale.

He replaced the handmike. 'Mr Foley. Get me the light-keeper on VHF. I'll bring him up to date.' Crutchley knew it would not help, but it was something which had to be done. He looked at the flashing light just on a mile away. There were men and women in that little community, safe and secure, the gale no more to them than a boisterous disturbance of wind and water. Many of them would be in their beds, snug and warm; some, no doubt, would be watching the lights of *Ocean Mammoth*, wondering what was going on in the supertanker, how those on board were standing up to the disaster. It was strange, he reflected, that a mile could mean so much in terms of safety and danger.

As the Captain's broadcast finished Abu Seku, busy with Gareth Lloyd easing nuts on the seawater circulating casing, let go a hollow laugh. 'The Old Man sure has a great script writer.'

'Indeed he has,' said the Welshman. 'I liked very much the bit about "the shore authorities will no doubt be taking action to assist us". That really got me. For Christ's sake, Abu, what can they do in a full gale?'

'You got him wrong, man. He didn't say *what* action. Jesus, this nut's tight. A tough bastard. They'll be taking action all right, Gareth. Plenty of it in the pubs and clubs tonight.' The

130

Ghanaian cackled merrily. 'Woosh! whoof! This goddam nut won't shift anyway. It don't want to flood the ship, man.'

When he went to the engineroom to supervise the flooding, Mr McLintoch left Malim with a crewman at the site of the fracturing welds and buckling plates.

Foley, looking down from the bridge, could see the two men crouching fifty feet below him, their backs braced against the pipelines to starboard of the catwalk. Their hard hats and oil-skins, dripping with water, reflected the light from the signal lamp. From time to time they ducked as clouds of spray swept over them. In spite of the signal lamp they were still using torches and looking down on deck where the beams were focused he thought he saw the buckling, along it a spidery crack, and he shivered involuntarily. At that moment Malim's voice came through on the bridge R/T. 'Wheelhouse! Wheelhouse!' He was shouting to make himself heard. 'The plating is buckling and opening. There's a fracture along a line of welds above the transverse bulkheads between seven and eight tanks. We can hear metal straining and breaking in seven.' The third engineer's hoarse shouting conveyed his fear. He went on. 'The break runs from the starboard side, across to amidships where it disappears under the pipelines. Probably stops at the centreline bulkhead. Some of the pipeline brackets are beginning to buckle. Not safe here any longer. We're going up to the walkway on the foreside of the housing. Okay?'

'Do that, Mr Malim,' said Captain Crutchley. 'And be smart about it.' With remarkable speed for such a big man, he moved to a telephone and called the engine control-room.

In the wheelhouse the Captain and the chief engineer were discussing the crisis.

'The after part of the ship is breaking away from the hull along the transverse bulkheads between seven and eight tanks,' said Mr McLintoch. 'The fractures and buckling have continued past the centreline bulkheads. Aye, and to starboard the break on the maindeck and down the ship's side is opening. It's the stresses imposed by wind and sea and tide. Compounded, you see.' As he spoke the sound of plates and frames buckling and parting, sometimes a shrill complaining squeal, at others a subdued

131

rumble, could be heard above the noise of the storm.

The Captain was silent. Too many things were happening. There were too many distractions. He must concentrate, he told himself. Should he sound emergency stations, get everybody up on deck, or would it be better to have them under cover on Deck One, just one level below the bridge? As a result of the flooding, steam had been lost on both boilers and the auxiliary generator was now supplying electric power. The throb of the 2500 BHP diesel, situated high up in the engineroom and well above the flooding level, was becoming a familiar background noise in the housing aft.

What made the problem so difficult, he explained to the chief engineer, was uncertainty as to how the after part of the ship – the stern section, about a fifth of her total length – would behave if it were still buoyant when the break came. The chief officer had fed the relevant information into the cargo loading computer – including estimates of the tonnage of floodwater in the engineroom – and reported that it should be reasonably stable. Captain Crutchley and Mr McLintoch were, however, by no means sure. There were too many imponderables: the effect of gale force winds and seas on the high superstructure if it were afloat on its own; the list which would develop since the engineroom was not subdivided into watertight compartments and floodwater would flow to the lower side. Once the stern lost buoyancy and sank the nature of the sea bottom would be important. If it were level the after part would settle evenly; if it shelved steeply or there were rock ledges there would be problems. Finally, if the break occurred while there was positive buoyancy the stern would drift before the gale and defeat the object of the flooding which was to get it aground on an even keel as soon as possible.

'If I get everybody up on deck,' said the Captain, 'they'll be exposed to the gale and God knows what'll happen to them if the after part floats free and takes a heavy list.'

'Aye, it's a terrible problem, Captain. Maybe better to get them up to Deck One. They'll be higher up then and . . .' Mr McLintoch shrugged his shoulders, spread his hands in a gesture of desperation. 'Well, if the worst comes to the worst, they'll be able to come up the stairway to the bridge deck. The Lord knows it won't help them in this weather, but at least they won't feel trapped like drowning rats.'

Mr McLintoch, who came from Glasgow, pronounced it

132

'tr-r-apped like dr-r-ooning r-rats' which made the prospect seem even more dreadful to Alan Simpson who was in the shadows on the far side of the wheelhouse.

In the semi-darkness the Captain's face was drawn, the red-rimmed eyes behind the dark glasses more than usually inflamed. 'I don't think it'll come to the worst, Chief,' he said, believing it probably would but conscious of the need to stiffen morale. 'Nevertheless, we'll bring them up to Deck One. They can assemble in my office and dayroom.'

'And in mine, Captain.'

Crutchley nodded. 'Yes, of course. That will help.'

'Any news from the shore?'

'A sea-going tug left Cape Town at one o'clock this morning. In this weather she'll need all of twelve to fourteen hours to get here. Gordons Bay is sending a rescue launch. ETA between ten and eleven in the forenoon. And the South African Navy is diverting a frigate. It's on passage from East London to Simonstown. May be here soon after daylight, they say.'

'Thank the Lord for that,' said Mr McLintoch. 'They won't be able to do anything in this gale, but it'll be good to see them. What about helicopters?'

'The weather's too much for them just now, but when it shows signs of moderating they'll no doubt be along. It's the best way to get men off a ship.'

'Aye, it is. And women.' Mr McLintoch was a stickler for detail.

Captain Crutchley moved along the console. 'Right, Chief. I'll do that broadcast now.'

The chief engineer took the hint and made for the engineroom.

Shortly before two o'clock in the morning, when it seemed the gale could do no more, its severity increased. The wind shrieked and screamed and incoming seas hurled themselves against the ship with unbelievable ferocity. Flashes of lightning revealed a foaming maelstrom, the wind snatching wave crests into flying spray so dense that despite mechanical wipers it was often impossible to see through the wheelhouse windows.

Foley was reporting that the anemometer had recorded a wind speed of 102 mph, when the after superstructure shook convulsively. There was a loud rending noise, a screech of steel, as plating and frames on deck and in the tanks below gave way, followed by the dull boom of an explosion and a flash of light which temporarily blinded those in the wheelhouse. The explosion seemed to have taken place at the point where the bridgehouse met the maindeck. The stern section wobbled as if a giant hand had pushed it off balance, before listing over to port.

Captain Crutchley, wedged into the gap in the console which housed the compass binnacle, shouted, 'Hold on as best you can. She's broken away.' As he reached over and grabbed the hand-mike of the ship's broadcast system, the wheelhouse lights flickered and went out. He pressed the 'speak' button but the mike was dead. All power had gone.

'Mr Simpson,' he shouted. 'Take a torch, double down to Deck One and get everybody up on to the starboard side of the bridge deck.'

When Simpson had gone the Captain tried to speak to the engine control-room by voicepipe. There was no reply and he assumed the engineroom had been evacuated. The list had increased to thirty degrees and from the staggering motion of the stern it was evident that the after part of the ship was drifting down wind away from the stranded forepart. The whole stern section carrying the accommodation housing, the engineroom, the funnel, the bridge, the very heart of the ship, was now a separate unit; a huge unwieldy structure with a beam of 190 feet and a length of 230 feet. It was listing heavily to port and was down by the bows – if the jagged stub of deck over the compartments and bulkheads which made up number eight tank could be called a bow.

The Captain suspected that the explosion had taken place in the pumproom. The pumpman had been there doing a last-minute check that pipe and gas line valves were shut when it was clear that a break was likely. Crutchley had tried to communicate with the pumproom but the phones there and in the cargo control-room were out of action and there was no response to calls on voicepipes and R/T.

From the violence of the explosion and the bows down trim of the after part, he concluded that fore and aft and athwartship bulkheads in the vicinity of the pumproom had collapsed and extensive flooding was taking place. He derived grim satisfaction from this because the sooner the stern sank and found bottom in shallow water the better. If it remained afloat for any length of time it would drift into deep water. With the wind blowing a full

134

gale it wouldn't take long for that to happen, and it would be disastrous.

The absence of the chief officer was something which nagged at the Captain. Where was the man, he kept asking himself, hoping that Jarrett had not been in the control-room or with the pumpman. He badly needed the chief officer to take charge of the crewmen and passengers who would be coming up to the bridge deck. Crutchley had no doubt they would need a strong hand to control them. There was certain to have been a great deal of alarm – even panic – over the last few minutes.

The third officer made his way through the chartroom towards the stairway to Deck One. He didn't relish the task the Captain had assigned him. Even with a torch it was frightening in the dark, and with the stern so heavily listed, its movements so haphazard, a sickening unrhythmic lunging and rolling, it was difficult to keep one's feet. He could hear the wind shrieking and feel the seas buffeting the after part, very close at hand they seemed now. He had a vivid mental picture of what the remnants of the bulk-heads to number eight tank must look like and he was terrified not only by that and by what was happening, but by the possibility that he would betray his fear. With these thoughts in mind he reached the top of the stairway and started down it when he was almost swept off his feet by a rush of men coming up. A torch flashed from the bottom of the stairs behind them and he heard Jarrett's shout, 'Carry on to the starboard side of the bridge deck. Hold on there until we know what's happening. Don't panic. It won't help. Figureido will look after you for the time being. I'm going back to see how things are with the engineers.'

The third officer breathed a sigh of relief. His mission was no longer necessary. He turned and joined the hurrying stream of terrified men and women struggling up the heaving stairway.

135

Chapter 21

Ocean Mammoth's stern section or after part, broke away from the stranded forepart at eight minutes past two in the morning. Eleven minutes later it had settled on the bottom with a fairly steep list to port, having come to rest upon shelving rock; the sounding to port gave twelve fathoms and that to starboard eight and a half.

During its eleven minutes afloat the stern section, driven by the gale, had travelled more than a mile. Listing over to port the superstructure had acted as a great sail which drove the sinking hulk down wind. It had grounded heading south. The light at Cape Agulhas, bearing 268°, slightly over two miles distant, was just visible through the rain and spindrift. The port side of the stern section was awash at maindeck level; to starboard the tops of waves at times reached the level of the maindeck though the freeboard was close to forty feet.

With the hulk aground the superstructure still stood high out of the water, but seas were flooding the port side up to Deck Three, one level above the maindeck. Deck Three had, as a result, been evacuated.

Flooding combined with the list had put the greater part of the engineroom under water. On the port side it had, with wave action, reached sufficiently high to put the auxiliary diesel generator out of action. Mr McLintoch had ordered everyone out of the engineroom when water began to pour through the bulkhead on the foreside of which lay the pumproom. That bulkhead had been breached either by the explosion under the bridge, or by stresses transferred from collapsing bulkheads and frames in the pumproom. Eventually it had more or less opened to the sea.

For those in *Ocean Mammoth* the eleven minutes of drift had been a time of unremitting terror. Even when the hulk had finally grounded circumstances continued to be fearsome coming on top of a night of endless crises, one piled upon the other until it seemed that body and mind, worn out by fear and exhaustion, could bear no more.

Throughout the drift, and for some time afterwards, the crew had gathered in darkness on the starboard side of the bridge deck. They had been sent there because it was the high side of the list; but it was also the weather side and they were exposed to all the rawness of the gale. Soaked by rain and spindrift, cold and wretched after hours without sleep, they kept close to each other for warmth and mutual protection, their backs to the sloping side of the bridgehouse, clinging to anything they could lay hands on. Horror and uncertainty were aggravated by the darkness, the staggering motion, the spray from the seas breaking against the side, and the shriek of the wind.

Captain Crutchley had ordered the women to take shelter in the chartroom. There, though protected from the worst of the elements, they sat on the deck in a state of mindless terror, without light but for the occasional flash of a torch wielded by a passing officer. At times they would break down and Sandy would put aside her fears to comfort them.

As soon as it was possible Jarrett set out to look for Jonathan Malim and the crewman who'd been with him on the walkway above the cargo control-room at the time of the explosion. With a lifeline round his waist, tended by Fernandez from the high side of the walkway, he searched along it with a torch. There was no sign of the missing men. The walkway was buckled and torn amidships and he imagined they'd been killed or injured in the explosion and carried away by heavy seas.

He tried but failed to reach the control-room. It had been badly damaged by the explosion and flooded by seas from the port side where the maindeck was awash. He was satisfied that the pumpman could not have survived.

As he made his way back, he was swept off his feet by a sea and dashed against the guard rails. The lifeline held, and when the sea receded he got to his feet and staggered back to Fernandez who was hauling on the line. The quartermaster saw the gash on the chief officer's forehead and the limp arm hanging at his side and helped him down to the radio office – the only lighted space left.

There the catering officer did what he could with bandages, splints and brandy. Jarrett asked for more brandy, but refused a sling.

'Can't do without the arm just now.'

'Not much use to you as it is.'

Jarrett shook his head. 'You'd be surprised.' He drank another tot of brandy and went off to report the casualties to the Captain.

The catering officer and Piet Pieterse – the only volunteer for that duty – were down in the saloon pantry on Deck Three. By torch-light they collected biscuits, cheese and apples which they offered to crewmen and passengers. But there were few with appetites and most refused.

'Pity we couldn't have given them some hot coffee,' said the catering officer. 'But what can one do without heat?'

'Yes, sir.' Wet to the skin, Pieterse shivered. 'You said it.'

When the power failed, Tim Feeny switched on the batteries which supplied lighting for the radio office and power for the emergency transmitter. Soon after the stern section broke away he was able to let Cape Town and the signal station at Cape Agulhas know what had happened.

He had kept in touch with them throughout the drift, and when the hulk grounded he had obtained a position from the second officer and passed it to them. The light-keeper told Feeny that in the intervals between rain and squalls he could see the stranded hulk in the flash of the Agulhas light.

Soon after dark Feeny made contact with the South African frigate *Simon van der Stel*. Positions were exchanged and the captain of the frigate gave his ETA at the wreck as 0730.

'Two and a half hours after sunrise,' added Foley as he passed the message to Captain Crutchley.

Of those on board, the Captain was probably the least appalled by the prospect of death. It was not something he contemplated with equanimity; death remained for him, as for all, the ultimate terror. Yet in the present circumstances – the problem of his eyesight, the certainty of unemployment, his future more than ever imperilled by the loss of *Ocean Mammoth* – death held certain advantages. His personal insurances were substantial and he would be worth more to his young wife and family dead than alive. Throughout the gale, desperately worried though he was, he found some comfort in this knowledge.

Chapter 22

By ten o'clock in the morning with the barometer rising and the gale showing some signs of abating, morale in the hulk was improving. The sky was clearing and to starboard colour was returning to the rocky coastline which had for so long been hidden. The red-and-white-ringed lighthouse tower once again stood out boldly, a solitary but reassuring sentinel for those still aboard.

In the foreground without its stern, *Ocean Mammoth*'s stranded hull, almost a thousand feet of it, looked like the beheaded corpse of some primeval sea monster. Now acting as a huge steel breakwater it lay astride the view of the headland, seas breaking against its far side constantly throwing up clouds of spray like puffs of white smoke.

Less than a mile away to port the frigate lay head on to the gale, its bows, rising and falling to meet the seas, capped at times with bursts of foaming water.

On the starboard wing of the bridge, wedged between the gyro binnacle and the screen, the second officer examined the headland through binoculars. Next to him Captain Crutchley, his hands on the bridge coaming, steadied himself against the wind.

Foley saw a small, mothlike object moving on the high land behind Cape Agulhas. 'I've picked up the helicopter, sir,' he said. 'Just to the right of the lighthouse. It's coming in low over the land.'

'Good. I'll talk to the pilot when it's down.' The unfamiliar hoarseness of the Captain's voice, the slight sag of his shoulders, were the only outward signs of exhaustion. He had not slept for almost thirty hours. The second officer had been without sleep for thirty-six. His bloodshot eyes had dark pouches beneath them.

They waited in silence until Foley said, 'He's going to land now, sir. Hovering over the houses to the right of the tower.' The Captain nodded. Foley wondered why he didn't use the binoculars which hung from a strap round his neck. Was he too tired to take off the dark glasses?

'It's landed, sir,' said Foley. 'He's put it down behind the houses.'

Captain Crutchley made for the wheelhouse.

The frightened groups of men who had spent the night huddled together on the bridge deck had long since broken up. Crewmen were now moving about the drenched windswept deck looking at the land, pointing to the stranded hull inshore, exclaiming at its grotesque aspect, ducking as spray swept the deck and making a joke of it; then, moving down the slippery slope to the port side, they would look at the frigate, admire its elegant lines and comment upon the way it was riding the seas. The men, dishevelled, their faces drawn and haggard, their eyes red-rimmed from long hours of strain, had taken on new life and they laughed and shouted together like schoolboys on a playground. They had been quick to see the helicopter arrive and now they were on the starboard side looking towards the lighthouse, speculating as to what would happen next.

The four women were out on the bridge and they, too, were sharing in the relief and excitement the morning had brought. Once daylight had come and with it news that the glass was rising and the worst was over, they had asked permission to go down to their cabins. There, despite the gale, they'd washed, changed into clean clothes, done their hair and tidied themselves. Now back on deck in raincoats with scarves about their heads they stood up to the wind, smiling bravely. Tired though they were, they looked less worn than the men.

A good deal had happened that morning since the coming of daylight. Captain Crutchley had spoken by radiophone to the captain of the frigate and to the agents in Cape Town, and a number of decisions had been made. The frigate would continue to stand by until the gale had abated; the helicopter would arrive at Cape Agulhas at about ten o'clock; the pilot would decide when weather conditions were suitable for lifting off the survivors; the sea rescue launch from Gordons Bay had been recalled – the frigate and the helicopter could do all that was necessary. Those arrangements made, it was a matter of waiting for the weather to improve. The hulk was still taking a battering from the gale, and from time to time the superstructure would shudder and jar as if

140

to warn those on board that their ordeal was not yet over.

It was Friday. The Foleys had not been alone together for the best part of thirty hours, not since the Thursday morning when he'd come off watch between four and five o'clock. The ship had run aground less than two hours later. He had seen her in the chartroom several times during the hours of darkness when the gale was at its height. He had ignored her at first but later relented. She had looked so miserable – and she was trying so hard to put a brave face on things and help the other women – that he'd gone to her, spoken a few words of encouragement and touched her cheek with awkward affection.

At noon on Friday she came to him on the bridge deck to say that she was going down to the cabin to pack. The Captain had passed word that survivors would be allowed to take off a small bag with essentials but no more.

'Is there anything I can do for you, George?' She looked at him uncertainly.

'No thanks. I'll get my own things.'

She had gone then, but she'd looked so hurt that he followed her a few minutes later. He found her sitting on the bed weeping.

He put a hand on her shoulder. 'What's the trouble, Sandy?'

'Oh, I don't know. Everything. I'm so tired I can't think.'

He sat down beside her, kissed her. 'Come on,' he said. 'The worst's over now. It's still blowing a bit but before long the chopper'll be lifting us off. Better put a few things in a bag. I'll do the same.'

As if to belie what he had said, the superstructure trembled and from somewhere deep in its bowels there came a prolonged rumbling.

'It's not over,' she said. 'Not here or anywhere. There's all sorts of problems ahead.'

He put an arm round her. 'Come on, Sandy. That's not like you.' For the next few minutes he did his best to comfort her and when she'd dried her eyes and pulled herself together they got on with putting essentials into airline bags. When they'd finished he said, 'Like something to eat, Sandy?' It was well past midday and a long time since a meal had been served.

'No. I'm not hungry. God, you look tired, George. Are you all right?'

141

'Yes. I'm okay. But bloody tired. Look, the stewards have put out cold meat, cheese and bread rolls in the pilot's cabin. We can have a drink there, too. What about it? Have a G and T? Do you good.'

She could see that he was worried, concerned for her. She nodded. 'All right. But – one thing?'

'Yes. What's that?'

'Will Freeman Jarrett be there?'

Foley stiffened. 'Why?'

'Is he okay? His head and arm, I mean?'

He noticed that she'd dodged the question. 'Nothing much wrong with him. Cut forehead and a fractured forearm. Wandering round a bit dazed smelling of booze.' His eyes challenged hers. 'Why do you have to bring him up at this time?'

'I suppose because it could be awkward.' She was nervous, hesitant. 'Because you're not talking to him. It'll be noticed, if it hasn't been already.'

'Too bad. I'm sure a lot's been noticed already, but I'm *not* talking to him.'

'George, don't think I'm asking for forgiveness – for him or for me. I've been crazy. What's been done, has been done. But is it necessary to go on with the hate now? Can't we behave like civilized human beings after all we've been through?'

He stood back, his eyes hard. 'Civilized human beings. My God! You could fool me. Your boy friend having seduced you, is now doing his best to saddle me with responsibility for running the ship aground in *his* watch.'

'George!' She looked horrified. 'How? He can't do that. Surely he can't?'

Foley's pent-up emotions were suddenly too much for him; he forgot his resolve to be kind. 'Better ask him when you're next together. No doubt he'll enjoy telling you.' He turned his back and left the cabin, slamming the door behind him.

By mid-afternoon wind and sea had moderated sufficiently for the helicopter pilot to inform the ship by voice radio that he was ready to lift off survivors.

Captain Crutchley at once ordered a general muster on the bridge deck. This done he spoke to the pilot and soon afterwards the big Sikorsky S61N came out from the shore. The sound of its engines and the flop-flop of its rotor rose as it grew larger, reaching a crescendo as it came in close and hovered nose down over the hulk, the down draught from its rotor blades blowing on to the bridge deck with the force of a gale. The pilot turned the Sikorsky in a tight circle as he checked what lay below and conducted a laconic exchange with Captain Crutchley by voice radio. Evidently satisfied with what he saw he said, 'Okay. We'll begin now.'

A line came down from the Sikorsky and the task of winching up the survivors – two at a time – began. Two men who'd suffered steam burns in the engineroom were the first to go. They were winched up in stretchers; the women followed and then the crew. With the wind still blowing hard it called for nerve and skill to hold the big helicopter in position to leeward of the signal mast while the winching took place; but the pilot was no newcomer to the task and the lift proceeded without hitch, the number of survivors on the bridge deck steadily diminishing until only the Captain and Mr McLintoch were left. It was not long before they too had been winched up and the Sikorsky with its heavy load roared its way towards the shore.

In addition to a canvas grip with personal items, Captain Crutchley had with him a small suitcase. In it were the deck and Decca logbooks, his standing orders and night order books, two charts which included the Cape Agulhas area, the course-recorder graph for the twenty-four hours to 0200 on 29 October, and the written reports by Jarrett and Foley.

Immediately after the landing the injured men had been transferred from the helicopter to an ambulance and driven into Bredasdorp, some thirty miles away. There the survivors were to spend the night before going on to Cape Town.

As the helicopter deposited its load behind the cottages near the lighthouse, they were met by the light-keeper and his aides, taken into their houses and given coffee and sandwiches. Captain Crutchley and Mr McLintoch went to the signal station where they were soon engaged in lengthy discussion with the marine surveyor and salvage expert.

The light was fading when the survivors boarded the coach which was to take them all into Bredasdorp, save Captain Crutchley and Mr McLintoch who went in by car with the salvage expert and the marine surveyor, Captain Summerbee.

As the car drove away from Cape Agulhas, Captain Crutchley

looked back for the last time at the broken remains of the great ship he'd once been so proud to command. Clouds of spray were still leaping from the long black hull; a mile beyond it, just visible in the gathering dusk, the white superstructure stood out of the water, a huge and ghostly sepulchre, the sea surging and foaming about its base.

In that moment he knew he would never again command a ship at sea and behind the dark glasses his tired eyes filled with tears.

Most of the thoroughly exhausted survivors had gone straight to bed on reaching the hotel, forgoing the evening meal for the sleep they so badly needed. But not all of them, for a few of the hardier souls were to be found in the hotel bar celebrating their survival. Among these were Gareth Lloyd and Abu Seku. The Ghanaian's presence in the bar had been tacitly approved by the proprietor notwithstanding the proscriptions of apartheid. The two men were at a table in a corner discussing their experiences over a long succession of beers.

'To think,' said Gareth Lloyd, 'that we wouldn't be here at all but for that bearing failure.'

'That's life.' Abu Seku poured a generous draught of lager down his throat. 'Poor old Jonah. He didn't know what he was letting us in for.'

'Maybe it was not his fault. Electronic alarm systems are fine once the teething troubles have been ironed out. I don't think we'd yet done that.'

'It would have to be Jonah that lost his life, wouldn't it. Unlucky to the end.'

'Maybe it was better that way. His wife's death was too much for him.'

'Yeh. Could be.' The African drank thoughtfully. 'My Welsh friend, I must tell you something. This beer is great. Really great.' He looked round the room, leant forward, his manner conspiratorial. 'Can you imagine. Me, a black from the Ghana bush, sitting here *illegally* drinking it. Now isn't that wonderful?'

'Indeed it is, my friend. Talking as a white from the wrong side of the Cardiff tracks, I am astonished.' Gareth Lloyd raised his tankard.'But anyway, here's to two great marine engineers.'

'Yes, sir. I like that.' Abu Seku clinked his tankard against the

144

Welshman's. 'You know, it's not so many hours since I thought
we'd have to swim for it. Jesus, I was praying then. Asking for
pardon for all the lousy things I've done. Promising never to do
them again. Just like that I was.'

'Tell you something for your black ears alone. Very confidential
it is.'

'What's that, man?'

'I cannot swim.'

'So you can't swim. Now isn't that something. Hey, you know,
you had a great chance to learn out there, Gareth. Anyway,
there I was praying to the Lord to save me, and at the same time
thanking him that he had me born in Ghana. You know, surf
boats and the surf. That was my life. Swim like a bloody black
fish, I could. I tell you, man. Big waves coming in like they want
to eat you up. But nice and warm that West Coast water. Very
warm. And good sand to land on. I didn't fancy making that
swim last night. Cold water and big black rocks. Jesus. And
maybe the Lord too busy with all the other guys because they
couldn't swim like me. You know he has to be fair to all.'

The Welshman looked up from under shaggy eyebrows. 'He
has indeed, Abu.' He grabbed the empty tankards and stood up.
'Let's have some more beer.'

Chapter 23

Three days after the crew arrived in Cape Town a preliminary enquiry into the stranding of *Ocean Mammoth* was held on the orders of the Secretary for Transport, acting in terms of Section 264 of the Republic of South Africa's Merchant Shipping Act No. 57 of 1951.

At the preliminary enquiry Captain Crutchley, the chief officer, Freeman Jarrett, the second officer, George Foley, the chief engineer, Hamish McLintoch, the second engineer, Benjamin Benson, and others involved had attended and sworn statements before the presiding officer.

Soon after the enquiry summonses were served on Crutchley, Jarrett and Foley ordering them to appear before a Court of Marine Enquiry four weeks later, to answer charges in connection with the stranding of the VLCC *Ocean Mammoth* off Cape Agulhas on 29 October. Subpoenas having been served to those who would be required as witnesses, the remainder of the crew were flown back to Rotterdam, London or their home countries, whichever they elected, at the expense of the owners.

An exception was Piet Pieterse, the coloured steward. He was not offered the choice as he was already in his home country. Paid off in Cape Town, he was left to his own devices.

In the weeks following the preliminary enquiry Captain Crutchley and his chief and second officer had been busy discussing their defence with their legal advisers. In view of the conflict of interests evident at the preliminary enquiry, each had his own lawyer and counsel. These appointments had been arranged by the Merchant Navy and Airline Officers' Association in London, the professional body to which the three men belonged and which would bear the costs of their defence. This enabled them to secure the services of three well-known barristers, all State's Counsel, the equivalent of a Queen's Counsel in Britain.

The summonses to appear before the court were couched in the briefest terms: Captain Crutchley was to meet a charge of 'by wrongful act or default stranding the VLCC *Ocean Mammoth*, then under his command, off Cape Agulhas on 29 October' – Freeman Jarrett and George Foley were each charged with 'contributory negligence or default or ineptitude leading to the stranding . . .'

The night before the enquiry Captain Crutchley left his hotel in The Gardens for an after-dinner walk. That walk, his only relaxation and exercise, had become a custom over recent weeks; it was most useful therapy at a time when he was beset with the gravest problem of a long career.

As always when he reached Orange Street he set off down it, crossing to the right-hand side shortly before reaching the gates of the Mount Nelson, then continuing along the pavement until he turned into Government Avenue, the beautiful and historic pedestrian way which led down between the botanical gardens and the Houses of Parliament to Adderley Street.

It was a warm night and the southern sky was bright with stars. A gentle breeze stirred the leaves of the oaks lining the Avenue and brought with it the scent of flowers.

Behind Captain Crutchley as he walked, Table Mountain loomed large above the city, the lights of residential areas glittering about its lower slopes. Ahead, at the far end of the Avenue, he could see the neon lights of Adderley Street and the constantly changing patterns of light from traffic moving along it.

He wished once again that his wife could be with him. The beauty of the Cape would have meant much to her. More than that, she would have given him the comfort, support and companionship he now so badly needed. On three occasions he had telephoned her and they'd had long and tense discussions. She had tried to encourage him, to be optimistic but he could tell that she, too, was deeply worried. The telephone was no satisfactory way of bridging the six-thousand-mile gap between Farnham and Cape Town.

Halfway along the Avenue he found a bench and sat down. His mind was a discordant jumble of thoughts until he concentrated it on the overriding problem – the Court of Marine Enquiry which would begin its sitting the next morning. It was going to be a nasty, messy business – he had no doubt about that. The incorrect course steered, Jarrett and Foley's attempts to implicate each other, the failure of the electronic systems, the missing

147

chart, pages torn from logbooks and the trace from the course-recorder. Finally, and to him most important of all, his absence from the bridge, enormously complicated by Jarrett's alleged phone conversation and his denial of it. All these things had emerged at the preliminary enquiry.

Ocean Mammoth was the biggest ship ever to have been wrecked on the South African coast. The press, alerted by rumours and conflicting statements at the preliminary enquiry, had sensed something sensational and made the forthcoming enquiry news long before it began.

As he thought once more of Jarrett's behaviour, the muscles in Crutchley's stomach contracted and he felt a spasm of pain as if he'd been stabbed with a burning knife. The recollection filled him with an overwhelming sense of helplessness. There was nothing he could do. All now depended on his counsel, James Goodbody.

Goodbody was a large ample man with a florid complexion and a deceptively genial manner. He was noted at the Cape Town Bar for the disarming smile he affected when about to destroy a witness, and for the red carnation he habitually wore out of court. After their first meeting, Crutchley had decided that he would rather have this formidable man with him than against him. Yet he was troubled by Goodbody's casual manner, his absence of concern when difficult aspects of evidence were under discussion. On these occasions he would state some unpalatable truth with brutal frankness, as he had done that morning in their final discussion.

'You will of course be Frans Lourens's principal target. The master of the vessel is always responsible. Your ship was in fog in busy waters, close to land, about to round Cape Agulhas and you, my dear sir, were not on the bridge.' Goodbody had smiled with his mouth and teeth but not with his eyes. 'That will appeal to Lourens as a fairly open and shut case of wilful default and gross negligence. Yes, he'll have a good deal to say about that. You see, it makes you pretty fair game. A sitting duck one might say. But only . . .'

'I have already told you that the onset of the fog was not reported to me,' interrupted Crutchley with unusual sharpness.

'Quite, my dear Captain. But Jarrett has sworn on oath that it was. However, I was about to say – when you interrupted me –' again the smile without the eyes. 'I was about to say, *but only if he can prove you were called.* That, I believe, he cannot do.·

'Cannot? In spite of Fernandez's sworn statement?'

Goodbody held up a large pink hand. 'I know. I know. Fernandez has sworn that he heard the telephone conversation. I propose to upset that evidence.'

'How?' challenged Crutchley, pushing the dark glasses further up the bridge of his nose.

Goodbody looked out of the window, then at the clock on his desk and finally at Crutchley. 'That, I think, is something you must leave to me. Now, Captain, if you'll excuse me, I have a luncheon appointment. One of these tiring Johannesburg mining men in litigious mood.' He got up from the desk. 'I'll see you in court in the morning. In the meantime try to relax. There is an excellent café in the docks. You know it? No. A most improbable place with quite superb shell-fish. Do try it. The crayfish thermidor is something of an experience. By the way, Frans Lourens is an old friend and adversary of mine. We play golf together. I look forward to meeting him once more in battle.' Goodbody's eyes gleamed.

Crutchley regarded him uncertainly. 'Very well. Until tomorrow then.' As he made for the lift he was thinking that it might be all right for Goodbody to regard the enquiry as an interesting battle of wits, with fees assured at the end of it, but it was neither interesting nor profitable for him. Nor did he look forward to meeting Frans Lourens, the State's Counsel who would represent the Secretary for Transport in a role equivalent to that of prosecuting counsel in a criminal court. Captain Crutchley knew that his livelihood and his family's future were at stake.

'When did you hear this?' The chairman frowned at the managing-director. Raustadt smoothed his hair with quick nervous gestures. 'This morning. Kostadis phoned me from London.'

'More than two weeks ago you told us there had been another gale. That both the hull and stern sections were breaking up.' The chairman's tone was critical. 'You said the marine surveyor and salvage expert in Cape Town had reported that the ship was a total loss. You confirmed that the brokers had submitted our claim, that the insurers were preparing to settle on a constructive total loss basis. Why this sudden change?'

'That was the position this morning – until Kostadis phoned.

149

He said that late yesterday afternoon our brokers informed him that there was likely to be some delay in settlement.'

The deputy-chairman patted an ample expanse of stomach which overhung the waistband of his trousers. 'Is this because the court of enquiry only begins its sitting tomorrow?'

Raustadt shot a quick glance at the chairman. 'Kostadis says it's been hinted that it *might* be the reason. That they may feel it's better to await the outcome of the enquiry. But that's only a hint from an unofficial source. The insurers apparently say no more than that they regret there is likely to be *some* delay. They give no reasons.'

'I don't like it, Raustadt.' The folds of the chairman's face drew in upon each other. 'It is a clear case of stranding in fog. There's nothing unusual about that in the maritime world. The consultants out there have reported that the ship is a total loss. *Lloyds List* have carried reports of the ship breaking up. What are the insurers waiting for?'

Le Febre's thin voice cut in. 'Perhaps for the court's finding. On the question of negligence on the part of the Master or his officers, for example.'

'Why? Their negligence is an insurable risk and we've insured against it.'

'Yes,' said Raustadt. 'That's covered.'

'Has Kostadis suggested anything else?' The chairman's eyes never left the pad on which he doodled with a gold pencil.

Raustadt gave him a long searching stare as if waiting for a signal; the chairman looked up. 'Has he?'

'Not directly. He did say that the marine surveyor from Cape Town – a Captain Summerbee – has been in London for some days. Apparently he has had discussions with the insurers. He returns to Cape Town tomorrow. It is possible . . .'

Le Febre interrupted. 'It's surely not unusual for a marine surveyor to fly over to London to report to the insurers on a loss of such magnitude.'

'No. It is probably not unusual,' agreed Raustadt. 'I mention it only because Kostadis did. He was surprised Summerbee had not been to see him.'

'We must continue to exert pressure,' said the chairman. 'Early settlement is essential. We have extensive commitments to meet. We don't want liquidators knocking at the door.'

Neumann took a cigar from a leather case with elaborate care.

'It is little more than a month since the ship stranded. It is only two weeks since we submitted our claim for settlement on a constructive total loss basis. The insurers are faced with paying out fifty-five million dollars, plus the Durban costs. Naturally they are going to delay. There is surely no need to become agitated.'

The chairman returned the gold pencil to an inner pocket. 'Of course not, my dear Neumann. But the company's liquidity problem *is* something to become agitated about.'

Chapter 24

THE FIRST DAY

Wynberg, eight miles down the line from Cape Town, is an old and mellow suburb lying in the shadows of Table Mountain and Constantiaberg. It is the seat of a long-established magistracy and it was in the Magistrate's Court there that those concerned assembled at 9.30 a.m. under the chairmanship of the Chief Magistrate to enquire into the stranding of *Ocean Mammoth*.

The beamed ceiling, the dark woodwork of the doors and furniture well worn with wear, the parquet floor from which rose walls of red brick to eye level, then cream to ceiling height, the smell of polish and disinfectant, combined to provide 'C' court with an atmosphere as cheerless and forbidding as any Captain Crutchley could remember. Looking round the court he saw nothing reassuring except perhaps the ample figure of James Goodbody beside him at the large table around which sat the defendants, their counsel, and Lourens the prosecuting counsel.

The clerk called for order and all stood as the Chairman entered followed by two Assessors and took his seat in the centre of the raised dais. He was a big-boned, bronzed man with bushy eyebrows and a black shade over his left eye; a relic, Crutchley had been told, of a shooting accident when he was a young man. For a moment after he sat down their eyes met and Crutchley found the single-eyed impersonal stare unnerving. He recalled that only the day before Goodbody had said, 'We're lucky to have Jan van Reenen as Chairman. Looks fierce but he's a decent fair-minded chap. He'll keep a firm grip on proceedings.'

The two Assessors, both master mariners, sat with the Chairman, one on either side. To Crutchley they looked like seamen and to that extent he was grateful. In the middle of the courtroom, immediately behind the large table at which counsel and defendants sat, was the dock. Goodbody had explained that it would not be used since this was a court of enquiry not a criminal trial. For that concession, small as it was, Crutchley was thankful. Forward and to the left of the dais was the witness box, provided on this occasion with a chair. Near it two shorthand writers sat at a table. Immediately beneath the dais the clerk of the court was at another.

There were twenty-five or thirty people on the benches of the public gallery which occupied perhaps half the courtroom. Crutchley had little doubt that the media men were among them, for several photographers had clicked away at him outside the court on his arrival that morning. He had always avoided publicity of any sort and he found it particularly galling to be at the centre of it in the role of principal defendant; the man whom, he imagined, the public already regarded as guilty 'by wrongful act or default' of stranding *Ocean Mammoth*.

On entering the court he'd seen a woman in the public gallery; the only woman in the courtroom. As attractive as ever, impeccably dressed for the occasion, she sat alone. In spite of her dark glasses he'd recognized her when she raised a hand in a small gesture of greeting. It was Sandy Foley. Outside the court Crutchley had nodded distantly to her husband, but he had not acknowledged Jarrett's brief smile.

Another man he recognized in the public seats was Captain Summerbee the marine surveyor; small, rotund, with pink cheeks, he wore an expression of perpetual surprise.

The proceedings began with Lourens, counsel leading the enquiry on behalf of the Secretary for Transport, handing in various documents, including statements at the preliminary enquiry, which were recorded as exhibits. That done, he proceeded to outline his case in a rather tired way, conveying the impression that it was a boring but necessary formality. It was in fact a bald statement of events leading up to the stranding, based upon the statements sworn at the preliminary enquiry. Lourens was a tall, thin man with dark hair sleeked back on either side of a centre parting. His eyes, magnified by pebble-lens glasses, appeared too large for his face. A mouth which turned down at the corners gave him a mournful expression so that he looked rather more like the conventional idea of an undertaker than a State's Counsel of repute. Once again Captain Crutchley recalled Goodbody's remarks during the run down of persona the day before. 'Don't be taken in, my dear sir, by the languid manner and soft voice. He's as quick as a rapier thrust.'

Lourens had stopped talking and was fidgeting with the pebble-lens spectacles with his free hand. 'Before concluding,' he said, 'I must remark that the task of this enquiry has been immensely

153

complicated by the disappearance – the somewhat unusual disappearance – of the chart in use at the time of the stranding, the pages of the logbooks for that day, and the automatic course-recorder trace giving the courses steered.' He turned towards the three defendants, looking from one to the other with a lugubrious expression before again facing the Chairman. 'That, Your Worship, concludes my outline of the case.'

The Chairman ordered an adjournment to give the defendants and their legal representatives time for a brief discussion. Fifteen minutes later the enquiry was resumed; the clock on the wall above the entrance showed 11 a.m.

Immediately upon resumption, Goodbody rose. 'I must protest, Your Worship. According to the charge my client, Captain Crutchley, has been accused of stranding *Ocean Mammoth* "by wrongful act or default". My Learned Friend has had the advantage of the preliminary enquiry at which he took full statements from those concerned. That notwithstanding, he has failed to give us the particulars upon which the charge is based. In his outline he has done no more than amplify the charge against my client by saying that he has been guilty of gross negligence. In terms of Section 283 (2) (b) of the Act under which this enquiry is held, the particulars upon which a charge is based must be served on the defendant at least forty-eight hours before he is called upon to make his defence. That, Your Worship, has not been done.'

Complicated argument followed, incomprehensible to Crutchley, during which the Chairman intervened. 'This is neither a civil nor a criminal action, Mr Goodbody. It is a court of enquiry, no more. There is a vast difference. It is not clear to me whether you are lodging an objection or simply voicing a complaint.'

'With respect, Your Worship, although it is an enquiry the defendants' certificates of competency are at risk. I am not formally objecting – we have no wish to prolong these proceedings – but I am bound to say that if at a later stage I find my client is prejudiced I will have to apply for appropriate relief.'

Counsel for Jarrett and Foley rose to associate themselves with Goodbody's remarks. Jerome Bassett, counsel for Inter-Ocean Crude and Bulk Carriers Ltd., explained that the point did not concern his clients for whom he was holding a watching brief.

While Bassett was speaking, Goodbody whispered to Crutch-

154

ley, 'Nothing to worry about. Important to get the sympathy of the court at the outset. Puts Frans Lourens off his stride.'

Gomez, the quartermaster, was the first witness called. Wearing a well-ironed blue denim shirt and trousers, he sat bolt upright in the witness box looking ill at ease in what must for him have been strangely formidable surroundings. Lourens handed him the sworn statement made at the preliminary enquiry. The quartermaster confirmed that it was his and Lourens proceeded to examine him.

When asked what course he'd handed over to Fernandez at 0400 on 29 October he said he'd not handed over any course because Fernandez was late in relieving him. With the ship on auto-steering he'd left the wheelhouse at about five minutes past four when the chief officer told him to carry on below and 'chase-up' Fernandez. He'd gone down and found Fernandez asleep. 'I give him a shake, watch him put on gear and see him leave for the bridge,' said Gomez.

Lourens asked Gomez what course he'd been steering before leaving the wheelhouse. The quartermaster said he could not remember. The ship had been on auto-steering for the last two hours of the watch, and he'd been doing lookout, making coffee and assisting the officer-of-the-watch with compass comparisons and synchronizing clocks. As far as he could recall the course was 'a bit south of west'.

Lourens regarded him gloomily. 'Was it two-six-seven?'

'It can be, sir. I don't remember.'

Lourens said he had no more questions.

Foley's counsel, Arnold Kahn, the youngest State's Counsel in court, rose. He was a pale, slight man with a polio limp, a quiet voice and a deferential almost apologetic manner. He asked leave to reserve his cross-examination and the witness stood down.

Fernandez was called next. Dressed in a smart blue suit he went briskly to the box, took the oath, sat down and looked round the court with the ready smile of a man who knew he was among old friends. He confirmed that the statement Lourens handed him was the one he'd sworn and signed at the preliminary enquiry.

Lourens rose. 'Who did you relieve at the beginning of the morning watch on 29 October?'

'Quartermaster Gomez, sir.'

'Did you relieve him on time?'

'No, sir. About seven minutes late. I sleep too long.'

'What course did he hand over to you?'

'No course, sir. He come down and call me. When I go to the bridge, he goes to his cabin.'

'When you arrived in the wheelhouse, did you check the course being steered?'

'Not then, sir.'

'Why not then?'

'When I come to the wheelhouse, the chief officer send me for his jersey. It was cold, you know.'

'When you got back with the jersey, did you check the course?'

'No, sir. The chief officer tell me to go to bridge wing to keep lookout while he goes to chartroom. Afterwards he call me back to the wheelhouse.'

'When you got back to the wheelhouse from the bridge wing, did you then check the course?'

'No. First I make coffee, then the chief officer tell me to take wheel, and then I check course.'

'And what did you then find the course to be?'

'Two-six-seven degrees.'

'Are you quite sure?'

'Yes. The same was on the indicator.'

The Chairman intervened. 'What indicator?'

'Course-to-steer indicator, sir. Is on the console in front of steering position.'

'I see. Please proceed, Mr Lourens.'

'You say the course was two-six-seven degrees. That is a bit south of west, isn't it?'

'Yes, sir. West is two-seven-zero.'

Lourens was fidgeting with his spectacles again. Crutchley began to wonder if this were a danger signal.

Lourens gave the spectacles a final tweak, looked at his notes, then at Fernandez. 'Did you alter course later?'

'Yes. Few minutes afterwards the chief officer order easy starboard wheel. We come round easy and I steady on two-nine-five.'

'Why were you altering course?'

'The chief officer pick up a big ship ahead on radar. Coming for us.'

'Did your ship run into fog later that morning?'

156

'Yes, sir.'

'Did the chief officer call the standby man to go on lookout?'

'Yes. He call Cavalho. Put him on starboard wing of bridge.'

'Did the chief officer inform the engineroom that the ship was in fog?'

'Yes. I hear him telephone. He tell Mr Benson ship in fog. Mr Jarrett tell him to put engines on manoeuvring speed.'

'Was the foghorn being sounded?'

'No, sir.'

'Why not?'

'I hear chief officer tell Mr Benson that switch for auto-siren is broken. He ask for electrician to come fix it.'

Again Lourens adjusted his spectacles. 'Did you hear the chief officer report the fog to the Captain?'

'Yes, sir. After he phones engineroom.'

'What did the chief officer say?'

'He tell Captain we have fog. He says he put lookout on bridge.'

'Did he say anything else?'

'Yes. He tell Captain the auto-switch is no good. Electrician is come to fix it. He say he don't want to use steam whistle aft because too many people are sleeping.'

'Is that all you heard?'

'No, sir. I hear him tell Captain we alter course for big ship ahead. Also, chief officer tell him there is two small ships on radar on starboard bow. Trawlers, he thinks. Not close yet. He say he keep sharp eye on them. He also tell Captain about the weather.'

'Was that the end of the conversation?'

Goodbody intervened. 'Objection, Your Worship. The witness could only have heard what the chief officer said. That was a monologue not a conversation. The distinction is important.'

The Chairman nodded. 'Objection upheld. Please proceed, Mr Lourens.'

Lourens shook his head in silent protest, looking reproachfully at Goodbody before returning to the witness. 'Was that the end of what you heard?'

The quartermaster frowned at Goodbody as if associating himself with Lourens's displeasure. 'No, sir. The chief officer is listening on the phone. Then he says he is sorry for Captain's headache. He says good sleep will make it right. Then he is

157

listening again and afterwards he says Captain must not worry. Chief officer will keep sharp eye on everything, and fog can finish soon.'

'Was that the last thing you heard the chief officer say?'

'Yes, sir.'

Lourens then questioned Fernandez about the sequence of events after the chief officer's report to the Captain, in particular the successive alterations of course for the two trawlers on *Ocean Mammoth*'s starboard bow.

Fernandez could not recall the times of alteration or courses steered, but thought the first alteration to starboard was 'a bit after four-thirty' and the return to port 'close to five o'clock'. They'd altered course to starboard for the second trawler, 'about ten/fifteen minutes later' and back to port 'another ten/fifteen minutes after that'. Lourens asked him if he could not be more exact. Fernandez said, 'No, sir. There is too much fog. Plenty is happening.'

'You say plenty was happening. Can you explain what you mean?'

'I am busy on wheel. Five/six times we alter course. Five/six times I must bring ship round easy for new courses. Afterwards I must steady ship on new courses and make good steering afterward. All takes time, sir, with very big ship. The quartermaster has plenty work. Chief officer is also too busy. Sometime with radar, sometime in chartroom. Then electrician is coming up. Busy with auto-switch. Always when we alter course, the chief officer tells me why. Also what he sees on radar, he tells me. He speaks of the trawlers and says we must not foul fishing nets. Then Mr Feeny is come up to fix the radar. It is very busy time, sir. Not possible now to remember all times and courses. Such things are not staying in quartermaster's head.'

Lourens was sympathetic. 'And you knew the chief officer was recording the changes of course and the times in the logbook. So there was no need for you to memorize them.'

Goodbody rose at once. 'Objection, Your Worship. My Learned Friend is leading the witness.'

The Chairman looked up from the notes he was making and frowned at counsel for the enquiry from under bushy eyebrows. 'You must not lead the witness, Mr Lourens.'

Lourens nodded and the shadow of a smile flitted across his mournful face. He turned again to Fernandez. 'So you have no precise recollections of the times and courses steered?'

Fernandez hesitated, baffled presumably by the word 'precise'. 'No, sir. But just like you say. I know chief officer is putting in logbook when he goes to chartroom. But is not possible for quartermaster to remember these things. Too much is happening. I worry too much. Chief officer also worry too much.'

'I see. And how did you know the chief officer was worried?'

'Because of what I hear him say. Like when the Decca Navigator is no good after we alter course for the second trawler. Before that the chief officer is swearing because he say this trawler is doing funny things. Also he must phone Sparks – I mean Mr Feeny, sir – to come up to fix the Decca. Afterwards the radar sets are not working and he is swearing. There is a lot of problems for the chief officer.'

'At what time did the Decca Navigator break down?'

Fernandez scratched his head. He was obviously thinking hard. 'About seven/ten minutes after five o'clock. After we alter for second trawler.'

'At what time did the radar sets fail?'

Fernandez frowned, looked at his feet, tapped his forehead thoughtfully. 'About ten/fifteen minutes before ship hits the rocks.'

In response to further questions Fernandez explained what had happened in the wheelhouse during the period shortly before the ship struck and immediately afterwards.

Lourens looked once again at his notes, took off the pebble-lens spectacles and dangled them by one arm. With casual indifference he said, 'Was the Captain in the wheelhouse at any time between the ship encountering fog and running aground?'

Fernandez hesitated, looked momentarily at the massive, dignified figure of Captain Crutchley whose eyes were masked as always by dark glasses. 'No, sir. The Captain was not in the wheelhouse.' The nuances of sincerity and apology were there, but somehow the quartermaster's broken English emphasized the enormity of the Captain's offence.

Lourens having said he had no further questions, the Chairman adjourned the enquiry until 2.15 p.m. and the court rose.

It was almost time for lunch.

Chapter 25

During the recess Captain Crutchley, Goodbody and his junior, lunched together at the Palace Hotel in Kenilworth, a few miles down the main road from Wynberg. Goodbody had been talking about the origins of the hotel – a familiar Peninsula landmark – and its associations with the past when, with deep gloom and quite out of context, Crutchley remarked, 'I imagine Fernandez's evidence has just about finished me.'

Goodbody halted a forkful of cabbage and beef on its way to his mouth and regarded the Captain with astonishment. 'Finished you, my dear chap? Not at all. Good honest seafarer, our friend Fernandez. Telling the truth, no doubt. But I shall upset his evidence. Dear me, I shall. What did interest me was what he had to say about the various alterations of course for a ship and two trawlers. All in the hour before the stranding. All towards the land. Most interesting.'

'In what way interesting?'

'Ah. That may become more apparent as matters proceed. Now do change your mind and taste this wine. It's a Constantia cabernet. Rather closer to a burgundy than a claret, but really very good.'

'No thank you, Mr Goodbody. Not at the moment.' Nothing, including Goodbody, had succeeded in persuading the Captain to drop the 'mister'.

After that Crutchley tried to get the barrister to talk about the quartermaster's evidence, but Goodbody refused to be drawn. It was soon apparent that his appetite matched his size and he ate and drank with tremendous gusto. Crutchley hoped the wine would not dull the big man's wits by the time they got back to court.

In between courses Goodbody filled in time with questions about *Ocean Mammoth*: her handling characteristics, turning circle, responses to different degrees of wheel and various engine revolutions. He showed particular interest in the duties of quartermasters and men on standby duty, wanting to know what went on during a typical night watch. He was endlessly curious about the wheelhouse and chartroom, and the positioning of the Decca Navigator, the two radar sets and other equipment. He produced a notebook and ballpoint and got Crutchley to draw diagrams of the layouts. When the Captain had finished, Goodbody examined the diagrams closely, asking a number of questions, few of which seemed relevant to Crutchley. Very often Goodbody was going over ground they'd covered in previous consultations, but Crutchley realized from his questions that here was a man with an exceptional memory and a gift for getting quickly to the heart of the matter. He was learning, too, that Goodbody was by no means the genial *bon viveur* he sometimes held himself out to be.

When they got back to the Magistrate's Court with ten minutes to spare, Goodbody asked to be excused. 'Frans Lourens wants a word with me before the resumption.' He chuckled. 'Probably golf.'

Crutchley said, 'Of course,' and made his way down the wide red brick corridor to the entrance to 'C' court. With a heavy heart he opened the door and went in.

On resumption that afternoon Goodbody and Kahn were granted leave to defer their cross-examination of Fernandez to a later stage and the witness stood down.

Cavalho was called next. The necessary formalities completed, Lourens began his examination.

'Were you on standby duty during the first part of the morning watch on 29 October?'

'Yes, sir.'

'Were you at some time called to the bridge for lookout duty?'

'Yes. At about four-thirty.'

'Where were you stationed on the bridge?'

'In the starboard wing, sir.'

'Was the ship then in fog?'

'Yes. Thick fog.'

'Can you tell the court what happened between that time and when the ship ran aground?'

Cavalho explained that at no time had he been able to see anything. The fog had been too dense. But he had heard the sirens of other ships. One which had been approaching had passed down the port side, about two miles away. There had been others in the distance, also to port. He spoke of the two trawlers on the

161

starboard bow for which *Ocean Mammoth* had altered course. With some pride he recounted how he reported to the chief officer that he'd heard a car hooter, and been told it must be a fishing boat. A few minutes later he'd felt the ship turning to port under full helm, the engine vibrations had increased, 'emergency stations' had been sounded and the chief officer had broadcast a warning that there was land close ahead. He had then heard blasts from a foghorn close on the starboard bow. Almost immediately after that the ship had struck.

Lourens said he had no further questions. Goodbody and Kahn were granted leave to defer cross-examination to a later date and the witness stood down.

Benson, the second engineer, was the next witness. He testified that he had been in charge of the engineroom during the morning of 29 October. The chief officer had informed him that the ship was in fog and ordered 'manoeuvring speed' at 0430. Asked if he was sure of the time he reminded Lourens that it was recorded in the Engine Movements Book which had been handed in to court as an exhibit. Benson went on to say that the chief officer had at the same time reported the defective auto-switch and asked for an electrician to be sent up to fix it. This man, Jackson, had gone to the wheelhouse at about 0445 to examine the switch, and had subsequently come down to get the necessary spares.

The chief officer had later informed him, said Benson, that the radar sets were unserviceable and as they were still in thick fog had ordered the engines to be put on 'standby' at 0529. Finally, at 0536, the 'full ahead' signal was received from the bridge and at the same time the chief officer told him by phone that there was land close ahead, that the wheel was hard-a-port, but that the ship might get clear. Immediately afterwards 'emergency stations' was sounded. Soon after that the ship struck and 'emergency full astern' was signalled from the bridge. All these movements, with their times, had been recorded in the Engine Movements Book.

In response to Lourens's further questions, Benson told of what had happened in the engineroom when the ship struck and afterwards.

Lourens had no more questions, and defence counsel were granted leave to cross-examine at a later stage.

The witness stood down.

The next witness was Mr McLintoch, the chief engineer. Soon

after 0430 Benson had informed him that the ship was in fog and that the engines had been put on 'manoeuvring speed'. As to what had happened after that he had little to contribute since he had only gone to the engineroom when the engines were put on 'standby'. His answers to Lourens's questions about events from that time on confirmed Benson's account. Lourens announced that he had no further questions and McLintoch was excused.

Next came the Cape Agulhas light-keeper who gave evidence on the state of the weather at the time of and preceding the stranding. The first indication he'd had of what was happening was when he'd heard repeated blasts on the siren of a big ship close at hand at 0536. He had at once requested the signal station to sound the International Code signal for 'You are standing into danger' – a series of U's – and he had by VHF radio warned the invisible ship immediately to the east of the lighthouse that she was standing into danger. Soon afterwards he had heard the continuous ringing of an alarm system which he took to be the ship's. At 0541 he had spoken by VHF to the Captain of *Ocean Mammoth* who said that his ship was aground and that the DF bearing of the Agulhas radio beacon from the ship was 268°. He had offered to act as a communications link, but the Captain had said he was in direct touch with Cape Town.

In response to questions by Lourens, the light-keeper said that there was a radio beacon at Cape Agulhas which transmitted continuously night and day. A vessel equipped with radio direction-finding apparatus could get a DF bearing from the beacon at any time and in all conditions of weather including fog. It had been in working order throughout 28/29 October.

Lourens having questioned the light-keeper on the action he'd taken when the ship stranded and afterwards, announced that he had no further questions. Goodbody received permission to cross-examine the witness at a later stage if necessary.

Before the light-keeper left the witness box the Chairman commended him for the action he had taken in trying to prevent the disaster.

At this stage Lourens handed in to court statements sworn by Jackson the electrician, and Feeny the radio operator. He explained that both these men had left South Africa by air for Europe with most of *Ocean Mammoth*'s crew soon after the preliminary enquiry.

163

The Chairman asked whether the statements were to be read in court. Lourens said that copies had been made available to defence counsel but if it were desired the statements could certainly be read out. The Chairman consulted with the Assessors whereafter he ordered that this be done.

Jackson's dealt only with the auto-switch, the times he'd been called and gone to the bridge, the faults he'd found – the clipped leads and missing terminal panel – and his visit to stores to obtain spares, delayed because the storeman was asleep and had to be called. The ship had struck before he could carry out the repairs. After that he had abandoned the task for more urgent duties.

In his statement Feeny, the radio operator, recorded that the chief officer had reported the failure of the Decca Navigator at about 0510. Feeny had gone to the wheelhouse, carried out a quick check, then gone below for the manual. Later when he'd returned to the chartroom and was working on the Navigator, the chief officer had informed him that both radar sets had packed up. At Jarrett's request he had then begun to check them out since, with the ship in fog, radar was the higher priority.

He had checked the controls and circuits of the radar sets, then examined the inter-switch unit in the chartroom where he felt the fault might lie. At that stage the fuse on his circuit tester had blown. He decided to go to the radio office to get a replacement. As he left the chartroom he saw the second officer come in from the bridge deck. While he was in the radio office 'emergency stations' were sounded, so he remained there as it was his station. A minute or so later the ship struck. From then onwards, through the storm and afterwards until evacuation of the crew by helicopter, he had been busy with urgent communication duties. Since neither radar nor the Navigator were of use with the ship stranded and breaking up, he had made no further attempt to find the causes of their failure.

The statements were marked as exhibits and handed in to court.

Lourens now rose to inform the court that he would like to call his final witness – Ernst Rohrbach, an electronics engineer – at a later stage. He would give evidence on the functioning of the Decca Navigator and the radar sets. Lourens reminded the court that statements made at the preliminary enquiry had suggested

164

that their failure at a critical time had contributed in large measure to the stranding of *Ocean Mammoth*.

Dirk Ohlsson, counsel for the chief officer, rose to object. He was a tall, thin, undernourished man with sharp eyes and nose which moved in unison, training and pointing in varying directions like mobile antennae. 'I submit, Your Worship, that it is most inappropriate that this witness – who is evidently to give expert evidence in support of the charges – is to be called *after* the defendants have been examined by My Learned Friend.'

The Chairman looked towards counsel for the enquiry. 'Mr Lourens. Can you answer that?'

Lourens stroked his chin, regarded Ohlsson with a funereal air, sighed audibly and proceeded. 'Yes, Your Worship. I will explain my difficulty. I would very much like to have called Rohrbach now. But unfortunately I cannot. He flew to Europe on business almost three weeks ago, expecting to be back well in time for this enquiry. Soon after he arrived in Germany he was involved in a car accident and has only recently been discharged from hospital. He is now said to be recovered and will arrive in Johannesburg by air on Wednesday. He will be available here on the following day. I would suggest to My Learned Friends that his evidence may well be in their clients' interests and not against them. The alternative to my proposal is to delay these proceedings, something which I am sure My Learned Friends would not wish to do.'

Goodbody passed a slip of paper to Crutchley on which he'd scrawled. 'Lourens is a cunning old fox. Don't worry. I'm pro-Rohrbach.'

As he destroyed the note, Crutchley wondered if it meant that Lourens had some clever trick of advocacy up his sleeve, or whether it was simply that the eminent counsel in court, busy men with extensive commitments, would be anything but pleased if the proceedings were delayed.

It was the first time Ohlsson had gone into action and Crutchley watched him carefully. The barrister stood up, his forehead wrinkled as he considered the point while darting sharp glances from Jarrett to Lourens to the Chairman, his long nose aiming at each in turn like a pointer scenting. At last he spoke. 'In the circumstances, Your Worship, I accept My Learned Friend's explanation.'

165

Messrs Goodbody and Kahn rose to say that in the circumstances they, too, had no objections to the calling of Rohrbach at a later stage.

The clock on the wall above the entrance showed 4.55 p.m. when the Chairman adjourned the enquiry until the following morning.

Chapter 26

THE SECOND DAY
When the court resumed for the second day of the enquiry, Cavalho, recalled at Goodbody's request, was first to enter the witness box.

'In your evidence yesterday,' began Goodbody, smiling in a most friendly way, 'you said that while you were on lookout duty in the fog there were two trawlers on the starboard bow of *Ocean Mammoth*?'

'Yes, sir.'

'You also said that at no time could you see anything because the fog was so thick. Is that correct?'

'Yes, sir.'

'Did you that morning look into the radar displays?'

'No, sir. I was lookout man on the starboard wing.'

'In your statement at the preliminary enquiry you said you heard a long blast followed by two short blasts from the first trawler. Is that correct?'

'Yes, sir.'

'What did that signal mean to you?'

'I know this signal to be fog signal for trawler with nets in the water. I am fisherman before, sir. In Cape Verde Islands.' Cavalho's eyes glowed with pride.

'Yes, and I've no doubt an excellent one.' Goodbody, nodding in affirmation, smiled engagingly at the quartermaster. 'And the second trawler – what signals did you hear from her?'

Cavalho considered the question. 'Nothing, sir. She makes no signal.'

'So you could see nothing because of the fog, and no sound came from the second trawler. Is that right?'

'It is right, sir.'

'Then tell me, Mr Cavalho' – again the genial smile – 'How did you know there *was* a second trawler?'

'The chief officer tell me. He see it on radar. He asks me, "You hear signal from this trawler?" I tell him I hear nothing. He says, "Okay. Trawler has radar. He won't worry to make signal if he

167

sees other ship." '

Mr Goodbody turned for a moment towards the Chairman and Assessors, a look of mild surprise on his face. 'So the chief officer told you there was a second trawler on the starboard bow, but at no time did you see or hear it. Is that correct?'

Cavalho's expression suggested that an important truth had been revealed to him. 'It is right. I don't see or hear it.'

'And the big ship you spoke of yesterday – the ship that passed down the port side – before you altered course for the trawlers. You said it was about two miles away. How did you know it was two miles?'

'The chief officer tells me, sir. He says two miles.'

Goodbody was silent, nodding at the quartermaster. 'I see. The chief officer told you,' he repeated slowly, before turning to face the Chairman. 'No more questions, Your Worship.'

Cavalho was told he could stand down.

At Goodbody's request Fernandez was then recalled.

The quartermaster walked briskly to the witness box. Once in it he looked round the court with easy familiarity, bowing to the Chairman and Assessors.

Goodbody rose with a reassuring smile to cross-examine.

'In your evidence yesterday you told the court how you had, during the morning watch of 29 October, altered course for three ships. First for the big ship approaching from ahead, then for the first trawler on the starboard bow, and later for a second trawler on the starboard bow. Is that correct?'

'Yes. It is correct.'

'Were each of the alterations by *Ocean Mammoth* to starboard?'

'Yes. Every time to starboard, sir.'

'On several occasions in your evidence yesterday you used the word "easy" in relation to wheel orders and alterations of course. When you made these alterations to starboard and later back to port were they all on the "easy" basis?'

'Yes. They were.'

'I see. Now in your evidence yesterday, towards the end, you said you were worried that morning. That it was not good to be in the wheelhouse because, with the windows shut and the fog, you could not see or hear the other ships. Is that correct?'

'Yes, sir.'

'Did you at any time that morning look into the radar displays?'

'No. This is not a duty for the quartermaster.' Fernandez's tone

168

implied that such a suggestion was highly improper.

'So you could not see or hear other ships, and you did not look into any radar displays?'

'Correct, sir.'

'How then did you know about the big ship ahead and the two trawlers to starboard for which you altered course?'

Fernandez's friendly face clouded. 'The chief officer tells me, sir. He sees with radar.'

'And if he had not told you, would you have known they were there?'

Fernandez hesitated. 'No, sir.'

Goodbody consulted his notes, put them down, jangled some coins in his trouser pocket with one hand, while the other rested on the table at which he stood. He looked up suddenly at the quartermaster and his manner was now stern. 'You told the court yesterday that you heard the chief officer report the fog to the Captain by telephone. You told us of a number of different things you heard the chief officer say. Is that correct?'

'It is correct, sir.'

'When the chief officer was speaking into that telephone you were at the wheel?'

'Yes.'

'The telephone he was using was on the console in front of – and to the right of – the steering position. Is that correct?'

'It is correct, sir.'

'And the distance between the steering position and that telephone was about five metres, was it not?'

'I think it must be five metres.'

'Could you hear everything the chief officer said?'

'Yes. Everything.'

'How did you know he was talking to the Captain?'

'I hear him say "Captain", three, four times.'

Goodbody looked into the far corner of the court and half-closed his eyes as if he were focusing on a distant object. He took his hand from his trouser pocket and pinched his nostrils before looking once more at Fernandez. 'You also told the court that you heard the chief officer telephone Mr Benson to tell him the ship was in fog. Can you tell the court what Mr Benson said in reply?'

Fernandez shook his head. 'It is not possible, sir. I only hear what the chief officer say.'

'Yes, of course.' Goodbody smiled understandingly. 'So you could not hear what the Captain said when the chief officer telephoned him?'

'No, sir. It is not possible.'

'When you heard the chief officer making that report to the Captain he was standing at the console, about five metres from where you stood at the steering position. Is that correct?'

'Yes. It is correct.'

'It was dark in the wheelhouse, was it not?'

'Yes, dark.'

'Could you see the chief officer?'

'If I look maybe I see his dark shape by the console. I know this must be chief officer.'

'Just a dark shape. Was his back to you?'

'I am watching the steering compass. It is dark. How can I say?'

'Could you, in that dark light, see the telephone he was using?'

'No, sir. It is not possible. But I hear him dialling.'

'So all you were aware of was the dark shape of the chief officer at the console, and the sound of dialling and of his voice speaking into a telephone.'

'Yes, sir.'

'Did you have any means of knowing whether the telephone he was speaking into was connected to the Captain's telephone?'

'I don't understand.'

'Well, Mr Fernandez, it is possible to pick up a telephone, to dial, and to speak into it without being connected to anyone at the other end. Is it not?'

'But I hear the chief officer speaking to Captain, sir.'

'Yes. Indeed. But you have said you did not hear the Captain, and that it was dark, and you had no means of knowing if the phone on the console had made connection with the phone in the Captain's cabin. Is that correct?'

Fernandez looked across to where the chief officer was sitting and his eyes seemed to signal an apology. 'Yes, sir,' he said in a low voice.

'Thank you, Mr Fernandez,' said Goodbody. 'No further questions, Your Worship.' Ohlsson was frowning at the pad on which he was making a note, and Lourens was looking at Fernandez with a more than usually mournful expression.

Meanwhile, Foley's counsel, Arnold Kahn, had risen to cross-examine the quartermaster. Large horn-rimmed spectacles and prominent ears gave him an expression that was slightly owl-like, and this was heightened by the way in which his small wiry figure bobbed from time to time as he shifted weight from the good leg to the lame one.

'You said in your evidence yesterday that you were late in relieving Quartermaster Gomez – that you did not check the course being steered when you first reached the wheelhouse. Is this correct?' Kahn's manner was nervous, hesitant.

'Yes, sir.'

'When did you check the course?'

'When the chief officer tells me to take the wheel. Before we alter for the big ship coming up ahead.'

'How long after you first arrived in the wheelhouse did you take the wheel?'

Fernandez appeared to give the matter some thought, counting with his fingers and looking at the ceiling as if for inspiration. 'Must be ten/twelve minutes. First I fetch jersey for the chief officer. Then he put me on bridge wing lookout. Then I make coffee. Afterwards I take wheel.'

'And you had come up ten minutes late. So that makes it about twenty minutes past four o'clock when you first checked the course. Would you agree with that?'

'Yes, sir. About twenty minutes after four.'

Kahn shifted his weight from one foot to the other and pulled nervously at the lobe of his left ear. 'Quartermaster Gomez has told the court that he cannot remember what course he was steering when he left the wheelhouse soon after four o'clock to go below to call you. You told the court yesterday that, after he'd called you, you went to the wheelhouse and he to his cabin. Is that so?'

'Yes.'

'Did he at any time – in your cabin, or elsewhere – tell you the course being steered when he left the bridge with the ship on auto-steering?'

'No, sir.'

'Do you know what course was being steered when Gomez left the bridge?'

'Must be two-six-seven, sir.'

'Why "must be"?'

'I find two-six-seven on course-indicator when I take the wheel. Also ship's head is on two-six-seven.'

171

'Quite so. But can you say what the course was and what figures were on the indicator at four o'clock – when Mr Foley handed over the watch?'

'No, sir.'

'In fact you only know what figures were on the indicator – and what course the ship was steering – at about twenty minutes past four. Is that not so?'

'Yes. It is so.' Fernandez nodded unhappily at this further incontestable truth.

Kahn informed the Chairman that he had no further questions to ask and the witness stood down.

The Chairman then adjourned the enquiry until 2.15 p.m.

On resumption of the enquiry after lunch Kahn asked for the recall of Cavalho.

'You were standby man during the first part of the morning watch on 29 October?'

'Yes, sir.'

'What are the duties of the standby man?'

'If the officer of watch wants extra hand for anything, he calls standby man.'

'To do what sort of things?'

'Sometime for lookout. Sometime to clean and polish around wheelhouse and chartroom. Sometime to help officer check compass, check clocks. Sometime to make coffee for wheelhouse. Sometime to fetch or take something from engineroom, radio office, pantry. Any place. Sometime to take message or radio signal to wheelhouse or Captain. Many things like this.'

'Where do you wait until you're wanted?'

'If near the land, in recreation room on Deck One.'

'What do you do there when you're not busy?'

'Sometime read book, or write letter, or listen to music. Hi-fi you know. Sometime just sit to think.' Cavalho grinned. 'Sometime sleep till telephone rings.'

'You are called by telephone, are you?'

'Yes. By telephone.'

Kahn said he had no more questions and the witness stood down.

172

Chapter 27

To Captain Crutchley, in a court of law for the first time, the proceedings were entirely strange and much of the cross-examination incomprehensible. The only part of it so far which seemed relevant to the charge against him was Goodbody's attempt to throw doubt on Fernandez's evidence about the telephone conversation. To what extent that had impressed the court he had no way of knowing. Crutchley was impatient to get on with the main business of the enquiry. The testimony of the minor witnesses seemed irrelevant. Why didn't the court get down to the heart of the matter right away? Put Jarrett in the witness box first. He was, or should have been, the major culprit. The ship had run aground in his watch. For more than an hour and a half before that he'd been in sole charge. Why not hear his story first? And Foley's. There was another man who'd had a good deal to do with what had happened. The court should surely have heard his evidence early on. Sort out the story that he'd given Jarrett the incorrect course when handing over. Find out what he was doing in the chartroom before the ship struck. Why wasn't he heard before the quartermaster, the lookout man, the light-keeper and those others?

At lunch that day Goodbody had enjoined patience. 'A most interesting situation is developing, my dear Captain. Lourens has something up his sleeve, young Kahn smells a rat somewhere, and poor Fernandez has been sunk with all flags flying. Frans Lourens didn't like that one little bit, you know. Nor did that person Ohlsson. But of course he wouldn't. No, it's coming along splendidly. What you call "trivial evidence" is always heard first. But it's by no means trivial. Dear me no. Just you wait and see. I've had a chat with Kahn. He will call Foley to the box after lunch. That should see us through to the adjournment.' After that Goodbody had launched into a dissertation on cheese soufflés, and Crutchley had been unable to get anything more from him about the enquiry.

Putting aside these thoughts, he once more concentrated on the proceedings, sitting always with his back half-turned so that he

173

did not have to see either Jarrett or Foley who were some little distance away on his right. He had ignored them both ever since the preliminary enquiry.

To Sandy, sitting well back in court, the proceedings were absorbingly interesting. She didn't understand the legal procedures, nor could she appreciate the tactical subtleties of the various counsel as they examined and cross-examined, but she sensed – perhaps it was her feminine intuition – that the drift of the cross-examination was against Jarrett. If it was against him, she assumed it must be good for her husband and that helped relieve anxiety.

Slowly, painfully slowly, she was re-establishing her relationship with him. The traumatic experiences of the shipwreck and the storm had helped: since then they had, little by little, drawn closer together. She'd had to work hard at it. He'd been stern and unforgiving, deeply hurt, very conscious of the wrong done him; whereas she was aware that she was entirely to blame. At times when he rebuffed her she would cry herself to sleep, but she had never given up. Couldn't he see, she would ask herself, her affair with Jarrett for what it was? Proximity, mutual attraction, opportunity. Didn't he understand what a powerful though transitory weapon sex was? That when a man and woman with compatible chemistry were thrown together something was almost bound to happen, given the opportunity? Of course it was adultery; of course it was disloyal; but it was happening every day to thousands of people. Couldn't he accept the reality of that and forgive?

As for Freeman Jarrett – well, that was all over. Once she'd learnt he was doing his best to put the blame for the stranding on her husband, whatever feelings she'd had for him – and they were always more physical than emotional – had gone. Not that she hated him. That was too strong a word. What she felt was something closer to contempt. He was no longer the strong, compelling, attractive man, but a conceited, self-seeking individual who was determined to save his own skin at her husband's expense. Jarrett was, she reflected, a strange contradiction. It was he who had gone into the sea off Durban when the wire parted and swept Cadet Price over the side; it was he who, during the gale, had searched in the darkness for Malim and the crewman in the faint hope of finding them alive. And there had been no

174

audience then, except Fernandez. Yes – Freeman Jarrett *was* a strange contradiction and perhaps that was why she couldn't bring herself to hate him. Or was it because they had been so important to each other, even if only for a very short time?

Whatever it was, it was all over now. She wanted Jarrett to lose and George to win. However mixed-up she may have been, she was sure of that. And George so badly needed support, even if he pretended he didn't. She could see that he was desperately worried and uncertain about the outcome of the enquiry. To a far greater extent than she believed was necessary, since it was Jarrett who'd been on watch in the hour and a half before the ship ran aground, even if Foley had made a mistake in handing over the course – something he strenuously denied.

She could not help wondering what Jarrett felt about all that had happened; the sudden end to their relationship, and the awful worry of the enquiry with himself as a central figure. He was such an aggressively self-confident man, so certain always that he was right, that the situation for him must be a particularly trying one. To have his conduct, skill and judgement publicly questioned would, she believed, hurt him more than most men. And there was Captain Crutchley – that stern, unapproachable man of whom she had seen so little during the voyage, and with whom communication had been so difficult when she had. She felt dreadfully sorry for him. In spite of his reserved, highly formal manner, he had the reputation of being a fine seaman and a conscientious Master. She realized how galling it must be for a man like that to stand charged with 'wrongful act or default and gross negligence'; yet the fact remained that throughout the fog, right up to the time of the stranding, he'd not been on the bridge.

She knew it hurt her husband deeply that the Captain had cut him since the preliminary enquiry, scarcely acknowledging his attempts at polite greeting outside the courtroom. Of course Foley and Jarrett ignored each other but there were good reasons for that, as she well knew. She and Jarrett had had no contact since leaving the wreck, other than glimpses of each other entering and leaving court. He was always polite on these occasions, though in a rather distant way. Occasionally in court she would see him turn and look back into the public gallery, but if their eyes met neither gave any sign of recognition.

On the second afternoon of the enquiry she was getting used to the atmosphere of the court, beginning to identify those involved

175

and their roles and to sense the developing drama. She'd already established likes and dislikes. She admired Arnold Kahn whom she'd met several times during the weeks since the preliminary enquiry, and she was glad he was her husband's counsel. She knew that he was regarded as one of the brighter men at the Cape Town Bar in spite of his apparent youth, frailty and help-lessness. Another man she liked was James Goodbody whom she described to her husband as 'a lovely, big, huggable sort of man'. She'd become aware that he was anti-Jarrett and that commended him. She mistrusted Dirk Ohlsson, no doubt because he was Jarrett's counsel, and described him as 'that man with the sly, foxy look'.

She couldn't make up her mind about Frans Lourens, but decided he was probably neutral. The Chairman struck her as stern but just and she thought of him as a rugged, attractive man – her sort of man. The two Assessors hadn't yet said a word, so they were for her enigmas. Jerome Bassett, counsel for the company, had only spoken once and she had found him pom-pous.

Though what went on in court was interesting and even exciting in a strange way, she suffered from loneliness. There was no one with whom she could share the experience, no one with whom to exchange whispered confidences. The only person in the public gallery she'd recognized was a coloured man sitting at the back. On the first morning she'd seen him, she thought he looked familiar but couldn't place him. During the lunch adjournment that day he had spoken to her and she'd realized he was Piet Pieterse, the steward who'd joined *Ocean Mammoth* the day before sailing from Durban. She had not really been aware of him until the gale when he'd brought blankets, pillows and food to the women in the chartroom. She remembered how he had laughed and joked in an effort to raise their spirits, and how grateful they'd been.

When they met outside the court she asked him what he was doing. He said he was looking for work but it was not easy to find because of unemployment. She asked him why he was at the enquiry and he said, 'Nothing, madam. Just passing the time, you know. It was my first job in a ship. After three days we got wrecked. Then there's the gale and the helicopter comes and takes us off. Now there's this court of enquiry. It's been a fantastic experience. I thought I better see it through. Like watching the

176

big picture from the beginning to the end.'

She smiled. 'Of course. I understand. It is interesting. I just wish my husband wasn't involved.'

And he had said, 'Yes, madam. That's no joke for him, is it?' Since then they had done no more than exchange smiles.

After Cavalho's departure from the witness box, Lourens informed the Chairman that apart from Ernst Rohrbach – the electronics expert who would not be available until the Thursday – he had no further witnesses.

Kahn asked leave to call the second officer. Foley made for the witness box, walking with a slight stoop, his dark grey suit matching the shadows under his eyes. When he had taken the oath and testified that the statement handed to him was the one he'd sworn at the preliminary enquiry, Kahn began his examination.

In response to his counsel's questions, Foley gave a brief, matter-of-fact account of events leading up to the stranding. He confirmed that he had been officer-of-the-watch from midnight to 0400 on 29 October. At 0240 he had obtained and plotted a position by Decca Navigator which showed that the ship had, over the previous hour, been set just over a mile to the north-west, that was inshore. A radar bearing showed Cape Agulhas at that time to be bearing 275°, distant 36·5 miles. The ETA for a position 10 miles off Cape Agulhas was 0530, and with the Captain's approval he had altered course from 264° to 257° to counter a similar set of current over the next three hours.

Soon after midnight he received a meteorological report from the radio officer. He immediately phoned the Captain and told him it contained a fog warning. The Captain had come up to the wheelhouse soon afterwards, remaining there for about fifteen minutes before going below.

At five minutes to four he had been relieved by the chief officer to whom he'd handed over course and speed, details of traffic in the vicinity, and other routine information. He had told him of the fog warning, and the instructions in the night order book that the Captain was to be called in the event of fog and for the alteration of course off Cape Agulhas. He had then gone to the chartroom, established the ship's position by Decca Navigator at 0400, plotted the position on the chart and found that the course made good since 0240 was 261° which was correct for the ETA

177

position. Throughout his watch the Decca Navigator and both radar sets had functioned satisfactorily.

Kahn then questioned him about his movements after leaving the wheelhouse at 0400. Foley said he had gone to his cabin, undressed and got into bed. About an hour later – he was uncertain of the exact time – he got up because he couldn't sleep. He'd slipped on some clothes, gone up to the lower bridge deck and found that the ship was in fog. He had been surprised that no siren was sounding, but was not alarmed since he thought the Captain was on the bridge. Some time later he noticed that the ship was steering well to the west of the course he had plotted. He assumed they had rounded Cape Agulhas and altered course to the north-west to make for the position off Cape Point. Later when course was altered back to the south-west, he thought they might have been altering course for another ship, but as he'd heard no fog signals and since *Ocean Mammoth* herself was silent he became uneasy. He went to the chartroom, checked the charted course and noted the time – it was just after 0530. He then switched on the Decca Navigator and found that there was no display. He switched on the echo-sounder and saw that the depth of water was considerably less than it should have been at a safe distance from land. While comparing the readings on the echo-sounder with those on the chart he had noticed that the figure 257° which he'd pencilled against the course line during the middle-watch had been altered to 267°.

He was puzzling things out, trying to make sense of what had happened, when the chief officer came into the chartroom and demanded, 'in a most aggressive way', what he was doing there. He had replied that 'something funny was going on'; the Decca Navigator was dead, the ship was not sounding fog signals, and the figure he'd written against the course line had been altered. He'd then looked at the echo-sounder again and seen with a shock that the depth of water had shoaled to eight fathoms. He had at once drawn Jarrett's attention to that fact.

Jarrett had shouted 'Christ', run back to the wheelhouse, ordered hard-a-port, pressed the full ahead button and phoned a warning to the engineroom. After that the chief officer had sounded emergency stations on the steam siren and broadcast 'emergency stations – land close ahead'. Moments later Foley had joined him in the wheelhouse and it was then that Jarrett had told him that both radar units were out of order. At much the same time the Agulhas light-keeper warned by sound signal and voice radio that the ship was standing into danger. Within minutes *Ocean Mammoth* had struck. Almost immediately afterwards the Captain arrived on the bridge and ordered fire stations.

Foley completed his evidence with an account of what had happened between the Captain's arrival and his own relief by the third officer.

Kahn said he had no further questions. Ohlsson and Goodbody reserved cross-examination for a later stage and the witness stood down. After a brief consultation with counsel for the enquiry, the Chairman adjourned the proceedings until the following morning.

It was close to five o'clock when George Foley and his wife left the courtroom with Arnold Kahn to drive back to their hotel in Cape Town.

Chapter 28

THE THIRD DAY

The enquiry was fully reported in the Cape Town press and interest in its proceedings grew steadily. It was therefore not surprising that at the resumption on the morning of the third day 'C' court was full to overflowing.

The low hum of conversation ceased when the clerk of the court called for order and everyone stood. Moments later the Chairman and Assessors entered the courtroom and took their places on the dais.

When Ohlsson asked that Freeman Jarrett – the man he was defending – be called there was a ripple of excitement. In pretrial accounts of the disaster and in stories gleaned from interviews with crewmen, the media had inferred that the chief officer, the man on watch when the ship ran aground, would be the principal defendant. It had been freely rumoured in Cape Town that he and the Captain were at loggerheads about the latter's absence from the bridge; and it was common gossip that Jarrett and Foley were doing their best to saddle each other with responsibility for the disaster. These elements of drama had not been overlooked. Finally, the story of how Jarrett had rescued Cadet Price from the sea off Durban, and later risked his life in the gale in an abortive attempt to save Malim and a crewman, had been prominently featured in the newspapers.

Thus all eyes were on the tall man in the fawn suit who got up from the big table in front of the dais and walked quickly to the witness box. The livid scar on his forehead was a reminder if any were needed of the failed but gallant rescue attempt and added rather than detracted from the manly looks and strong features.

The preliminaries of oath taking and statement verification having been completed, Ohlsson began his examination by asking Jarrett to narrate events on the bridge of *Ocean Mammoth* from the time he took over the watch at 0400 on 29 October, until the stranding just over an hour and a half later.

Speaking in a firm voice, his manner composed and assured.

the chief officer embarked on his story and it seemed to those in court that the Chairman and Assessors listened with particular attention and sympathy to what he was saying.

He had begun by stressing the difficulty of reconstructing accurately such a complex series of events – compressed as they had been into a short space of time – without the relevant chart, the missing pages from the logbooks and the course-recorder trace; but he would, he said, do his best. At that point Ohlsson interrupted. 'When did you last see the chart and the other items you've just mentioned?'

'A few minutes before we stranded. When I went to the chart-room and found the second officer there.' Jarrett hesitated, looked for a moment at Foley who sat slumped in a chair at Kahn's side, before turning back to Ohlsson.

'What was the second officer doing?'

'Working on the chart, I presume. He was leaning over it with a pencil and had parallel rulers in his hand.'

'Did he have an eraser?'

'There is always an eraser on the chart-table.'

'Were you surprised to find him there – in his watch below?'

'Yes. To be perfectly frank, I was astonished.'

'And you never saw that chart or the missing pages of the log-books and the course-recorder trace again?'

Goodbody was on his feet. 'Objection, Your Worship. My Learned Friend is leading the witness.'

'You must not lead the witness, Mr Ohlsson.' The Chairman frowned.

'I'm sorry, Your Worship. An oversight.' He turned back to Jarrett. 'Did you ever see that chart or the missing pages of the logbooks and the course-recorder trace again?'

'No. There was no opportunity. The ship struck minutes after that. The Captain came to the bridge, ordered fire stations, and I had to leave the bridge to go to my station.'

'Leaving the Captain and the second officer there?'

'That is correct.'

Ohlsson began another question when the Chairman said, 'Mr Ohlsson, I suggest you deal with events in their chronological order. This switching about confuses the court. No doubt you will have an opportunity in due course to bring the defendant to what happened *after* the stranding.'

Ohlsson's sharp nose swung from his client to the Chairman. 'I am sorry, Your Worship, I wanted to emphasize the extent to which my client is handicapped by the absence of those documents.' He sighed audibly before looking again at Jarrett. 'You were about to tell the court what happened after you had taken over the watch.'

Jarrett went on to tell of the various alterations of course necessary – first for the big ship ahead then, successively, for the two trawlers on the starboard bow – his account according closely with the evidence of the previous witnesses. He dwelt on the difficulties created by the advent of fog so soon after altering course for the big ship.

Ohlsson again interrupted. 'When your ship encountered that fog what did you do?'

'I called the standby man, Cavalho, and put him on bridge lookout. Then I phoned the engineroom and told the second engineer of the fog and we put the engines to "manoeuvring speed". That was at 0430. I remember the time because he and I agreed it. Next I tried the auto-switch on the pneumatic siren – the forward one used for fog signals – but there was no response. I phoned Mr Benson at once and asked him to have someone attend to it. He asked me not to use the steam whistle aft because it would disturb those sleeping. I told him I would not. I reported the fog to the Captain by telephone. Told him of the steps I had taken and mentioned the trouble with the siren. He agreed with the decision not to use the steam whistle. He then asked me about traffic in the vicinity and the state of the weather generally, and I gave him the necessary information.'

'Was that the end of the conversation?'

Jarrett frowned, his expression a mixture of worry and embarrassment. 'No. The Captain said that he had a bad headache.' Jarrett's voice dropped. 'He said he'd taken some pain-killers so that he could sleep – and wouldn't be coming up. He asked me to keep a sharp eye on things and to let him know if I wanted him on the bridge at any time. I said I was sorry to hear of his trouble – that I was sure that a good sleep would help – I told him not to worry – I said we should be out of the fog before the end of the watch.'

Ohlsson's small eyes darted towards the Chairman and Assessors.

Goodbody passed a slip of paper to Crutchley. He'd scrawled

on it: *Here it comes.*

Ohlsson turned back to Jarrett. 'Were you surprised the Captain did not come up?'

Jarrett hesitated. 'Yes. To be frank, I *was* surprised.'

Ohlsson apologized for the interruption and asked Jarrett to go on with his story.

The chief officer said that no sooner was he ready to alter course back to port to regain the former course line – after altering for the big ship which had now passed safely to port – when radar showed a small vessel on the starboard bow to be a potential hazard. Under the Regulations for Preventing Collisions at Sea, he was required to give way and pass astern of the vessel. To do this he had to alter once more to starboard and, because it was a trawler, make a long detour astern of it. In response to a question by Ohlsson he said he knew from the fog signal that it was a trawler with her gear in the water. During this time Jackson the electrician had arrived on the bridge to check the auto-siren circuit. When the trawler was clear he'd altered back to port, to a course of 258° which would have taken the ship to a position at least five miles off Cape Agulhas. *Ocean Mammoth* had been on that course for some time – probably about seven minutes – when radar showed another small vessel coming out from the direction of Struys Bay. It was about five miles away on the starboard bow and was not then on a collision course. He'd gone to the chart-room to fix *Ocean Mammoth*'s position, only to find that the Decca Navigator was not functioning. That was at about 0510. He had immediately phoned the radio officer and asked him to come up and attend to it. Jarrett said he'd then gone to the wheelhouse and again checked by radar on the small vessel on the starboard bow. It had been steering a south-easterly course when first detected, but now it had begun to alter round to the south-west. This put it on a collision course. Once again he had given way by altering to starboard to pass astern of it. Worried about the ship's position now that it could no longer be fixed by Decca Navigator, he had taken a DF bearing on the radio beacon at Cape Agulhas and at the same time obtained readings of 34/36 fathoms from the echo-sounder. From this data he estimated the ship to be in a position just over seven miles south-east of the lighthouse. He had plotted that position on the chart and written the time of observation – 0515 – against it. It confirmed his impression that he had ample searoom in spite of the alterations of course he'd been obliged to make.

In due course the second trawler had passed ahead of *Ocean Mammoth* – at about twenty minutes or so past five, he thought – and he'd ordered port wheel to bring the ship back to the south-east once more – that was towards its former course line. He went to the radar to check the DF position he'd obtained at 0515 and found that both radar displays were dead. The radio operator was then in the chartroom working on the Decca Navigator, and he told him to leave it and attend to the radar which was the more urgent priority. Feeny had then begun to check out the radar circuits.

Not long after that he'd gone to the chartroom and found Foley there. Feeny had by then gone down to fetch a technical manual. Jarrett said his altercation with Foley had followed and soon afterwards the ship struck.

'When you took over the bridge at 0400, what course did the second officer hand over to you?' asked Ohlsson.

'Two-six-seven degrees.'

'What figures were pencilled against the course line on the chart when you took over?'

'Two-six-seven degrees.'

'And the figures on the course-to-steer indicator?'

'Two-six-seven degrees.'

'Had you known that the course on the chart was in fact two-*five*-seven degrees when you took over, would it have made any difference to your judgement during the next hour and a half?'

'A great deal. We were making good twelve/thirteen knots. A ten-degree error in course over an hour and a half's steaming at that speed would have put the ship three and a half to four miles closer inshore, even if there'd been no changes of course. As it was with the various alterations to starboard and the current setting inshore, the error was magnified and in the end disastrous.'

'Do you consider that the error of ten degrees was responsible for the loss of this great ship and the lives of some of its crewmen?'

Jarrett nodded slowly. 'Basically, yes. Of course failure of the electronic navigation aids at a critical juncture was a contributory factor – but only contributory. Had the correct course been given me, even their failure would not have been disastrous

184

because we would have had considerably more searoom. At least several miles more.'

It was 12.45 p.m. and the Chairman adjourned the enquiry.

Captain Crutchley felt that those present that morning were likely to have left the courtroom feeling that Jarrett had acquitted himself well. His lucid, unfaltering account of events during the early hours of 29 October left the impression that he had been confronted with an incredibly difficult situation: the fog, Foley's error in handing over the course, the absence of the Captain from the bridge, the three ships – hidden by fog – for which he had to take avoiding action, the failure of electronic systems at a critical juncture, and Foley's mysterious presence in the chart-room shortly before the ship struck – all this compressed into an hour and a half.

Crutchley was sure that Jarrett had won the sympathy of the court. He was almost sure that the chief officer's story of the telephone conversation was a fabrication. Yet there was still that nagging doubt – could Grundewald's capsules have obliterated the recollection? Foley had denied handing over a course of 267° and yet when Crutchley had looked at the chart and deck logbook shortly after the stranding he'd seen the figures 267° in Foley's neat hand against the course line. He'd also seen the 0515 position on the chart – the position which Jarrett said he'd obtained by means of a DF bearing of the Agulhas radio beacon and echo soundings. Much of Jarrett's evidence had been corroborated in advance by Fernandez, Cavalho and the other witnesses.

So was the man lying about the telephone conversation or was he giving an honest account of what had happened? Of course Jarrett had been negligent. To a seaman, that stood out a mile. Long before the Decca Navigator or the radar units had failed he could have fixed the ship's position; indeed, with radar right up to within ten minutes of the ship's stranding. Why then had he not done so? With this in mind Crutchley had passed a note to Goodbody suggesting the chief officer be questioned on the point. Goodbody had read it, nodded understandingly and put it in his pocket.

Crutchley had hoped he would be discussing the morning's proceedings with Goodbody over lunch, but to his dismay the barrister said he had to discuss certain matters with Lourens in the recess and would not be lunching at the Palace Hotel. He'd added, 'But don't worry, my dear Captain. Things are not going at all badly. Indeed, it may not be necessary to call you as a witness.'

Chapter 29

When the enquiry resumed on the afternoon of the third day, the Chairman informed the court that during the luncheon recess he had had a discussion with the Assessors. Since the evidence of the chief officer dealt with a number of complex aspects of ship handling and navigation, he felt it would help the enquiry if the Assessors – both master mariners of long experience – were without further delay to put certain questions of a technical nature. He had discussed the matter with the counsel concerned and they had agreed.

Jarrett then returned to the witness box.

Captain Wedderburn, a solemn cadaverous man with iron grey hair, put on spectacles, cleared his throat and looked at the chief officer. 'When you took over the watch at four o'clock on 29 October, did you check the course on the chart to see if it agreed with the course of two-six-seven degrees you allege was handed over to you by the second officer?' Wedderburn's manner was polite but unsmiling, his voice deep and abrasive.

'No. I did not.'

'Would it not have been a wise precaution?'

Jarrett thought about that for a moment. 'Yes. With hindsight I suppose it would. But the second officer is an extra-master. I had no reason to suppose the figures he'd written against the course line were ten degrees in error. As a pencil line on a chart, a course of two-five-seven looks much the same as two-six-seven. He'd given me two-six-seven verbally, the ship's head was on two-six-seven, and those were the figures on the course-indicator.'

'But you did not check the charted course?'

'No, sir.'

Captain Wedderburn looked surprised, put on his spectacles and consulted his notes.

'There have been a number of references in evidence to the TM and AC radar sets in *Ocean Mammoth*'s wheelhouse. Will you explain to the court the difference between them?'

Crutchley could see from the half smile on Jarrett's face that he liked the question. The chief officer was not a modest man. Here was an opportunity to show off his knowledge to an important audience.

'The TM set – that is True Motion radar – is intended primarily for coastal navigation. The AC set – Anti-Collision radar – for anti-collision work. The AC unit can in fact do the work of both since it is basically a TM radar, but its markers provide the relative motion reference essential for collision avoidance, thus giving both true and relative motion on the same display. This is very important for collision avoidance in close quarter situations. For this reason many deck officers prefer to use AC radar under most conditions.'

'In that case is there any advantage in having both sets? Why not just have AC radar?'

'Ah. It's not quite as simple as that.' Jarrett's smile was condescending. 'There *are* real advantages in having both. In close waters – the Straits of Dover for example, where there is a lot of traffic and very little searoom – both sets can be manned at the same time.'

He must have sensed a trap then, for he quickly added, 'If there are enough people on the bridge, that is.' He looked for a moment towards Captain Crutchley whose dark glasses were trained on the witness box.

Wedderburn nodded. 'Of course. Any other advantages?'

'When necessary,' went on Jarrett, rather more slowly now, as if weighing each word, 'one display can be used for checking the other. There's also an inter-switching device that makes it possible to use alternative wavelengths on either display. This is important. It makes possible improved detection in difficult weather and sea conditions and reduces interference from other ships.' He paused. 'Is that sufficient, sir, or do you want me to go further into the technicalities?'

'No. That will do very well, thank you.' Captain Wedderburn again looked at his notes. 'Could you not have checked the ship's position by radar once you could no longer use the Decca Navigator?'

'There just wasn't time for that.'

The Assessor adjusted his spectacles with bony fingers. 'I see in his sworn statement that the radio officer records that you reported the Decca Navigator failure at about ten minutes past five, and you told him of the radar trouble about fifteen minutes later? Was there no opportunity in those fifteen minutes to use radar or fixing the ship's position?'

'A lot was happening in those fifteen minutes. I'd already got a position by DF bearing and soundings at five-fifteen. We were taking avoiding action for the second trawler. I had Feeny on the bridge discussing the Decca Navigator problem with me. I was checking on the lookout and his reports, then going back to the wheelhouse to consult the radar displays and give wheel orders. After that came the radar failures and I had to discuss them with Feeny.'

'You have mentioned the five-fifteen position you obtained by combining a DF bearing with echo soundings; a position which you admitted in your statement to the preliminary enquiry may have been two miles south of the ship's actual position. Do you agree that a DF bearing combined with soundings is by no means a reliable way of fixing a ship's position?'

'I only resorted to it after the Decca Navigator had failed.'

'But you still had radar at that time?'

'I was fully employed using it to avoid a collision. It was dark, we were in dense fog. A close quarters situation had developed. It was necessary to keep the trawler under continuous radar observation if a collision was to be avoided. The trawler was changing course all the time – the situation was changing all the time.'

'How far off the land – that is Cape Agulhas – were you when you passed astern of the second trawler?'

'Without the chart and course-recorder trace to check on, it is very difficult for me to answer that question.'

'The ship ran aground at five-thirty-nine. That time is not in dispute. You have told the court she was steaming at twelve/thirteen knots. You passed astern of the trawler at about five-thirty, give or take a few minutes. At say, five-twenty, the land must have been within nineteen minutes' steaming distance at twelve knots. That is about four miles. Would not the land have shown up on your AC radar display – particularly on the six-mile range scale?'

'Not necessarily under those conditions. Thick fog. Moisture-saturated atmosphere.'

'My experience is that radar is good in fog.'

'Not always,' said Jarrett stubbornly.

'I believe that your radar had a range of up to sixty-four miles. Is that correct?'

189

'Yes. But I was operating it on the six-mile range.'

'Why only six miles?'

'It is the normal range for operating AC radar in a white knuckle situation.'

'What do you mean by a "white knuckle situation"?'

'A critical situation. When your ship and the target ship are on converging courses in the decisive four-to-six mile zone. Things are happening very quickly. Unexpected manoeuvring by the other ship, for example. It requires intense concentration to maintain safe control in fog under those conditions.'

'Could you not have switched on the TM set and consulted that display from time to time? I understand the two sets were mounted side by side in the wheelhouse?'

Jarrett shrugged his shoulders, spread his hands in a gesture of helplessness. 'Now – with all the facts before the court – with any amount of time in which to consider them, sitting in the security of this courtroom in bright daylight, it is not difficult to suggest what might have been done. But I had no such advantages. It was dark. The ship was in dense fog. I was totally occupied in dealing with three different collision-avoidance situations in the space of an hour. Due to the course error I inherited, I had much less searoom than I had been led to believe. I had no means of anticipating the failures of electronic equipment which occurred. Yes – of course it's easy to see now what I should have done. But I can assure you, sir, it was not easy under those conditions.'

To Captain Crutchley, listening to all this, it occurred that Jarrett should have been a lawyer, not a seaman. This prompted him to scribble a note for Goodbody: *If things were so difficult on the bridge why didn't he ask me to come up? He's already said in evidence that I told him to let me know if he wanted me on the bridge.*

Goodbody read it, scribbled on the reverse side and passed it back: *Good point. It won't be overlooked. Our friend is beginning to limp.*

Crutchley wished he could agree. Jarrett appeared to him to be doing rather well.

Captain Wedderburn told the Chairman he had no further questions. Captain Bronson, the other Assessor, a dark, sallow man with surgically cold eyes took over.

'Did you check the four o'clock position plotted by the second officer before he left the bridge?'

'No, sir.'

'When did you first use the Decca Navigator to fix the ship's position that morning?'

Jarrett replied that the Decca logbook had been entered with the 0400 position by the second officer. There was no reason whatever to suppose that it was an incorrect position. Although the Decca logbook was ruled for positions at twenty-minute intervals, it was customary to record them at forty-minute intervals, except in close waters like the Straits of Dover. The next fix by Decca would have been due at 0440, but he had not been able to attend to it because he'd been busy avoiding collision with the first trawler. It was after they'd passed astern of that trawler, and were returning to the south-west, that he'd gone to the Decca Navigator and found that it was not functioning. That was at about ten past five.

'It appears from the evidence that when taking collision-avoidance action you were giving wheel orders for long slow turns to port and starboard. Also that you were making large alterations of course.' Captain Bronson looked at the folio on the table before him. 'For instance the evidence shows that the first alteration of course – that for the big ship ahead – was from two-six-seven to two-nine-five degrees. Was it necessary to make such big alterations?'

Jarrett smiled confidently. 'Yes, sir. It has been drummed into our generation of ship handlers that when taking avoiding action, particularly in fog, large alterations are safer than small ones.'

'I see.' Captain Bronson, a man in the middle fifties, could scarcely have missed the inference that 'our generation' knew something his didn't. 'And why the long slow turns? *Towards* the land incidentally, each time you went to starboard?'

'I was beginning those turns when the target ships were several miles away. It is necessary when handling a VLCC for collision avoidance to begin your turn well in advance. These three-hun-dred-thousand-ton supertankers don't handle quite like ten-thousand-ton ships.' The way Jarrett said that made clear the tag he'd put on Bronson's experience.

'I'll take your word for it, Mr Jarrett.' The Assessor's cold eyes outstared the chief officer's. 'But they seem just as liable to run aground.'

Goodbody passed a note to Captain Crutchley. *How to win friends and influence people.*

191

Bronson considered his notes. 'Why, when you had these two trawlers crossing ahead of you from starboard to port, did you not reduce speed rather than alter course towards the land?'

'I thought I had ample searoom.'

'Presumably your generation of ship handlers has not been taught to keep away from the land in dense fog.' Having fired that shot across the chief officer's bows, Bronson announced that he had no further questions.

Goodbody rose with a friendly smile to cross-examine the chief officer.

'Mr Jarrett, from your evidence and that of the quartermasters, it is not clear during what period the course *was* two-six-seven when it *should have been* two-five-seven? Did that error begin at four o'clock when you took over, or are you suggesting it began at two-forty when the second officer fixed the ship's position and altered course to allow for the north-westerly set of the current?'

'It certainly was incorrect from four o'clock onwards. I've no means of knowing what course was steered from two-forty because the chart and other records are missing.'

'But when you took over the watch, right up to the time of stranding, the chart and other records were not missing. You could have seen the positions plotted by the second officer at two-forty and four o'clock. In other words you could have checked the course made good since two-forty, could you not?'

Jarrett did not answer at once. 'My first concern when I took over the watch was to check on traffic in the vicinity. To examine the chart I would have had to go to the chartroom. I did not want to leave the wheelhouse while Fernandez was down below. I was at that time the only person on the bridge.'

'But it was you who sent Fernandez below to fetch your jersey. Why did you not get Cavalho, the standby man, to fetch it?'

'We were not then in fog. I knew Fernandez would only be a few minutes.'

'Why did you not check the course – and the ship's position – when he returned?'

'The second officer had obtained a fix shortly before – at four o'clock. The next was due at four-forty. There didn't seem any urgency, and in any case I was already worrying about the ship coming up ahead.'

Goodbody plunged a hand deep into a trouser pocket and grasped the lapel of his coat with another. It was a gesture which somehow made him look even larger and more formidable than he was. He squinted at the Republican Coat-of-Arms on the wall behind the Chairman as if trying to discern some detail there, his face very serious. By the time he turned back to Jarrett he was smiling again – a warm, outward-giving smile. 'You have told the court that when you phoned the Captain to report the fog his last words to you were, "Let me know if you need me on the bridge at any time". Am I right?'

'Yes.'

'In your interesting and – if I may say so – erudite discourse on TM and AC radar, you said both sets could be manned at the same time. You quoted this as one of the advantages, did you not?'

'Yes, I did.'

'You added a rider – "if there were enough people on the bridge"?'

'Yes.'

'You have stressed in your evidence that you were so busy during the critical period – let us say between five and five-thirty – that you had no time to establish by radar where the ship was in relation to the land?'

'Yes. I have explained that I was fully occupied with three successive collision-avoidance situations in that time.'

'I see.' Mr Goodbody looked at the chief officer with a mildly surprised expression. 'Why then did you not ask the Captain to come up? Surely you *needed* him then?'

'There seemed no point.'

'No point, Mr Jarrett? You were too busy to plot the ship's position – too busy to check the ship's course – too preoccupied with avoiding collisions – too busy to use both TM and AC radars at once, though they were alongside each other in the wheelhouse. With the Captain on the bridge would you not have had time to do these things? How can you say there was no point in asking him to come up?'

'The Captain's presence on the bridge would not have helped.'

'Perhaps you might care to amplify that statement?'

Jarrett was patently embarrassed. He fidgeted with his hands, moved his weight from one foot to the other, looked from Goodbody to the Chairman, then at Ohlsson. 'You are forcing me into a corner where I may have to disclose something I prefer not to.'

'Come, come, Mr Jarrett. Be forthcoming.'

193

'I prefer not to.'

The Chairman leant forward, focusing his good eye on the chief officer. 'Is it something relevant to this enquiry, Mr Jarrett?'

'Yes, Your Worship.' Jarrett nodded slowly, looking very unhappy.

'Then I must remind you that you are bound to answer counsel's question.'

'Come, Mr Jarrett. Let's have it,' prompted Goodbody.

'I did not call Captain Crutchley because I knew his presence on the bridge could make no difference. It would have been for formal purposes only.'

The Chairman intervened again. 'Kindly explain yourself.'

'The Captain's vision is badly impaired.' Jarrett blurted it out. 'For most of the voyage – since we left Rotterdam – it has been so.'

Goodbody paused, looked down at the impassive figure of Captain Crutchley sitting beside him with folded arms, the dark glasses seeming now to be of enormous significance. The barrister turned back to Jarrett. 'That is a most damaging allegation. Perhaps you could explain how the Captain managed to take his ship from Rotterdam to Durban with such defective vision?'

'He used Cadet Middleton as his eyes. He was never on the bridge without him. He used to ask Middleton to take bearings of other ships, of shore objects. He always got him to examine the radar displays and report what he saw. While the ship was undergoing repairs in Durban, Middleton was transferred to another ship. Without him . . .' Jarrett gestured with his arms, shook his head and fell silent.

'I see.' Goodbody's lips parted in a smile which revealed moist white teeth. 'Did you read the Captain's night order book when you took over the watch at four o'clock that morning – or were you too busy?'

Jarrett's frown suggested he didn't like the sarcasm. 'Yes. I did. And I signed it.'

'Perhaps you could explain to the court how a man whose vision was as badly impaired as you say Captain Crutchley's was, could write up his night order book with entries which included, among other things, numerals of time, date and position?'

'I haven't said that he was blind. I said his vision was impaired. If you don't believe me I suggest you test it here and now in this

194

court.' A note of asperity had crept into Jarrett's voice.

'I have no intention of perpetrating such an impertinence. The vision of a lot of highly competent men who carry great responsibility may be badly impaired.' Goodbody paused, looked across at the Chairman – seeming to focus on the black eye-shield – and then at Lourens. 'You may have noticed that My Learned Friend – counsel for the enquiry – wears pebble-lens glasses. Presumably his vision is impaired. Would you care to suggest he is incapable of leading this enquiry?'

Ohlsson got up, his sharp eyes glinting. 'Objection, Your Worship. The eyesight of counsel for the enquiry has nothing to to with the stranding of *Ocean Mammoth*. My Learned Friend is endeavouring to lead us away from the point.'

'I can assure you I shall bring him back to it if he does,' said the Chairman. 'Objection dismissed. Please proceed, Mr Goodbody.'

'Your answer to my last question, Mr Jarrett?'

'Leading an enquiry in a courtroom in broad daylight is a very different matter from handling a ship in thick fog in a white knuckle situation.'

Goodbody beamed. 'Ah, our old friend the white knuckle. Admiral Lord Nelson seemed to handle such situations quite competently in spite of somewhat impaired vision. Now, Mr Jarrett, let me put to you the situation as I see it. You came on watch at four o'clock in the morning. You did not check the ship's course. You did not check the ship's position. The ship encountered fog half an hour later. You say you reported the fog to the Captain but . . .'

Goodbody stopped, looked towards the Chairman, then at Jarrett. 'In his statement at the preliminary enquiry, Captain Crutchley denied that absolutely. He said your story of a telephone conversation was pure fabrication. Indeed he said that had speed been reduced or the siren sounded he would have gone to the bridge at once without waiting for any report. That would, he said, have been the automatic response of the Master of a ship, particularly when close to land. It is a view which I have no doubt the master mariners in this court would strongly endorse.' Goodbody glanced at the Assessors, his face serious. 'But no siren was sounded. Jackson, the electrician, says the junction box had been interfered with.' Goodbody paused, adjusted his spectacles, looked up suddenly. 'I put it to you, Mr Jarrett, that there never was any telephone conversation – that you were determined the Captain should not come up to the bridge that night.'

'Objection, Your Worship.' Ohlsson was on his feet again, his sharp features switching left and right like a ventriloquist's dummy. 'My Learned Friend is addressing the court, not cross-examining the witness. I really must object.'

The Chairman's bushy eyebrows lifted in a frown. 'Counsel is perfectly entitled to put to the witness the situation as he sees it. I've no doubt he is coming to a question.'

'Thank you, Your Worship. Indeed I am.' Goodbody had a wonderful capacity for conveying respect, or indeed any other emotion necessary. He addressed himself once more to Jarrett. 'In your evidence you have painted a grim picture of the intolerable burden laid upon you in the hour and forty minutes before *Ocean Mammoth* ran aground. You had no time, you have said, to do those fundamental essential things like checking the course, fixing the position – the very things upon which the safety of that great ship and all those in her depended.

'I suggest . . .' Goodbody's smile froze and the hand that held the notes pointed accusingly, 'that for reasons best known to you, you had the arrogance to decide, at a time of crisis and danger, that it was neither necessary nor desirable to call the man responsible for the safety of the ship, the man who commanded her – the Master of *Ocean Mammoth*.

'Even if he were blind, it was your duty to call him. Even if he could not see at all, his judgement – the judgement of the Master, the most experienced seaman in the ship – should have been made available. And if his vision was indeed badly impaired – and Cadet Middleton was not there – who better to be his eyes than you, his chief officer?' For the first time since the enquiry had begun Goodbody glared contempt at the man in the witness box.

'What is the question?' Jarrett's manner bordered on the insolent.

'Was it or was it not your duty to call the Captain?'

'It depends on what you mean by *duty*?'

Goodbody gave the chief officer the sort of look reserved for bad smells. 'No further questions, Your Worship.'

Jarrett left the witness box and Foley was recalled at Ohlsson's request.

Chapter 30

To his wife, sitting well back in the public gallery, Foley looked a tired dispirited man as he got up from the table where he sat beside Kahn and made for the witness box. Knowing how much he disliked and feared Ohlsson, she could imagine his feelings at that moment. Her heart went out to him.

He mounted the steps to the box, looked for a moment towards her, his face quite expressionless, then turned wearily to face his inquisitor.

'There's one point I'd like to clear up before we go any further,' began Ohlsson. 'There have been a number of references in evidence to the failure of the auto-siren. Was it not your duty to test it before leaving harbour on each occasion?'

'Yes. It was.'

'Did you test it before leaving Durban?'

'No.'

'Why not?'

'It was a job I'd delegated to Cadet Middleton. He left the ship in Durban and I overlooked the matter.'

'So you failed to test the siren?'

'Yes.'

Ohlsson darted a quick sidelong glance at those on the dais.

'When you handed over the watch to the chief officer did you warn him that the current had set north-westerly during your watch?'

'No.'

'Why not?'

'A warning about the current is printed on the chart and in the Sailing Directions. Apart from that, the chief officer could have seen the set from the positions I'd plotted on the chart during my watch.'

'But you did not warn him?'

'No. I've just explained why.'

Ohlsson busied himself with his notes before looking up suddenly as if hoping to catch the second officer off guard. 'At what time did you leave your cabin, *because you could not sleep*, Mr Foley?'

The second officer hesitated. 'I can't say with any accuracy. About five o'clock perhaps.'

'Why the vagueness about the time?'

'I was not wearing my watch and I did not switch on the cabin light for fear of disturbing my wife.'

'Do you often have difficulty in sleeping?'

'Not as a rule.'

'Why on that occasion, then?'

Foley hesitated. 'I was worried.'

'Worried. By what?'

'It was a personal matter.'

'I see.' Ohlsson nodded slowly, staring at Foley. 'A personal matter. H'm. You have said that some time after coming up to the lower bridge deck and finding the ship in fog, you'd noticed she was steering well to the north-west of the course you'd plotted. At what time did you make this observation?'

'About ten minutes after I came on deck.'

'And how did you in fog, in the dark, without instruments, come to the conclusion that the ship was steering well to the north-west of the course you'd plotted?'

'Throughout the middle-watch there was a swell from the south-east. When I noticed that its direction relative to the ship had changed from four points on the port quarter to dead astern, I knew there had been a substantial alteration of course to the north-west. It was then I assumed we had already passed Cape Agulhas and were making for Cape Point.'

'You have said in your evidence that later, when course was again altered to the south-west, you became suspicious.'

'That is correct.'

'It was then that you went to the chartroom?'

'Yes.'

'Why did you not at once go to the officer-of-the-watch in the wheelhouse – the chief officer – and inform him of your fears?'

Foley hesitated, looked unhappy. 'I wanted to make sure first what was happening. I was under the impression the Captain was on the bridge.'

'How long was it between the arousal of your suspicions and the arrival of the chief officer in the chartroom?'

'About ten minutes, I suppose.'

198

'At twelve knots the ship would have travelled two miles in that time. With the current more. Do you agree?'

'Yes. That is so.'

'You were the ship's navigating officer?'

'I was.'

'So it would have been perfectly proper for you to have gone straight to the bridge and discussed the situation with the chief officer, or even the Captain had he been there?'

'I suppose so, but . . .'

'But what, Mr Foley?'

'I didn't want to make a fool of myself.'

'So you took your time about things although the safety of a fifty-five-million-dollar tanker and her crew were at stake?'

'I did not realize how close to the land the ship was.'

Ohlsson shook his head in disbelief. He looked at his notes before turning back to Foley. 'In his evidence the chief officer has said that when he reached the chartroom you were busy at the chart-table with parallel rulers and a pencil. He also said there was an eraser next to the chart. Now, Mr Foley – can you tell the court what you were doing on that chart?'

'While I was checking the echo-sounder readings against the soundings on the chart, I saw that the figure two-five-seven I had written against the course line had been changed to two-six-seven. To make sure I checked the course line with the parallel rulers. It was exactly as I had drawn it: two-five-seven degrees, but the "five" had been changed to a "six" making the figure two-six-seven.'

'And the pencil in your hand?' Ohlsson pinched his nostrils and poised for the kill.

'I had picked it up instinctively.'

'*Instinctively*,' echoed Ohlsson. 'Why instinctively?'

The second officer's drawn face twisted with worry. 'When you've spent years of your life plotting courses and positions on charts – well – it *is* instinctive to have a pencil in your hand.'

'It is of course not impossible that when the chief officer came into the chartroom that morning you were about to use the pencil and eraser to alter the two-six-seven to two-five-seven to cover up your mistake.'

'That is quite untrue.' Foley leant forward, gripping the rail of the witness box.

Ohlsson's eyes darted round the courtroom as if to check

199

whether the drift of his questioning had caught on. They settled once more upon the second officer.

'I take it that before handing over the watch at four o'clock that morning you had entered the course in the logbook?'

'Yes. I had.'

With the skill of one who had performed the operation many times before, Ohlsson removed his spectacles, wiped them with a silk handkerchief and returned them to his nose. 'Soon after the stranding the chart disappeared from the wheelhouse, pages in the deck and Decca logbooks – the pages for that day – were torn out, and the trace on the course-recorder was removed. In other words, all the evidence relating to responsibility for the incorrect course steered by *Ocean Mammoth* on her way to disaster had disappeared.'

Ohlsson paused to pinch his nostrils once more. 'I put it to you, Mr Foley – from your point of view the disappearance of those items of evidence was no bad thing?'

Foley's face turned a ghostlike white. His voice when he spoke was hoarse with emotion. 'I have testified on oath that the course figures I wrote on the chart and in the logbook were two-five-seven. Those figures were altered after I left the bridge.' He hesitated before blurting out, 'They can only have been altered by the chief officer – I'm quite certain he is responsible for the disappearance of the evidence. It would have shown up all the other mistakes he made.'

Ohlsson's eyes glittered dangerously. 'On the contrary, I suggest that your evidence is deliberately and with malice loaded against the chief officer – that you are making these reckless allegations in a desperate attempt to cover your own mistakes.'

'That is not true – it's a lie.'

Ohlsson lowered his voice, spoke more slowly, more deliberately. 'Were your personal relations with the chief officer not under intense strain because of an incident two nights before the stranding – that is on the twenty-seventh?'

Foley's hesitation, his anguished expression, seemed to answer the question. With difficulty he said, 'That had nothing to do with it. Nothing at all.'

'The chief officer will say that you and he had a fist fight in his cabin at about one o'clock in the morning, when you came down unexpectedly from the bridge. That you both bore the marks of that fight for days afterwards.'

200

Foley's colour was ashen. 'You have no right to drag that into these proceedings. It is a despicable thing to do.'

'Because of that fight, because of the incident which caused it, I suggest that much of your evidence has been hopelessly prejudiced and must be disregarded. I suggest that once you'd seen the fog warning, you deliberately falsified the course figures with the object of involving the chief officer in a situation which could destroy his career – that you were intent upon revenge for the humiliation you'd suffered when you went to his quarters that night and found him there with a passenger in highly compromising circumstances.' Ohlsson paused, looked round the court, before saying, 'That passenger being your wife.'

'You have no right to make these insinuations, Mr Ohlsson.' The reprimand came from the Chairman like the boom of a gun. 'This is a court of marine enquiry not a divorce court. We are trying to establish how this ship came to be lost through running aground and who was at fault. You must restrict yourself to the facts on the basis of the evidence led.'

'I apologize, Your Worship. I thought the point was particularly relevant since it established a motive. I have no further questions.' The gleam of satisfaction in Ohlsson's eyes suggested he had made his point.

Foley, white and drawn, his body trembling with emotion, stood like a man under sentence of death as the Chairman explained that he could stand down, there being no further questions.

In the highly-charged atmosphere which followed, Lourens rose to inform the court that Ernst Rohrbach, the electronics engineer, would be available in the morning to give expert evidence. It was almost five o'clock when the Chairman adjourned the proceedings until 9.15 a.m. on the following day.

Foley waited until most people had left the courtroom, before walking towards a side exit. He was halfway there, a dazed look on his face, when his wife came up from behind, slipped her arm through his and whispered, 'Oh God, I'm sorry. It's my fault.'

Chapter 31

THE FOURTH DAY

With the revelation in court of an affaire which had for weeks been the subject of informed gossip out of it, public interest in the enquiry had grown even more intense by the fourth day.

Cape Town's morning newspapers had featured Ohlsson's cross-examination of Foley and headline writers had had a field day: *Love Drama in Wrecked Supertanker* competed with *Sex Fight Strands Ship?*; one columnist got in his titillation with *Did Sex Wreck Supertanker?*; another with *Supertanker Sex Drama*. It was highly predictable stuff and no doubt sold newspapers.

Thus it was not surprising that on the fourth day a queue had formed outside the Magistrate's Court. It led into the building and down the passage to the entrance to 'C' court. Those who'd come early and managed to get into the courtroom sat on benches in the public gallery exchanging whispered confidences. A number who'd been present since the enquiry began had acquired the ephemeral status of 'Old Hands' and were listened to with due respect. The atmosphere was unmistakably that of an audience looking forward to a good day's entertainment.

While there was considerable interest in the two men primarily concerned in the drama of the previous day's evidence – Jarrett and Foley, who sat with their counsel at the long table – it was Sandy who stole the occasion. For the first three days of the enquiry she had sat well back but now, with feminine perverseness and not a little courage, she had moved to a front bench. Wearing a simple grey suit, her hair elegantly casual, her oval face with its fine bone structure scarcely concealed by dark glasses, she looked the sort of woman men could fight over.

The low hum of conversation ceased when order was called and the Chairman and Assessors entered and made their way to the dais.

Almost immediately Ernst Rohrbach was called, went to the witness box and was sworn in. He was a slight man with a skeletal face, large dark eyes and a pronounced German accent. Lourens's opening questions established that Rohrbach was an electronics

202

engineer whose qualifications included a doctorate from Munich University. He had, he said, received his practical training with Krupp-Atlas in Bremen. There he had specialized in marine radar and other shipborne electronic devices. In Cape Town, where he had been in business for five years, he headed a firm which installed and serviced maritime electronic equipment. In this way he had acquired considerable experience of Decca systems since they were widely used.

'I understand you inspected the equipment on board *Ocean Mammoth* a week after she was wrecked?' said Lourens.

'Yes. I did.'

'Why did you do that?'

'The marine surveyor acting for the insurers, Captain Summerbee, asked me to go on board the after part of the ship to evaluate the electronic equipment for salvage purposes. Most of the superstructure was still above water but there had been two gales in close succession and he wished to know if it was still worth salvaging. He also said that if I had time I should try to find the cause of the failures.'

'Did you find the cause of those failures?'

'Yes.'

'Can you tell the court what you found?'

'In the case of the Decca Navigator, the insulated aerial wire which leads into the chartroom through a gooseneck on the monkey island . . .'

The Chairman held up his hand in a traffic-stopping gesture. 'What is a *gooseneck* and what is a *monkey island*?'

Rohrbach's face showed surprise. Surely, his expression conveyed, everybody should know these things. 'A gooseneck is a tube with the top bent round through one-eighty degrees to face the deck . . . this keeps the water out. The monkey island is an open space on top of the bridgehouse. Its primary purpose is to provide a platform for the magnetic compass.'

'Thank you. Please continue.'

'This gooseneck I was talking of is on the starboard side of the monkey island, immediately above the chartroom. I found that the aerial wire had been pulled out of the gooseneck, cut with pliers and pushed back again.'

'Would that put the Navigator out of action?'

'Yes. Completely. It would also take some time for the cause of the trouble to be found.'

'You are quite certain that the aerial wire had been cut?'

'Absolutely. With cutting pliers.'

'How do you know that?'

'It was a clean, two-dimensional cut. Not a single cut as with a knife.'

'Could it have been done with scissors?'

'I don't think so. The wire was too thick.'

'Could the aerial wire have been kicked or pulled out accidentally by someone on the monkey island?'

'I don't think so. In any case there would not then be the clean cut.'

Lourens frowned at the notes on his clipboard. 'And the radar sets. The TM and AC sets, both of which failed. What did you find there?'

'There was an inter-switching unit on the after bulkhead in the chartroom. In a steel cabinet. From it multi-core cables led to the transceivers and radar displays. This unit makes switching possible. Gives the operator a choice of ten-or-three centimetre signals at each display, and other alternatives. I found that it had been short-circuited.'

'How had this been done?'

'A pocket-knife blade had been thrust between the two multi-core cables just beneath the unit.'

'How do you know it was a pocket-knife?'

'The end of the blade had broken off and was still embedded.'

'Would a short circuit on the inter-switching unit put both radar sets out of action?'

'Absolutely.'

'You are telling the court that both the Decca Navigator and the two radar units were deliberately sabotaged?'

'Well, they had been interfered with. Yes. This is sabotage.' Rohrbach's guttural accent made the word more sinister, and exclamations of surprise came from the public gallery. The Chairman called for order. 'If that happens again,' he threatened, 'I will have the court cleared.'

Lourens, fidgeting impatiently with his spectacles, scowled at those in the gallery before turning back to Rohrbach. 'How is access gained to the monkey island?'

'A ladder leads from the bridge deck on to the after end of the island.'

'How long would it take a person to go from the chartroom up

204

on to the monkey island, carry out the act of sabotage you have referred to, and return to the chartroom?'

Sandy saw her husband wince as the question was put, and her heart thumped against its rib cage.

'Two minutes at the outside. Probably less.'

Lourens said he had no more questions.

Kahn at once rose to cross-examine Rohrbach. 'Were you alone when you went on board *Ocean Mammoth* to make this examination?'

'No. Sergeant van Jaarsveld of the South African Police at Bredasdorp was with me.'

'Why was that?'

'In terms of the South African Shipping Act the wreck falls under the jurisdiction of the Secretary for Transport. Local responsibility for it had been delegated to the S.A. Police at Bredasdorp. Sergeant van Jaarsveld accompanied me.'

'Did he watch you making the examination?'

'Yes. All the time.'

'Did you show him what you found?'

'Yes. I did.'

'Why did you not at once report to the authorities?'

'I left the next day for Europe on urgent business. The police at Bredasdorp knew what I had found. Captain Summerbee had flown to London that day. I wrote to him there from Germany to say the equipment was in good shape and still worth salvaging. I mentioned that failure of the electronic systems had been caused by interference. I understand that when he returned to Cape Town recently, Captain Summerbee informed Mr Lourens and I was then subpoenaed as a witness. I had expected to be back here well before the enquiry began. I did not know that I would be detained abroad as a result of a car accident.'

Kahn said, 'No more questions,' and sat down.

Ohlsson leapt to his feet. 'Your Worship, I must object. Counsel for the enquiry, in providing particulars of the charge, failed to mention that evidence would be led to show there had been sabotage. We have had no opportunity to consider this point, or to prepare any sort of defence in relation to it.'

The Chairman called on Lourens to explain.

'Your Worship, the report we received from Captain Summerbee indicated that the failure was due to "interference". We took that word to mean interference caused by atmospheric conditions.

We did not realize until Mr Rohrbach gave his evidence this morning that it meant sabotage.'

'That seems to me a reasonable explanation, Mr Ohlsson. Your objection is overruled.'

Ohlsson's dark eyes flashed angry signals of resentment and when he returned to Rohrbach his manner suggested that some of this displeasure was reserved for the German. 'You went on board *Ocean Mammoth* a week after she was wrecked?'

'Yes. That is so.'

'How do you know someone did not go on board during that week and interfere with those wires? Commit those acts of sabotage?'

'In the first place weather, and the police guard on shore, would have made it difficult. But in any event the sabotage took place *before* the ship ran aground. First to the Decca Navigator and after that to the two radar sets.'

'How do you know those failures were not due to some other causes?'

'I tested the circuits after I'd found the faults. There was nothing wrong with the Navigator or the radar units.'

Ohlsson hesitated, seemed about to say something, shook his head, announced that he had no more questions and sat down.

Lourens asked leave to address the court. He said they were now confronted with an entirely new factor. Sabotage was, he explained, a criminal act and as such a matter for investigation by the police and trial by a criminal court.

'We are here,' he said, 'to enquire how *Ocean Mammoth* came to run aground. The failure of the electronic navigation systems was certainly an important factor but it was contributory and not necessarily decisive. We have already heard evidence which suggests that serious errors of judgement, of commission and omission, played a major part in the disaster. I trust that Your Worship will feel that we should restrict ourselves at this enquiry to the purely maritime aspects – the mistakes and errors of judgement in navigating and handling which led eventually to the loss of this great ship – and leave the sabotage aspect to the police and criminal courts where it properly belongs. That is my submission, Your Worship.'

Lourens sat down and Goodbody got to his feet. 'May I reply to My Learned Friend's submission, Your Worship?'

The Chairman nodded. 'Please proceed.'

206

'We have known all along,' said Goodbody, 'that the electronic systems failed at a critical juncture. We are now told that those failures were due to sabotage. That, Your Worship, is an extremely important and disturbing development, and it is one of the utmost importance to those answering charges here today. For the witness Rohrbach to have testified that sabotage took place is one thing. To establish by whom it was committed and for what purpose is quite another. There are considerations of access, motive and corroborative evidence. We know that certain persons had access to the monkey island and chartroom during the critical time of approach to Cape Agulhas. There may have been others, for it was a dark night and there was dense fog. If so, who were they? Short of a searching and thorough investigation these questions cannot be answered. There is, I submit, good reason for adjourning this enquiry until such time as the proper authorities have completed their investigations. I do not see how we can usefully or justly proceed with the matter now. That is my submission, Your Worship.'

Goodbody sat down. The Chairman had just begun to consult with Lourens on the question of adjournment when a man stood up at the back of the public gallery and called out, 'Your Worship, I can give you important information about the sabotage.'

There was a surge of excitement in 'C' court. Heads turned to see who was speaking, the Chairman called for silence and two policemen converged on the speaker.

'Bring that man before me,' ordered the Chairman.

The policemen brought the interrupter forward and stood one on either side of him beneath the dais.

'Who are you and what do you mean by interrupting these proceedings?' demanded the Chairman who looked very fierce, his good eye glaring at the man.

'Piet Pieterse, sir. I am sorry I had to do this but I was a steward on *Ocean Mammoth* when she ran aground and I know quite a bit about the sabotage. I can help you, Your Worship. That is why I spoke out.' Pieterse's voice was hoarse, querulous, and he appeared to be extremely nervous.

The Chairman frowned. 'If you have such important evidence why did you not come forward at the preliminary enquiry, or during the weeks since?'

'I didn't know that I had this evidence until today, Your Worship. It was only when I heard the German gentleman talking about sabotage . . . and then the other gentleman . . .' he turned and nodded towards the table where counsel sat. 'When I heard the talk about motives, I knew I could help you. It would be wrong if Your Worship didn't know what I know.' Pieterse's voice trailed away as if he didn't really think his message was getting through.

The Chairman had a discussion with the Assessors after which he said, 'Mr Lourens, I would like to discuss this matter with you and with counsel for the defendants. We shall now withdraw briefly for that purpose. In the meantime the court will remain in session.' He looked at the young coloured man beneath the dais. 'You, Pieterse, must stay here until we return.'

The clerk of the court called for order and everybody stood as the Chairman left the courtroom followed by the Assessors, Lourens and the various counsel. The Chairman led the way down the passage to the Chief Magistrate's office, additional chairs were brought in, and when everyone was seated he said he would like to have the views of those present on whether or not Pieterse should be heard.

During the discussion which followed, Ohlsson, Kahn, and Jerome Bassett – counsel for the company – came out against hearing the steward. They made the point that since the information he claimed to have concerned sabotage, and no such charge was before the court, it was a matter for the police.

To the surprise of his colleagues, Goodbody believed that Pieterse's evidence should be heard. It might be irrelevant, he said, but that could be decided when its content was known. Certainly as far as his client Captain Crutchley was concerned he had no objection; he felt sure his Learned Friends who represented Jarrett, Foley and the shipping company would, on reflection, feel that their clients, too, stood to lose nothing by hearing what Pieterse had to say. Having cleverly lobbed the ball into the opposing court, he left it to Lourens to say that he was in favour of hearing Pieterse without delay. The proceedings, already protracted, were nearing their end, and the steward's evidence might well assist the Chairman in deciding whether or not the enquiry should be adjourned indefinitely. 'We have already heard from Rohrbach that there was sabotage. Now let us hear what Pieterse has to say about that sabotage. I believe it can only help the enquiry, not hinder it.'

Chapter 32

Fifteen minutes after the Chairman, the Assessors and counsel had left 'C' court for their discussions in the Chief Magistrate's office, they came back and the proceedings were resumed.

The Chairman informed the court that after consultation with those concerned he had decided that Pieterse should be heard. The steward was then called to the witness box where he took the oath.

Lourens rose to examine him. 'You must now tell us what you know about the sabotage on board *Ocean Mammoth* before she ran aground. I must remind you that you have sworn to tell the truth, the whole truth, and nothing but the truth.'

Pieterse nodded. 'Yes, sir. I understand.' He began by explaining that he had joined *Ocean Mammoth* as a steward the day before she sailed from Durban. On the morning of the first day at sea he was cleaning officers' cabins when an envelope in a wastepaper basket he was emptying caught his eye. He collected stamps and this envelope had on it some beautiful Surinam stamps. 'Birds and flowers in bright colours, sir,' he explained. So he put the envelope in his pocket. In his cabin later that day he looked at the envelope again and saw that the reverse side had some figures scribbled on it. There were three columns headed Z, G and B, and the figures were conversions from Swiss Francs to US dollars and British sterling. The sums were large, over three hundred thousand dollars in all. An item '10%', with a ring round it, reminded him of a conversation he'd overheard some nights previously.

Once launched into his story, Pieterse grew more confident and his voice became firmer. He stood stiffly to attention while he spoke, looking straight ahead, his hands at his sides as if he were on parade.

Lourens asked where the envelope was. Pieterse took it from his wallet and handed it over. Having examined it briefly, Lourens placed it on the table in front of him. He then asked Pieterse to tell the court about the conversation he'd overheard.

Pieterse said it had taken place in a Durban restaurant, the

Beau Rivage, where he'd been employed as a waiter. He was at a serving table beside a drawn curtain, close to where two guests he was looking after were having dinner. The men were talking softly. 'When they talk like that you listen, sir,' he explained. 'That's when it can be interesting. Like talk about horse racing and women.' He grinned sheepishly at this admission of human frailty. 'The foreign gentleman – he spoke with a strong foreign accent, you know – told the English gentleman how he could do himself a lot of good if he fixed things the right way for these people, and he explained that, properly handled, there was no risk.'

Pieterse said he'd been obliged to leave his vantage point then to attend to customers at another table. When he returned the foreign gentleman was handing a slip of paper to the Englishman and saying, 'That's the Zurich receipt for the ten per cent. Numbered account. Already in your name. It's a guarantee of my client's good faith.' Then, said Pieterse, the foreigner had gone on to say something like, 'When the matter is settled a third of the balance will be paid into the Zurich account and the other two-thirds into numbered accounts in Geneva and Berne.'

At that time, said Pieterse, he assumed it was a conversation between two businessmen and he'd thought no more about it. He'd heard many like it before. Later, when he joined *Ocean Mammoth* as a steward, he had recognized one of the officers as the Englishman. When he saw the figures on the back of the envelope he realized they were in some way connected with the Beau Rivage conversation. He imagined it was to do with freight rates and oil shipments, or something like that. Only when he'd heard Rohrbach's evidence that morning had the real significance of what he'd stumbled on come to him.

In telling his story Pieterse had shown himself to be either extremely naïve, or a master of suspense. He had succeeded in holding the attention of everyone in the courtroom, and all must have been waiting for him to name the officer. Lourens, who'd been seen to examine both sides of the envelope, refrained from putting the key question and thus added to the suspense. He did, however, at last say, 'Do you know the name of the "foreign gentleman" you waited on that night?'

'Only his first name, sir. The Englishman called him "Stefan", sir.'

And then at last it came, or began to – the name everybody in court was waiting to hear – as Lourens fidgeted with his spectacles, his mournful face somehow sadder than usual, his smooth dark hair reflecting light from the lamp bowl above counsel's table. 'The Englishman you waited on that night,' he said quietly. 'What was *his* name?'

The silence in 'C' court was electric. All eyes were on the coloured man standing stiffly to attention in the witness box, staring ahead at no one in particular.

'The same name as what's on the envelope, sir.'

The Chairman leant forward, clasped his hands on the table in front of him. 'You have the envelope, Mr Lourens.'

Lourens picked it up and peered at it as if he were doing so for the first time. 'It is addressed to Mr Freeman Jarrett, sir.'

Sandy, sitting within twenty feet of the table which accommodated the defendants and their counsel, had watched with agonized interest the faces of her husband and Jarrett as the German electronics expert gave his evidence.

Jarrett had looked confident and relaxed as he concentrated on what Rohrbach was saying. It was her husband who seemed then to wilt, his head bent forward, his body sagging deeper into his chair.

But as Pieterse's story unfolded the demeanour of the two men changed. Foley pulled himself up in his chair, sat bolt upright, his attention riveted on the coloured man in the witness box, his face showing sudden relief from strain. Jarrett's frown deepened, his face twisted, and from time to time he would look sideways at Ohlsson and tap nervously on the notepad in front of him.

When at the end of Pieterse's evidence Lourens read out the name on the envelope, Jarrett's head sank between his shoulders and he seemed to have shrunk and aged before her eyes. The bounce, the confidence, the arrogance had gone and he looked a frightened man.

Pieterse's evidence, coming on top of Rohrbach's, created something of a shockwave in 'C' court. It was evident that the direction of the enquiry had now taken a new and irreversible turn. The first indication of this was the Chairman's acceptance of Ohlsson's request for an adjournment so that he might discuss the matter with his client.

When the court resumed some twenty minutes later, Lourens

rose to ask leave to re-examine Jarrett. Ohlsson at once objected. There was a possibility, he said, that arising from evidence heard that day his client might have to face new charges in another place. He thought it improbable but nevertheless the possibility remained, and to submit him now to examination and cross-examination on the evidence of Pieterse and Rohrbach – without having given him the opportunity of preparing a defence – would not only be most improper but could gravely prejudice him in any proceedings elsewhere. He reminded the Chairman that evidence had to be tested as it arose. In this instance that was not possible because it had been sprung upon them without prior notice.

Pieterse's evidence of a conversation overheard in a restaurant was, continued Ohlsson, *ex parte* and without corroboration. The envelope addressed to Jarrett might well have been 'planted' in the wastepaper basket, said Ohlsson, pointing his sharp nose like a gun-dog's to where Foley sat with Kahn. It would require handwriting experts, he went on, before the slightest credence could be attached to the allegation that the figures scribbled on the envelope were Jarrett's. 'I submit, Your Worship, that the evidence of Rohrbach and Pieterse should be struck from the record and that the enquiry be adjourned *sine die* until such a time as these allegations have been properly investigated and resolved.'

Lourens lost no time in getting to his feet. 'I can understand My Learned Friend's anxiety to protect his client from the evidence of these witnesses. I will not press the point but I would with respect remind Your Worship that there are three defendants before the court. If the proceedings are adjourned *sine die* while the sabotage allegations are investigated, innocent men may be kept waiting many weeks, if not months, before they are free of those charges. I have no doubt Your Worship will have this consideration in mind in coming to a decision.'

As Lourens sat down the Chairman looked at the wall clock over the entrance. He must have noted with relief that it showed ten minutes to one, for he thereupon adjourned the proceedings until 2.15 p.m.

When the court resumed the Chairman ruled that Pieterse's evidence should be struck from the record and that Jarrett should be excused further examination. He told Ohlsson that he could

212

not accept the plea that the proceedings be adjourned *sine die*.

The various defence counsel having then indicated that they had no desire to recall any witnesses, the Chairman asked them to proceed with their closing addresses.

Goodbody and Kahn addressed the court briefly, both emphasizing that the evidence heard during the enquiry had failed to support the charges against their clients and they asked for their discharge.

They were followed by Ohlsson who said he trusted that the court would put out of its mind the sabotage allegations and confine itself to questions of fact. He believed that his client had been seriously prejudiced by the sensational and uncorroborated evidence heard that morning although it had been struck from the record. He appealed for its 'expunging from their minds', and for 'that innate sense of fair play and decency without which justice cannot be done'.

'That, Your Worship, is my submission,' he concluded, sitting down and pressing his hands to his eyes as if to shut out the light.

Poor Ohlsson sinks without trace, scribbled Goodbody on a slip of paper which he passed to Captain Crutchley.

Lourens, as counsel for the enquiry, was the last to address the court. He said it had been a long and exhaustive enquiry during which much detailed and highly technical evidence had been heard. 'Fortunately,' he continued, 'this Marine Court of Enquiry is so constituted that it has the benefit of Your Worship's legal knowledge, wisdom and experience, combined with the maritime knowledge and expertise of the Assessors, both master mariners with long experience at sea.'

He then turned to the evidence and the direction in which he was heading was at once apparent. The burden of it, he said, suggested that the chief officer's story of phoning the Captain to report the fog was improbable. On his own admission Jarrett had failed to ask the Captain to come up when the situation had become critical. He dismissed as impertinent Jarrett's defence that he'd not done so because the Captain's vision was impaired. The chief officer alleged that he'd been given an incorrect course by the second officer on taking over the watch, but Foley had denied that. The chart and other relevant information were missing so there was no way of resolving that contradiction. But Jarrett, again on his own admission, had failed to check the ship's course or position on taking over the watch. Either of those routine precautions would at once have revealed the error, had Foley in fact made one.

Jarrett had failed to obtain a position by Decca Navigator or radar at any time while those units were serviceable – in the case of radar, right up to within ten minutes of the stranding. Jarrett's answers to a number of questions put by the Assessors were unsatisfactory. Why, for example, had he not reduced speed when avoiding the two trawlers which were crossing from starboard to port, instead of turning towards the land on each occasion? It was inconceivable that – with the ship in dense fog, approaching a notorious maritime hazard such as Cape Agulhas – he had kept turning inshore and yet failed to ascertain the position of the ship relative to the land.

There had been a series of failures of electronic equipment between 0400 when the chief officer came on watch and 0539 when the ship struck. The equipment had been working throughout the middle-watch – the second officer's watch. The auto-siren switch had been interfered with. That, too, had been discovered in the chief officer's watch.

'We have been told by the witness Rohrbach – the electronics expert – that the Decca Navigator and the two radar sets were sabotaged. I have no intention of speculating as to who might have committed those acts of sabotage, and for what motive. That is a matter which will be dealt with at another time and in another place. It is sufficient for me to say that at five-thirty-nine on 29 October, the new supertanker *Ocean Mammoth*, three hundred and twenty thousand tons deadweight, valued at fifty-five million dollars, returning to the United Kingdom to be laid up, ran aground on Cape Agulhas and subsequently became a total loss.

'I submit, Your Worship,' concluded Lourens, his voice low pitched, his manner bleak, 'that the loss of this great ship and the lives of three of her crew was the result of gross negligence on the part of the chief officer, Freeman Jarrett, who was officer-of-the-watch at the time.'

Lourens returned to his seat and sat blinking owl-eyed as he polished his spectacles with a silk handkerchief.

The Chairman announced the conclusion of the proceedings adding that the court, consisting of himself and the two Assessors, would have to consider the evidence and come to a finding. He then adjourned the enquiry until the following Tuesday at 10 a.m.

when the court's finding would be made known. The clerk of the court called for order, those present stood, and the Chairman and Assessors made their way out.

The public gallery emptied slowly as if the onlookers were reluctant to accept that the performance was over. They stood about uncertainly, talking in low voices, before leaving in twos and threes. At counsel's table the legal men and their clients were collecting their papers, putting them into briefcases and exchanging small talk.

With Lourens's closing address had come Jarrett's final disintegration. He had sat loose-lipped and bewildered, dabbing at his forehead with a handkerchief and drinking innumerable glasses of water as Lourens spoke. Sandy, watching him, had shrunk from the sight of the man she once so much admired, who had so infatuated her, being publicly humiliated. In that moment she felt deeply sorry for him.

Now, waiting in front of the public gallery to join her husband, she saw a man she did not know go up to where Jarrett was sitting, lean over and show him a piece of paper. Jarrett's drawn face seemed to collapse as he read it. Then Ohlsson joined them and there was a short discussion after which Jarrett took his briefcase from the table, got up slowly like an old man with arthritic joints and left the courtroom with the stranger.

Chapter 33

The news of Jarrett's arrest in court was too late for the evening papers, but it got mention in the SABC news bulletin and headlines in next day's morning newspapers.

On Friday when the enquiry adjourned, Kahn had told Foley that the court would almost certainly discharge him with a clean sheet. Thus it was with light hearts that the Foleys went down to St James the next day, swam and sunbathed, ate an enormous lunch at a local hotel, and relaxed for the first time in weeks. That evening, back at the hotel in Cape Town, the receptionist handed Foley a letter which had arrived in the morning mail. It was from the Iranian National Oil Company in Abadan and had been forwarded on from his London address.

He read it quickly, put it in his pocket and went upstairs. Later that night when they were having a drink before dinner, he passed the letter to Sandy. 'Might interest you,' he said.

She looked at him quizzically, opened and read it. 'George! How fabulous.' With scant regard for the people in the lounge she threw her arms round him and kissed him. 'You didn't even tell me you'd applied.'

'Wasn't any point. I've tried for so many jobs and not got them I thought I'd keep this one under my hat.'

'Well, well.' She looked at him with shining eyes. 'You are a clever boy. What is a Loading Master?'

'Bloke who controls tanker loading at an oil terminal.'

'Is the pay good?'

'Fabulous by our standards. Tax free, plus car, house, free holiday travel to Europe, education allowance for kids.'

'If any.' She looked at him guardedly.

'And other fringe benefits. Three years there and we'll have saved a packet. Even with your tastes.'

'Don't be a bastard, George.' She sighed. 'You'll miss the sea, won't you?'

'I'll get over it. Still be mucking about with ships. It'll be a lot better for us.'

'Tell me about Abadan and what life's like out there?'

He stood up, held out a hand. 'Come on. I'll tell you over dinner and a bottle of bubbly.' He pulled her up. She put her hands on his shoulders and looked at him in a puzzled way. 'When did you apply for this one?'

'Saw the advertisement the day before we sailed from Durban. Gave the letter to Kostadis to post when he left the ship.'

'You secretive brute.' She squeezed his hand. 'Come on, let's go.'

Tuesday came and the small courtroom was packed as usual when the Chairman and Assessors took their seats.

Jarrett was the only absentee when the Chairman began to read aloud the court's finding. After a fairly lengthy preamble, its real meat was commendably brief:

The Court having carefully examined the circumstances attending the matter find, for the reasons stated in the appendix hereto, that the stranding of the Cyprus registered VLCC Ocean Mammoth *at Cape Agulhas on 29 October last was due to the gross negligence and default of the chief officer, Ian Freeman Jarrett, as more fully set out in the Court's findings on the questions formulated by the Secretary for Transport.*

The appendix recorded, among other things, the cancellation of the chief officer's certificate of competency in respect of all waters and ships within the jurisdiction of the Republic of South Africa, the finding of the court to be conveyed to the United Kingdom's Department of Trade and Industry, the issuing authority for the certificate.

The Chairman and Assessors withdrew and the courtroom soon emptied. The proceedings had occupied less than twenty minutes.

It was after ten-thirty when the Foleys, escorted by Arnold Kahn, slipped away from the Magistrate's Court and made for a small café in a side street near the railway station. It was empty but for a man who sat alone in an ill-lit corner. They ordered coffee and Kahn began explaining some of the behind-the-scene activities at the enquiry. He'd not got far when Sandy interrupted. 'Look. That's Piet Pieterse sitting over there. Shouldn't we ask him to join us?'

Foley looked at Kahn. 'Any problems?'

'No. Ask him over if you wish.' Kahn hesitated. 'Don't discuss the sabotage business. It's *sub judice* and you're both likely to be called as witnesses.'

Foley went over, brought Pieterse back with him and greetings were exchanged. Pieterse, looking mildly embarrassed, sat down. A coloured girl brought coffee, another cup was ordered and Kahn got some sort of conversation going. Pieterse's coffee arrived, he sipped it, found it too hot and the conversation dried up. The silence which followed was broken when the steward in a shy and rather halting way congratulated Foley on the outcome of the enquiry. Sandy Foley then asked him if his search for a job had produced any results.

He shook his head. 'Not yet, madam. I've been too busy for that.'

'Of course. I'd forgotten.' She smiled sympathetically.

'But the prospects are not too bad.' His grin revealed a missing tooth. 'All that stuff in the papers about Piet Pieterse. My goodness. You'd think I was an important guy. Now the press boys are making me offers for my story.' He laughed, a kind of cracked cackle, one hand over his mouth to hide his teeth. 'Not that it's much of a story. For three days in my life I'm at sea, then I'm wrecked. Jesus!'

They laughed with him and Kahn warned against accepting the first offer. If he needed help and advice, he could put him in touch with a reliable agent. Addresses were exchanged and Pieterse was about to go, when Kahn congratulated him on what he had done in the interests of justice.

Pieterse looked at him doubtfully. 'It wasn't that, sir. Because you're white you wouldn't understand. But that man called me a coloured bastard.'

Pressed for his story, Pieterse said, 'The first day at sea – after we left Durban – I came round a corner in the alleyway outside the bar-lounge. The ship was doing some big rolls and I was carrying a loaded tray. I wasn't used to doing it under those conditions. The chief officer comes round the corner and we collide. It's then he says, "You stupid coloured bastard. Why don't you look where you're going".'

Pieterse watched his audience through hurt, bloodshot eyes. 'It was only a little coffee that spilt on his white uniform. Not much, sir. Just a few drops really.'

Instinctively Foley knew then who it was had phoned him on

the bridge that night to tell him his wife wanted him urgently in their cabin.

The easy chair in the bay window of the hotel bedroom in The Gardens gave Captain Crutchley a view over Table Bay. It was a beautiful aspect, the lights of the city spread like a glittering quilt before him, the long lines of mercury and sodium vapour lamps marking the main thoroughfares leading towards the foreshore and the sea, then swinging left and right to the suburbs. He could see the lights of the ships in the Duncan Basin, beyond them those of vessels at anchor in the outer harbour. Most of his life had been spent at sea, and the ships and the harbour filled him with nostalgia for other times and places. He thought of all the great ports he'd seen at night: Sydney, Rio, Montevideo, Bombay, Hong Kong, Tokyo, Marseilles, Hamburg, Genoa, New York, Baltimore, San Francisco, Liverpool, Southampton – and many others. Pictures of them passed through his mind's eye, taking him back to the romance and adventures of his youth.

His thoughts returned to the events of the last few days. The enquiry was over, the charges against him had been dismissed, but he knew that he had not come through unscathed. Some of the mud would stick: impaired vision, absence from the bridge in fog, missing charts and logbooks, officers fighting over a woman, lives lost . . . these were the things that would be remembered, however rational the explanations, however innocent the man. Jarrett's treachery had destroyed him.

He poured himself another stiff tot of whisky, added a little water. No point in brooding about that now. It was all over and done with. Like his life at sea. Like everything else. He thought about his family in Farnham. He'd already told Emma the result of the enquiry. Phoned her that night before dinner. She had been so thrilled. The relief in her voice which sounded over those thousands of miles had told so clearly of the strain she'd been under, and he was doubly sad. She said how much she and the boys were looking forward to his return. Told him not to worry about the future. Things would come right. They always did, she insisted. He'd agreed, said he hoped to be back in a few days – that his thoughts were, and always would be, with her and the boys.

He drained the last of the whisky, looked at his watch, put on the dark glasses, took an ash walking-stick from the cupboard and made his way downstairs.

At the front door the hall porter said, 'Going for your constitutional, Captain?'

Crutchley nodded. 'It's a fine night,' he said, and walked out into it.

As always when he reached Orange Street, he set off along it until he came to the place, shortly before the gates of the Mount Nelson, where he usually crossed. He stood waiting at the lights, making no effort to press the pedestrian button. It was after nine and there was a good deal of traffic in both directions but he watched the stream coming down on his right from the direction of de Waal Drive. He waited until a fast-moving phalanx of vehicles had almost reached him before stepping into the roadway ahead of them. His last recollection was the fierce glare of headlights, the shrill screech of brakes, and a voice behind him shouting.